THE

PALACE

Wiesław Myśliwski

THE PALACE

TRANSLATED FROM
THE POLISH BY
URSULA PHILLIPS

PETER OWEN
LONDON & CHESTER SPRINGS PA

PETER OWEN PUBLISHERS
73 Kenway Road London SW5 0RE
Peter Owen books are distributed in the USA by
Dufour Editions Inc. Chester Springs PA 19425–0449

First published in Great Britain 1991

Peter Owen Limited gratefully acknowledge the assistance of the Arts Council
of Great Britain in the publication of this book.

British Library Cataloguing in Publication Data
Myśliwski, Wieslaw, *1932–*
The palace.
I. Title
891.8537[F]

ISBN 0–7206–0790–6

Typeset by Action Typesetting Gloucester
Printed in Great Britain by Billings of Worcester

THE WAR WAS ALREADY LONG OVERDUE. We were expecting it year after year, month after month, day after day. At New Year, Easter, Whitsun, Christmas, on every saint's day, and on every other day. People went on and on about it, predicted when it would be, prayed for it. And from a certain moment you could even hear it. All you had to do, on a clear day, was put your ear to the ground and listen hard to the east, and it would reverberate with distant rumblings, booms, the occasional odd explosion. You could even catch a glimpse of it sometimes, from a hilltop on a dark starless night. Far, far away, as if on the very edge of the night, divers and wondrous flares, brilliant flashes of light, red glows, would appear before your eyes, seeming like an ordinary storm in the distance, but people said this was war all right. They said it wasn't far off at all now, and estimated the days. But if you went on watching, it came so close it looked as though it would arrive today, in the middle of the night, at daybreak, tomorrow at the latest, the day after tomorrow. But before it, it also brought fear.

Some people had already set out on long journeys to meet it half-way, to sound it out, to see from which direction it was most likely to come. But others said this wasn't war yet, only a presentiment. However, they'd already dug their pits, bunkers, shelters, in the cliffs, in the slopes, in the hillsides, carried out their possessions, buried them in the ground. And some were already spending the night in the open, taking their animals out into the orchards, down to the river, into the fields, into the woods.

So too in the palace, ever since the first rumours of impending war, they had been making preparations for a journey. Nobody knew where to, however, because everything took place in the greatest of secrecy. Even the valets could say very little, except that the young ladies had already been removed, that her ladyship wandered around in floods of tears giving away her dresses to the maids whilst his lordship just stood by the window, thinking. That trunks, cases were being loaded up and transported somewhere at night. That carriage and pair were ready and waiting to whisk their lordships away. And that they too were expecting the war any day, only no one was allowed to mention it out loud.

But the war was somewhat reluctant to come. It was on its way, yet not on its way. One night it was closer, the next further away. It just kept deceiving us.

So when, after all these omens, it eventually did come, it was upon us so suddenly and unexpectedly, it was hard to believe it was really the war. What's more it came in the middle of the afternoon when people were expecting the gong for lunch, not a war. And it was so swelteringly hot that everyone was wondering how to skive off work, at least for a moment, and take a breather in the shade.

Blazing heat poured down from the sky. The warmth seemed to radiate not only from the sun but from the earth as well, from the buildings and trees, so that even the animals driven into sties and stables projected this sultriness, even people did. The oppressive, baked air seemed to billow forth from the green wall of the park as from a furnace, sticking to your body, stifling your breath, stinging your eyes like smoke. In this heat wave it was torture simply to walk. It was torture even to see people fighting their way forward as if it were some kind of punishment. The palace guard-dogs too were drained of all their aggression and slunk about dejected, more like sheep than dogs, basking in the shadows and letting the village children rattle their sticks along the fences of the estate.

The world seemed about to expire. You didn't feel like looking at anything, or hearing anything, or thinking. A kind of uncanny drowsiness hung in the air, heavy with the sweet scent of lime blossom. But such a time is not the right time for a war. War ought to come at night, heralded by the howling of dogs, by the restlessness of all creation, by signs in the sky, when people stay up sensing its imminence, amidst lightning, thunderbolts, conflagrations. For only the night and the menace of danger are deserving of human terror, tears, loss.

I was sitting on the step of the sheep-fold when suddenly there was a shrill screech through the air, a flash and a terrifying bang in the tops of the wayside poplars. Before I had even managed to duck, it was all over. Wailing broke out, yelling, lamentations.

People rushed to get away, to the gates, though the fences, running blindly wherever their legs would carry them. Everything teemed, seethed. I'd never seen such a lot of people on the estate before all at once. I'm sure there had never been so many, unless it was once upon a time, long ago; but this sudden panic somehow increased their number, for there was no telling where they all came from and where they were galloping off to, as usually happens when people have no defence other than their own misery. Even the drowsy guard-dogs rose to their feet and joined the human chorus in their weeping and bewilderment.

It was somehow unreal, as though simply dreamed up out of the scorching heat, the sultriness, the drowsiness, the sweet scent of the limes. I couldn't believe this was the war already. It wasn't how I had imagined its arrival. Just a single missile, which landed moreover in a poplar tree and brought disaster only to some crows, and this was meant to be the war already. The war! The war! Those crows circling up there in a black cloud above the poplars, turned out of their nests, cawing their hearts out, embittered, were the most real thing about this war. Furthermore I was angry with people for adopting this war so readily. I had no desire even to be noticed in the fearful panic. Though somebody there was yelling to some Jacob, mournfully, like a dog calling to a bitch:

Jacob! Jacob! Where are you, Jacob? Oh, you stupid oaf, Jacob! You're always the same!

But on the estate there was more than one Jacob. His lordship, too, who could never remember anyone's name, called everyone Jacob, because he liked the name. Her ladyship, who generally speaking didn't know anybody, followed his lead and also called everyone Jacob. And because their parents did, the young ladies called everyone Jacob, too.

I don't know myself why I didn't run away. Maybe I was so exhausted by the oppressive heat I imagined I'd still make it. But maybe it was due to disbelief. For I wanted there to be at least another raid somewhere, perhaps on the palace, then it really would be the war.

The valets were still fleeing from the palace, ridiculous in their terror, in their black frock-coats, all the more ridiculous as they attempted to flee with dignity. After them came the chefs, the cooks, the parlourmaids, the other servants. The chambermaids had gone quite berserk like swallows before a storm, so that you could have clutched them in your grasp and ravished them.

I was still looking up at the sky, listening out for another screech somewhere, when all of a sudden the park rose up ahead of me and a carriage drawn by two grey stallions, their heads thrust back against the sky, sped out of the drive on to the highway. His lordship running away. So fine a lord, but running away in panic, in terror, just like ordinary mortals, still goading the coachman impatiently with his cane to stretch the horses to their limit. So fine a lord, that he alone could be his only downfall as well as his only solace, yet he was running away along with everybody else. Beside him her ladyship quivered in fright beneath her fancy sunshade, dabbing her eyes with her handkerchief. I got to my feet and bowed, but they took no notice of me.

And then everything fell silent. In fact calm descended rather than war.

At first I even experienced a sense of relief after all the wailing, yelling, lamenting. I even felt a blissful sweetness come over me in that calm, in that emptiness, devoid of people. I still had to water my sheep, toss them some hay, as once again they'd eaten very little while out grazing. But what were they supposed to eat when the sun had scorched the grass right down to the ground and I'd been chasing them, more to drive them on than to let them graze? I didn't feel like moving, however. I watched the crows suspended above the poplars, curious whether they'd also settle on their nests, or whether they'd fly away, though after that missile silence had descended. The mugginess got worse and worse, soporific, cloying. If it weren't for this weird emptiness all around, you'd think the war had tried to avoid us. Besides, I imagined that people would soon start to return to the emptiness, furtively wiping away their tears, ashamed of their fear. But above all his lordship would return, and on his return he'd order the carriage to stop in the emptiness and he'd say to his lady:

Look, my darling, how empty it is without us.

Maybe he'd even notice me and reward me copiously, because I stayed behind.

Though gratifying, the thought was nevertheless disturbing. I sprang to my feet, glancing around hesitantly. There wasn't a living soul anywhere. Even the dogs, which not so long ago would have attacked people, lay hidden in shady retreats, subdued. You couldn't even hear a cow lowing, a horse whinny, the screech of a peacock.

In this emptiness I suddenly felt as if I myself didn't exist at all, let alone other people. I wanted to shout to someone but didn't know to whom; I wasn't sure my shouting would reach anyone. I wanted to run away but didn't know where, and it was too late to follow the others.

Suddenly I grabbed the whip lying abandoned on the floor and made for the cowsheds. I flung the doors wide open and began to chase the animals outside. I cracked the whip, screaming and lashing at the walls, but the animals, being animals, were in no hurry to get out. They crept out slowly, stood in the doorway, had a look around. But I was in a hurry, I don't know why, but I was in a hurry. I was in such a furious temper I took the whip and began thrashing their backs, heads, eyes, legs, wherever the blows landed. I didn't feel the least pity, just rage, remorse, bitterness, as though those cows, God's innocent creatures, had done me some great wrong. Then I drove out the horses. I even turned loose the stud, though my courage deserted me once I found myself among those glistening hides, long necks, eyes big as fists, gawping at me in amazement for having dared to come near them with a whip. But I opened the paddocks, cracked the whip once, twice, and they charged towards the door one after the other. Then the sheep, though they were the closest to me among both men and beasts. But something had so affected me I felt no pity for the sheep either, and I chased them outside. There I swept them forward with the whip into the throng of creatures, lashing their fleeces in my rage, until they squeezed themselves compliantly among the legs of cows, horses, dogs.

I was exhausted by it all; I almost felt drunk from exhaustion. Perspiration trickled into my eyes, and I didn't even have the strength to raise the hand in which I held the whip. I leaned my back against the pigsty wall, gasping for the sultry, roasted air with my mouth wide open.

And there before my eyes the animals surged and eddied, careering into one another, seeming to rush off somewhere neighing, bellowing, bleating, but remaining in the same spot like an agitated pond. Bewildered cows swam against other cows, gored each other, tore the fleeces off the sheep with their mouths like they were juicy green grass, as angry with their own calves as with the yapping dogs lunging at their legs. But the horses in their despair managed to wrest themselves from this maelstrom, climbing on top of one another. Only the horses with their long necks kept above water. The sheep were bleating, crushed underfoot.

I looked on with unseeing eyes; in fact it was all just an image reflected in my eyes, for I stood there absorbed in my own exhaustion and couldn't give a damn.

Until the moment when I suddenly came to my senses, realized what I'd done, and was gripped by a terrible fear. I flung aside the whip and began to run away from the surging animals towards the park. Then on through the park, taking short cuts across the lawns, through the shrubs, as fast as my legs would carry me, without looking round, without pausing for a moment – until I collapsed out of breath, fainting from exhaustion, in front of a summer-house covered with wild vine not far from the pond.

Here it was cool and shady; you didn't want to believe in the sweltering heat of the world outside. Also the stillness here was somehow unreal, concentrated, paralysed, fragrant from the vegetation, alive with the warbling of birds. I looked about suspiciously because the stillness seemed queer to me, as though it was lying in wait for me, but all around there were just trees, trees, an impenetrable wall of green. Only through the trees to the north could you see the grey sheet of the pond, where the swans sailed by without a care in the world. I was sorely tempted to sprawl out beneath one of those thick old trunks, close my eyes, forget about the world around me, drift into my day-dreams, fall asleep. Something, however, didn't feel quite right. I imagined any moment I'd hear carefree, rippling laughter from behind the trees, and their lordships would appear walking down the avenue, arm in arm. He grave, wrapped up in his thoughts, she laughing by his side, bubbling over with her birdlike chatter, beaming her angelic smile. For who cared if I'd seen them running away? Their appearing in the avenue seemed much more real to me than their running away. Or some cousin leaping out from behind the trees with a young lady, she in flight, he in pursuit, certain they were quite alone. Or whispers suddenly reaching my ears from the summer-house. Maybe there'd be a splash of water and a boat would appear before my eyes on the pond. And in the boat would be ladies, gentlemen. I had always found the park a somewhat mysterious, inaccessible place, harbouring strange surprises.

I heard a blackbird singing above me. My heart trembled with joy. I looked up. But it had already moved on to another tree, further away. Without making a sound, I went after it, trying to spot it amongst the foliage. But it was already singing somewhere else, another two, three trees ahead of me. Again I went after it, trying not to crunch the twigs beneath my feet. It hopped across to the next tree. I stood still and waited till its song rang out anew. Then again I moved forward a few steps, holding my breath. Without a sound. So softly. I almost had it. But then it fell silent. Vanished along with its song.

Oh, the singing of the birds in the park was quite different from their singing in the woods, down by the river, in the village orchards. Somehow more refined, more noble, the same yet not the same. You could listen completely absorbed, oblivious to all else. And in that singing the blackbirds reigned supreme. I used to know by heart all the birds in the park. I knew what tree they were nesting in, whether they were sitting on their eggs, whether they had babies. If they were singing for a mate, or for rain, or out of fear. At one time, as a boy, I often used to sneak into the park with my catapult and search among the leaves for the most beautiful song, that song before which all other songs fell silent. And then I'd lie in wait for it, stalk it, seek it out, until I managed to track it down and kill it. Then I'd pick up the tiny corpse in my hand and walk sadly over to the palace to show the young ladies that yet again someone had killed a little bird in the park – I'd just come across it as I was walking by. And they would mourn it with great remorse, and their tears were so beautiful I could never take my eyes off them.

I was still in pursuit of that blackbird, searching among the trees in the hope that it would show some sign of life or that I'd catch it as it flitted from tree to tree, when suddenly to my right, a peacock began to screech loudly in the brushwood. A moment later a deer crept out of the thicket before my very eyes. It hesitated, watched, and then shot off into the park. I glanced around trying to get my bearings, when I realized I was near the palace. I was utterly amazed, terrified, at how the palace had got there, in the park, in the silence, so suddenly, unexpectedly. As though I'd stumbled upon it by accident, straying unwittingly into the thickets, heedless of warnings that somewhere among the old oaks, beeches, hornbeam, spruce, the perpetual warbling of the birds, there stood a palace, white and immense as the light of breaking day. And I knew the palace well; after all, I used to go there on errands as a boy. A little voice whispered to me, urging me to run away, run away. That blackbird had led me astray. That accursed blackbird. I tried quickly to find some justification for my being so near. But at the same moment I remembered that everybody had fled, that the palace stood empty. This brought me to my senses, even spurred me on.

Scared and unsure, I gradually moved towards it, stealing from tree to tree, straining my ears for the slightest sound. I walked round it in a semi-circle, sneaking up on it from the main drive so it looked as if I was coming from the farmyard. But when I crept out into the forecourt, my heart missed a beat in panic. I felt suddenly exposed as I found myself bang in the middle of the dazzling brightness radiating from the palace. And in my head the terrifying thought just kept pounding away – what would I say if someone discovered me here and asked in amazement:

And what might you be doing here, Jacob?

For I too was amazed at myself, that here I was standing in front of the palace. Me in front of the palace.

Opposite me were the great doors with the broad marble staircase leading up to them, guarded on either side by two naked, curly haired youths leering down at me with their sniggering smiles. The doors were bigger than many a peasant hovel, and ornate like the high altar in the church. The two wings stood wide open.

I was embarrassed. I felt as if I was standing before a palace dreamed up by myself, and the real me was far away tending my sheep on the hillside, under a hawthorn bush, hands behind my head, staring into the open sky, bathed in tranquillity, listening intently to the sound of grass under the sheep's muzzles, and immersed, immersed in day-dreams of myself standing before a palace, an empty palace, a palace devoid of life.

It crossed my mind that I ought to deny my presence here, refuse to admit it to myself, make up some excuse, even pretend I'd got lost following that blackbird or I'd come here out of common concern to see if any doors or windows needed shutting now that the palace was deserted. A storm could blow up, or someone might take advantage of a war being on to steal roses from the flowerbeds. But at the same time something tempted me, persuaded me tentatively, guardedly, to mount that marble staircase, at least to step on to the first stair, the nearest stair. Just to step on to it. Me. Jacob. Me, the real me. And those great doors were standing wide open just for me. The whole vast, empty palace was standing there just for me. And I saw myself mounting the staircase. First one step. Then a second. And from out of the doors came two rows of footmen, who lined the stairs, bowing respectfully, lighted candles in their hands. And I walked up slowly, with dignity. On and on, as though the stairs were without end.

I looked about distrustfully in case anyone was watching, then went round to the other side of the palace. The doors here were easier to cope with as they were for the servants, for those who came to beg his lordship's favour or her ladyship's mediation, or who dropped in to the kitchen in search of scraps. Darkness enveloped me as I went inside, for the corridor was long and windowless, and light only ever entered when someone opened a door. But I knew the corridor by heart. The kitchens and pantries were located on the left, the servants' rooms on the right, whilst straight ahead led to the Rooms.

Whenever I came here as a messenger and it happened to coincide with some function, I'd sneak into the corridor so I could savour the smells of the dishes being carried past. All I had to do was squat in a corner and an endless array of fragrances would run rings round me like a cocoon, oppressive, piquant, pungent, worming their way into my eyes, into my thoughts, into my blood. And the smells were so powerful I could not only feel them, but hear them. Even the darkness where I slunk reeked of venison, mushrooms, marjoram and all sorts of other delicacies. Even the flustered voices of the cooks were redolent of fried goodies, sauces, warmth. But above all there was the aroma of footmen carrying trays of sizzling game through to the Rooms. Tears sprung to my eyes, the saliva flowed freely, my hands, belly, legs itched as if I had scabies, but I would surrender myself to these smells till it hurt – sometimes I would feel the urge to burst out laughing, sometimes I wanted to whine like a dog. Someone somewhere would be calling me, but I could never tell if I'd really heard it, or if I was only remembering it.

Jacob! Jacob! Where are you, Jacob!

I knocked tentatively on the doors to the Rooms. Then again, more boldly. But my knocking failed to provoke the slightest response on the other side. I waited for a bit just in case and only then pressed down the handle slowly. Amidst the protracted creaking of the door, which sent shivers up my spine, I found myself in a broad, spacious corridor stretching the entire length of the palace. Here it was bright and sunny like outdoors. At both ends of the corridor enormous windows reached from the ceiling right down to the parquet floor, and in front of the windows, on either side, wide marble staircases wound their way up to the floor above. Innumerable doors led off the corridor into the Rooms. On the walls hung paintings, chandeliers, everywhere paintings, some bronzed with age, others as if the paint were still fresh. The hunt. A lord shooting a stag in flight. It must have been a good shot because the poor beast is besieged by dogs. It still tries to get away, but its eyes are already bulging. And here again, a forest clearing, ladies, gentlemen. Having something to eat. Laughing, joking. Life must be treating them well. Winter. A long trail of haggard figures. Trudging on and on. Where might they be going at such an icy, unpropitious time? Alongside them riders with rifles slung across their shoulders, wearing some kind of weird caps. And now – a battle. Immense. All twisted in pain like the roots of a tree. Red with blood. Men and horses intertwined. Screams, curses, moans, the gurgles of the dying. In the end the sight of it made me feverish and I couldn't bear to look any more.

I took stock of the doors. I had no idea where to go now. No idea, what for. As if the palace no longer interested me. I even began to regret I'd come here at all, and then when I realized I'd almost reached the Rooms, I started to feel uneasy. Quite unexpectedly the thought struck me that I could perhaps stay here and sit out the war. The safest place would surely be within these ancient solid walls. Maybe it'd even be possible to forget the war. Sleep through it in a quiet chamber somewhere and wake up when it was all over, rather like waking up to a sunny morning after a long night, having a good stretch, yawning and stepping out into a world which was once again at peace. And even if someone discovered me asleep, I could always say I was guarding the palace. How many wars had this palace lived through before now! They used to say wars were humbled before it just as people were, skirting round it from afar, making detours to avoid it. And apparently these wars got successively more and more gruesome. Some were evil and vindictive, flattening everything in their path, some short but vicious like the passage of a hailstorm. They were bitter, jealous, insidious, and every time people dropped like flies and no one batted an eyelid. But no war ever touched the palace. It was quite uncanny. It inspired awe, yet trust at the same time. Only once was the palace struck by a stray shell, which lodged itself in the wall and failed to go off, and his lordship ordered it to be set into the brickwork as a memento.

I coughed as I looked from door to door to see if any of them stood ajar, or in case a handle started to creak somewhere. But apart from my coughing, which echoed throughout the palace peculiarly loudly, no sound reached my ears.

I was encouraged by this. I opened the nearest door a little way and stuck my head round. I was dazzled by a blinding light. I was in the drawing-room. Streams of sunlight poured through the huge windows, which occupied one whole wall. I retreated. Hovered for a moment clutching the door-handle, not sure whether to enter or not, for that bright light had slightly unnerved me. But what business had I in a drawing-room? Me in a drawing-room. My God. In this brilliant afternoon light. Lolling in an armchair like a lord. Me. Laughter. Conversations. We're enjoying a joke. Ugh, frightfully hot today, wouldn't you say, Cousin? A real scorcher, awfully stuffy, and now the war on top of everything else. Then all of a sudden someone announces a sheep is giving birth. I can hear them sniggering behind my back.

I let go the handle and moved on to the next door, but gave it a miss. I passed over the next one too. Only somewhere on the other side of the corridor did I push one ajar and peep inside. A musty smell wafted towards me. Gloom permeated the whole room. Even through the window, draped with a heavy curtain, a murky pallor penetrated instead of light. But after a while, armchairs began to emerge out of the gloom, a sofa, a coffee table, and on the right a cupboard as high as the ceiling full of books. On the opposite wall hung two portraits side by side: an old man and an old lady. They looked as if they were still alive. I imagined they were watching me menacingly, as if chastising me for defiling them with my presence.

Fear got the better of me. I retreated all the faster. I didn't even shut the door properly. And as I placed my hand on the door-handle of the next room, I could still feel my heart pounding away in my breast. Because of this I even knocked before I entered. And for a long time afterwards I couldn't shrug off that fear. It welled up in me again every time I opened a door or even touched a handle. There was nowhere I could just sit down for a bit and have a rest. Here it was too bright, there it was too spacious, somewhere else I remembered something which immediately stripped me of my courage, yet elsewhere I could in no way convince myself everything would be all right.

I had already begun to lose my way among the Rooms. I had no idea which wing I was in, though I'd once known the palace like the back of my hand. I imagined this would be the room where they usually rested after one of their stuffing sessions, sitting in their huge soft armchairs over their wine, tea, conversations, or playing cards. Or it would be that bright, spacious room where they used to sit in the May evenings by the open windows listening to the pearly song of the nightingales in the park. But I found myself in her ladyship's bedroom.

Here all was whiteness, like white linen drying in the sunshine, or apple trees in bloom in the orchard. There was a beautiful fragrance. And it was somehow cosy and reassuring. Somehow very nuptial. Veils, everywhere veils. In the windows, over the bed. Even the huge mirror on the wall opposite had veils flowing down either side, fixed at the top with a golden rose. The whole room exuded a strange, blissful well-being. As though enticing you back into childhood. As though awakening a longing for your immature self, small, wretched, a baby bird, a bunny-rabbit, a tiny spider hanging somewhere in the veil over the headboard, wandering over the puffy quilt as if across mountains, valleys, not even aware of its own existence. A longing for something so private you're ashamed not only to think about it, but also to feel that shame inside yourself. A longing to experience yourself through this whiteness, softness, cosy security.

At one point I even caught a glimpse of myself in the distant mirror as a small, insignificant little boy, scared stiff, as if waiting for somebody to feel touched by him, take him by the hand, nuzzle up to his cheek – perhaps it would be her ladyship – and make him feel braver.

That made me ashamed. I would have given anything not to have recognized myself. But I drew my hand across my face involuntarily, and the small, insignificant figure deep in the mirror did exactly the same. I grabbed hold of my hair, and it grabbed hold of its hair. I seized my ear. And it did too. I made threatening gestures. It copied me. Then I stuck out my tongue at it, so it flung out its own tongue back at me. Overcome by spite I thrust out my arse in defiance, looking over my shoulder to see what it would do. It stood there just as defiant with its arse stuck out at me and looking over its own shoulder to see what I would do. It clung to me like a leech, it was impossible either to catch it out or to get rid of it.

I began to walk towards the mirror step by step. I felt a desire to attack that insignificant figure with my fists, to pull its shaggy hair, treat it to a mouthful of such abuse it would lower its eyes. But as I drew near a sense of shame swept over me for behaving so spitefully towards myself. I almost felt intimidated by this self in the mirror. I wanted to give myself a friendly smile, gently touch my cheek, even if it was just with one finger, say some kind word, but I was afraid that I might scare myself away, vanish, maybe withdraw into the depths of the mirror and return to my terrified insignificance waiting there for someone to feel touched by it, afraid that I wouldn't even be able to recognize myself.

So I stood there astonished that this was me, wondering at my sunburnt face, my hesitant eyes, my yellow mop, at my arms dangling limp by my sides as if they didn't belong to me, at my great hands out of place, at my whole self, wondering that this was me. And the longer I looked at myself the more amazing it seemed to me, that this was me. That I could stand like this in front of myself as if I was one person and somebody else at the same time, that I could order him in there to raise his arm, run his fingers through his hair, do this, do that, but that at the same time, enslaved by him, I was forced to repeat his movements. Eventually I began to be tormented by the suspicion that maybe there were two of us, as though we were split into soul there and body here, or the other way round, into thirst for oneself and fear of oneself, into amazement and joy. Here we were, perhaps having found each other at last, perhaps having longed for our union – but in reality there were two of us, only neither of us knew whether he was the one standing before him or the one watching him. Something even warned me to be wary of the one in the mirror, like you'd be wary of someone if you couldn't tell whether a smile afforded him pain or sadness hilarity, if you could tell almost nothing about him. Despite this, a secret joy welled up inside me, for here I was standing before myself.

Had I not been so afraid I was aping myself, making a fool of myself, I would have grabbed hold of that yellow head and hugged it to my breast. Clasped it, caressed it, buried my fingers in it as if it were grass, so I could feel its softness, its yellowness, its fragrance. I felt I wanted to plant these hands right there and do something, do something, if it was only to stroke myself at a distance without even touching myself, delicately, tremulously, almost as if with rabbit's fur, with the mossy down of a sheep's fleece, with the warm tongue of a cow soothing her new-born calf not yet cool after delivery – or no, with claws rather, with teeth, in order to experience until it hurt the amazing joy which was coursing fearfully through me, to stifle that fear which made me feel shy in front of my own self and prevented me from believing that here I was, me, and that I could see myself.

For I had never examined my whole self like this in a mirror before, really looked into myself. When I used to come here as a messenger, terror would usually get the better of me whenever I accidentally came face to face with my own reflection, and I would run away scared out of my wits in case anyone had seen me. For there was always someone who'd suspect me of some crime.

Therefore perhaps that old boyish fear awoke within me now as a temptation, an irresistible temptation, to reach out to myself with my arms, to lay down my head on my own breast, to yield my hair to my own fingers and my trusting ears to my own whispers full of comfort, kindness, sleepiness, to nestle into myself.

But now, suddenly, out of the depths of the mirror there looms the white figure of a woman in a long dress reaching to the floor, with bare arms, obscuring my image. I can't believe my eyes but can't let her out of my sight lest she should vanish. I think I even whisper something in disbelief or perhaps in admiration, for she lifts her eyes as though she heard my whisper, but she is unaware of me, shows no hint of surprise in her serene, unseeing gaze. I feel my heart galloping wildly in my breast; I can't control my trembling. I hold my breath so as not to frighten her or offend her with my presence. I stare at her as though at an apparition, but she is real all right, I can see her, she is so real that I could stretch out my hand and touch her white dress, I could bow to her if she deigned to notice my presence and remind herself that it's me, who used to come to the palace once upon a time as a messenger. Doesn't she recognize me? Well yes, I've grown up. Become a man. The wind has lined my face with wrinkles. The sun burned my skin. The rains lashed over me. But I can remember her. I can still remember her hand on my head all those years ago, when she stroked my hair as she passed once in the corridor, smiling out of her sadness, and it was as if she cast a spell on me with that hand, that smile, for I stood transfixed, gazing after her with my eyes, my thoughts, my whole body trembling, ashamed, until she disappeared through some door. But I stood and stood and stared after her, till I was awoken by the voice of a valet.

And who might you be dreaming about, Jacob?

She must have been on her way to bed because she sat down and began to unfasten her hair-slides. Then with a capricious gesture she tossed her loose hair back over her shoulders and arms, so she sat there completely drenched in its glorious sunshine. But not satisfied with that she ran the palms of her hands through the length of it, from top to bottom, fondling it to her face as if she couldn't get enough of it. Then she stared at her face, not yet past its first youth but already slightly marked by the passage of time, and at her doe eyes, sad yet spattered with her sleepiness. She must have noticed fear in their dark depths for, full of uncertainty, absorbed in her own countenance, she suddenly leaned forward towards herself as much with burning hope as with regret. She was close to tears almost, childish tears of self pity, but also to mockery of herself, desperate derisive mockery. It seemed to me that in a moment she would slip off her chair, kneel in front of herself and start to pray to this face of hers, to her own eyes, hair, her long white hands held up to herself in the iridescent radiance of her rings. And maybe in that short moment of doubt she might notice me standing before her.

But gradually pensiveness or maybe sleepiness returned to her eyes. She began to run her fingers delicately over her face, observing herself now from the side, now from above, from close by, from a distance, now considerate towards herself, now astonished, then again full of the affection you'd show a child. Then she smoothed out the creases under her eyes, fondled her eyebrows, stroked her forehead with the back of her hand, tossed back her loose hair, stood up and began to undress.

I didn't know which way to turn. I didn't know whether I was supposed to watch her or not. I was seized with pangs of conscience that I was watching her in such a defenceless state without her being aware of it. But I couldn't restrain myself; it was beyond my will-power. I felt I was going to burst. She, meanwhile, bent closer to me than ever before, so close that had I bowed, our heads would have touched. She unravelled one leg from her dress, then the other, rolling down her gossamer stockings. Then she stood up straight, undid the glittering brooch on her breast, and the dress just fell off her of its own accord. I covered my eyes with my hands and fled from the room.

I didn't stop till I reached the end of the corridor. I was so burning with shame I would have dearly loved to escape from the palace. I pressed down the handle of some door. Went inside. A pleasant coolness wafted over me.

I was held at bay by some swords covering the walls, ornate daggers of some sort, rifles, belts studded with nails, antlers, the head of a wild boar. I withdrew.

I suddenly remembered the room that hardly anyone in the palace knew about, but where I used to hide sometimes, where there reigned eternal semi-darkness and a stillness so sensitive you could hear rustling sounds in the walls like whispering, weeping, or water murmuring. There was no furniture, just chests and trunks; sacks stuffed with something or other; skins – fox, marten, hare – lying all over the place; old chandeliers piled in a heap in a corner; books strewn about in disarray, their bindings broken, torn, nibbled by mice. Stuffed birds hung on the walls: hawks, buzzards, an owl that seemed to be still alive, quite tiny birds too, in another corner a heron on a pedestal, all of them already moulting with age. And there used to be a human skull lying about on the floor. At first that skull aroused in me feelings of abhorrence, of dread almost. I tried not to look at it, but then it would torment me all the more, thrusting itself before my eyes of its own accord, rolling towards my feet, laughing in its empty eye sockets. Until I got used to it. Then I would even pick it up, rock it to sleep, sing to it, chatter away to it. I used to ask it what it would like to be, a girl, a priest, a musician. It would reply, Whatever I wanted to be.

That room must be somewhere here, I didn't dream it up out of nowhere.

I opened more and more different doors as I walked on and on through the palace, but there was still no end to the rooms and chambers. I no longer had any idea if I was really looking for anything. It seemed that there were never as many rooms before as there were now, even taking them all into consideration, both upstairs and down. I no longer believed in myself very much. But the worst thing was I constantly lacked the courage to sit down for a moment and have a rest. I already felt exhausted, like after a long journey, weary of these chambers, rooms, this inaccessible emptiness, opulent, emanating from almost every corner. I was all the more exhausted because everywhere I went there were armchairs, sofas, various chairs, some bigger than others, some more comfortable than others, and all beckoning to me, imploring me to sit down, sprawl out, let myself go. Also, there was such a deathly hush that I wanted more than once to whisper, shout, in order to hear my own voice at least. I imagined, however, that if I sat down something would happen, someone might appear, catch me red-handed, and I wouldn't even know how to explain myself. Or sleep would overpower me and I'd fall asleep for ever.

Once again I opened some door and stopped dead in my tracks. Here luncheon was still in progress. It made such an impression on me I bowed though there was no one there; but the white table, sumptuously spread, warm aromas still wafting from it, indicated that luncheon was only half-way through. Perhaps their lordships had stepped out on to the terrace for a rest before the next course. Hunger awoke within me, so intense I even forgot my fear. I felt nothing but this hunger, flaring up angrily inside me, beginning to suck at me, gnaw at me.

I went up to the table. I had a good look at the dishes; I hadn't a clue what several of them were, but my mouth began to ooze saliva like I was a dog. I even caught sight of myself sitting at the table where his lordship usually sat, in the most important place, and eating whatever was put in front of me, a bit of everything in turn, until I'd guzzled my fill. I'm not even aware of the taste of the food, only that I'm eating it; I feel nothing but my greed, my insatiable craving, my joy.

I didn't, however, have the courage to sit down. I felt rather as if I'd come in only because some urgent tidings had brought me running to his lordship. And I stood there waiting until they'd finished eating, ready to bow again in gratitude should someone notice me from the table and address me.

Perhaps you'd care for a drop, Jacob?

I looked round the room, then picked up a fork and struck the first plate that came to hand. I listened for the ringing to stop and then to a bit of the silence which followed, then I offered myself a glass and poured myself some golden-hued liquor from the heavy, cut-glass decanter. I drained the glass. It was fine. Oh, it was fine. Neither sweet, nor bitter. I felt a warm glow inside me. My hunger deserted me. I poured myself another, examined the glass under the light. What, I too was drinking such stuff. And I even allowed myself to utter a few words:

Well, Jacob, cheers!

That time it was even better. It no longer burned so much, it had become mellow instead, sweet. But after the third or fourth glass a feeling of weariness came over me as if this whole palace where I'd been wandering were suddenly bearing down heavily on my legs. I had to grip the chair in order to get up from my seat. I had to keep going. Here, and there too. However, I only just made it into the neighbouring room, and there it all caught up with me, so much so that I collapsed into the first armchair that presented itself.

Immediately I was overcome by inertia. I closed my eyelids because I was dazzled by the light, but I had no intention of falling asleep. I even kept watch over my eyes under their lids so they didn't slip away into darkness. I cast them around as though in a waking dream. I saw the rooms, chambers, park, pond, and on the pond swans, the palace shimmering through the trees like the light of breaking day. Even the crows wheeling in a great cloud overhead. Thus I couldn't tell when and whence drowsiness began to obscure my blind stare; maybe it was because of those crows multiplying above me, cawing, cawing. So here I am, feeling myself sinking into the softness of the chair. And I have no strength to move either arm or leg. I am being covered with sheep-skins. Someone is placing silver coins on my eyelids. My thoughts are dying within me. But I have no desire even to shake them up. Only fear comes to my aid. A sudden and dreadful fear. At the last minute I dig my hands into the arm of the chair like a drowning man clinging to the bank, and wrest free my eyes, which have already taken root in a dream.

I look about mistrustfully, adjust my position in my chair and rest my head against its back, but drowsiness attacks me once again. Pins me down as if I'd been crushed by a tree felled in a storm. I can't free my legs. Wooden, numb, lacking in all sensation. And from my legs upwards I can feel my body gradually stiffening, as far as my groin, my waist, then my chest, arms. My hands are already lifeless. Only in my head a mouse still scuffles about, trying to wrench itself free from this wooden clamp, but I can't do anything to help it, I'm completely crushed by the tree.

Not far off I can hear the rattle, muffled as it is by the thick walls, of a carriage, maybe a *britzka*. It's growing louder, getting distinctly closer. I can already hear it coming up the drive, across the park to the palace, then stopping after a while in the forecourt right underneath the windows. I can't make out who on earth it could be. Perhaps I might have recognized it, but the rattle suddenly dies on me. Obviously someone from the town, maybe the *starosta*, for the placidity of the driving suggests someone with dignity. And I could recognize anyone from the rattle of his carriage, his style of driving, his horses.

But now I can make out a new rattle. Then the next. Then another. All coming from the same direction. Like echoes of the one before. The one now approaching even hobbles on a single wheel, but this makes it all the louder, a nagging pain, boring its way into my drowsiness like a light piercing darkness. Oh, I'd recognize that one three miles away. It's the Squire from the neighbouring estate. The wheel on his *britzka* gives him away. That ever-limping wheel. He can never bring himself to repair it. The old beggar, hardly a squire. But he has a damn good sense of smell, oh, the nose of a hunting dog. He always gets wind of everything going on in the palace, even if it's just some cousin's birthday or somebody returning home from abroad. He drops by right away to pay a visit as though on the off-chance, on his way somewhere else, with his limping wheel and his two emaciated, mangy horses. It's a disgrace to receive such a man. A disgrace to admit he's an acquaintance. Though he's supposed to be sitting on a packet. Miser. And he's a glutton, the bastard. My God, what a glutton! Scoffs like a pig yet can't bear to see others eating, he's so jealous. It wouldn't be so bad if he just came on his own for once. But no such luck. He never forgets to bring along those two decrepit maidens of his. And all he ever bothers about is how to marry them off. He'd palm them off on the Devil himself as long as he was rich. One a witch, the other a saint. God knows who'd want them. And yet he still goes on saying to them:

My little daughters, my little angels, my sweet little birds. Eat. Eat. Then you can play us a tune.

So what am I supposed to do? I smile and lie. Please do. Please do.

What's this, they're all gathering for a ball? The very thought raises my spirits. There's going to be a ball in the palace. A ball! Ball! It's been such a long time since there was a ball. And there's nothing quite like a ball. All you've got to do is stand by the gate, direct them to the right into the park, and they're already handing you money. Hold their horses' heads steady, and they hand you money. Bring the tired horses a bucket of water, and again they hand you money. Bow, and they just hand it out. Rush to open the carriage doors before the valets get there, and they hand you money. And when the ball is over and they all go their separate ways, drunk, they don't even count the sum.

They are driving up now one after another. From every direction. It's difficult even to make out who is the nearer, who further away. Before one carriage has come to a halt in the forecourt the next comes hurtling out of the distance, hastily transformed from the indistinct burble of water into cooing doves, the clatter of sticks along the fences of the estate, a hailstorm of horses' hooves, the swishing of whips, coachmen's cries, wheels bouncing along the bumpy roads. All thrown together in confusion, overtaking one another.

From time to time I can just make out somewhere in the din the shy, lesser rattle of a ramshackle *britzka*, shaken to bits with age, barely audible, soothing almost amid the general frenzy. It approaches slowly as if returning from a long journey, overtaken by all the rest, and the closer it gets the more frequently it's lost among the clatter of coaches driving up, the carriages, the waggonettes, still resounding with their own echoes long after they've drawn to a halt in the forecourt. But as I listen to this lesser rattle I'm almost moved to the verge of tears. I know it well. Hardly had it made itself heard somewhere out there when my keen ear picked it out among the riot of vehicles like a grasshopper's chant amid grass abuzz with swarming insects. It's my old friend from my childhood days. He's the only one who comes to pour out his heart, even though he's poorer than the others. Out of the vast property he once possessed he has scarcely a peasant holding to his name, though not because he ate or drank his way through it, or lost it at cards. Yet he doesn't seem at all perturbed by it. At least one man has come down in the world like a true gentleman. Perhaps time is to blame for his downfall. He even has the bearing of a peasant, but no doubt prematurely. He occupies only one room in the crumbling manor-house, and even that's too much, so he says, for all he does is read books, sleep and wait for death. In the remaining rooms he stores grain, tools. He's even got rid of his coachman and does all his own driving. But he's the only one I don't resent for being poor. I always welcome him as a most distinguished guest, going out to meet him on the steps in front of the palace. I myself help him to extricate himself from the *britzka*, then I usually embrace his huge, musty body for a long time, longer than custom dictates. And I order the valets to show him deference among the other guests, to be at his every beck and call, to address him as Count even though he's not a count.

But somehow I can't hear whether he's finally dragged himself into the forecourt, or whether he's still on his way.

And now there's that young dandy charging up. I'd recognize him miles away. He's making up to the elder of the young ladies, though she's got a long way to go before she's of age. But he's already got her earmarked like a hawk singling out a chicken, or more likely it's her dowry he's after. Any time of day is good enough for him. He turns up in the afternoon, at sundown, in the evening, uninvited, unexpected. It's just as well he's an amusing fellow, clever talker, wit, so nobody objects too much to these perpetual visits. And he speeds along as lightly as if travelling through the air, not along the road. And his carriage is always just so, a different one for every visit. He sells land to buy carriages, amasses debts on carriages. Mad about carriages just like his father. Another profligate. Tearing along as if he were racing across open country, across fields, ravines, hills. Even mowing down the sheep. God Almighty!

And that must be the Bishop driving into the forecourt. Straightway into the forecourt. Because I didn't hear him earlier either. But this entrance of the Bishop is somewhat ineffectual, noisy yet sluggish, dignified yet at the same time apprehensive, as if the Bishop was restraining the driver from a more spritely pace, even though he has four horses in harness. He doesn't give the impression of driving up in style, rather of staggering up a hill, panting and complaining about the road, blaming his blameless horses, constantly tormenting the driver with the question, Have we still got far to go? Constantly mopping the sweat from his brow with his white kerchief, as though there was nothing of the gentleman about him. Like an ordinary parish priest, whose whole life passes by in a single parish, at christenings, marriages, funerals. Oh, the Bishop's seen better days. And when he sits at table, you'd never guess he was a bishop. Drumsticks, wings, whole birds disappear into his slobbering mouth, as if he was shoving them as a penance into the fathomless depths of his stomach.

Oh, what fine cooks you've got! Fine cooks.

Suddenly I hear the Bishop's carriage starting up afresh from the undying echo of its own emergence, from all roads at once, deafening, shaken to bits, relentless, sweeping up the drive along with the whole earth, the sky, the lowing of cattle, the crying of birds. I gulp with fear. Another moment and I'll see the Bishop before me mopping the sweat from his brow, and lamenting, lamenting.

Oh, I tell you, my dear, it gets more and more difficult to be a servant of God.

And what will I say in reply? I see myself falling on my knees, clasping his legs, whimpering:

Spare me, Reverend Father, I didn't mean to do it. I was tempted. You know better than anyone that temptation is stronger than will, wisdom, conscience.

No, no, it's not the Bishop. It must be a peasant wedding on its way back from the church, in their innumerable festive carts, traps, waggonettes. They come charging towards the palace in an enormous circle which clouds the whole horizon, outstripping one another in the commotion of wheels, cracking of whips, curses of drivers, in their local tongue, their songs, the squeals of the girls. They push one another off the roads, scraping wheel against wheel, hoof against hoof, setting their exasperated horses against each other, as though the wedding had ceased to matter and all that mattered was the honour of the drunken drivers. Their driving is making my head split. A wedding! A wedding! They're already invading the yard. I can hear them right on top of me, right on top of me. Forging their way into me. Crushing me to bits, trampling me with their hooves. Driving their wheels over my ribs. Someone slashes me across the face with the end of his whip. I leap out of my chair. Hurl myself into the mouths of the oncoming horses.

Stop! Stop!

I'm unable to grasp what's happening. I see my hands, which only a moment ago had been stuck in the horses' muzzles, raised above me in supplication. I lower them tentatively. Hold them before myself hesitantly, examining them, terrified. I glance around the room in case anyone is watching. And then I hear the blasts exploding, menacing. Here. There. Drawn out into one long uninterrupted thunderclap, which recedes somewhere beyond the horizon, fades away into the barely audible rumble of hungry bowels, into distant murmurs, then again bursts forth, gathering might, closing in with perpendicular bounds, almost reaching the palace, rending the tree-tops in the park, venting itself against the walls, the roof. Reminding me of a storm after a heat wave, brimming with God's chastisement. I cross myself involuntarily.

And the Word was made flesh....

Terror presses on the pit of my stomach, crawls under my ribs, reaches my larynx. I feel my heart swell in my breast, trying to force its way to the surface, hammering, hammering, hounded by fever. I place my hands over my ears, but the blasts seem even closer. I hear them rocking the palace, making the window-panes rattle, the furniture pulsate. I hear fire-balls screeching across the sky above me, sluggish at first, breathless, long drawn out, but now intensified, vexed, unrelenting as they whistle in mid-air and suddenly explode, as though they were tearing the world to shreds, out there in the park, in the village.

The idea occurs to me, half consciously, of opening a window, of darting throughout the palace and opening all the windows. Let the whole palace fill with terror till it falls silent. And suddenly, almost without knowing what I'm doing, I cry out:

Is anyone there?! Hey, is anyone there?!

At this very moment the whole room resounds to the striking of a clock. Vast, majestic, sonorous, stabbing my brain. Like an alarm bell. I'm not counting the strokes. Not counting. Anger takes possession of me, an almost uncontrollable rage. I clench my fists hard as rock. Advance towards the wall where this clock scoffs at me, ready to smash it to pieces, clobber that booming inside it, so unconcerned in its ridicule.

Only a few paces separate me from it, but all of a sudden my anger deserts me, my hands hang limp by my sides.

And so the clock rises up before my eyes, enormous, a lot bigger than me. Taking up more than half the wall. I have to crane my neck to look at its white face bordered with markings. It even has a little roof adorned with some sort of crown, a coat of arms in the middle, a kind of winged horse, yet not a horse, on the very top, little turrets guarding the corners. And its sides, from top to bottom, are carved in vines, convolvulus, birds, animals and other wonders.

An altar, not a clock! God shut away within himself. Glass-fronted as well. And behind the glass, beneath the face, two brass weights on gossamer chains. I'd rather not believe it's they who weigh out time inside the clock. Just ordinary brass weights, and it's their job to weigh out your lifetime? And don't you get any say in the matter? Can't you even guard against them deceiving you, ripping you off? Don't you even get the chance to stand up for yourself, question what kind of life it's meant to be? For you'll never eat to the full, sleep to the full, enjoy to the full. You'll always long for much more than you'll ever get. As though you never existed. So what is it they're weighing out that's so wonderful? Oh, if only you could get your own back for this one small thing – for your own life, nobody else's, at least argue your case if you felt you'd had a rotten deal, at least grab an axe and not allow yourself to be hard done by. Human life, after all, is unequal. For some it's poor, for others rich; for some it's degrading, for others exalted; some are singled out by birth, others by destiny. So how can life be weighed out to everyone in equal measure, whether you have it good or bad?! How come these weights can't see what's so obvious, what's crying out to be avenged, don't comprehend what they ought to comprehend, don't even listen to your complaint, but chop your life off like just another notch in the measuring stick, and that's it? So you can't even insist that you deserve to live longer in return for all you've suffered. That you deserve eternity. How can it be so? That they weigh out your life for you without your volition, without your consent? How can it be so? Ordinary brass weights?

As I study them, they are motionless, paralysed, uncommunicative, unfeeling. And yet they're supposed to possess such omnipotence. But where is it? Where is it? I wait patiently. Maybe it'll be revealed to me if one of them gives a start. But perhaps they don't, in fact, weigh out time. Or perhaps they've cut themselves off from me in this motionlessness. Oh, I'll make you move!

I open the glass doors and pull on the lower weight like on a sheep's nipple, but it shows no sign of life. I draw up a chair, clamber on to it, and shift the longer hand forward with my finger as best I can. I watch the weights. They've moved a little. I shift the hand a little further, more boldly. Then further still, watching the weights come together, when suddenly the clock hits back at me with a tremendous loud strike, so that I almost fall off my chair. I hear nothing except this terrifying, clamouring resonance. The din reverberates through my head. I glance around petrified lest people come flying from all over the palace, woken by the loud booming. I imagine them outside the door already. I hear the patter of their feet, their breathless gasps. Panic-stricken I move the hand back; I can't remember where it had been but I move it back just to get it as far away as possible from this striking. But then the clock begins to strike again, this time from the other direction, all the more loudly, relentlessly, as if it were crying for help. So once again I hurriedly bring the hand forward, and once again the clock strikes. No longer able to control myself, I turn it full circle. Once. Twice. Three times. If only to throttle that striking. Suffocate it. Strangle it. I go on turning till the longer of the weights approaches the face itself. Something tells me the clock has already stopped. But I force it, force it. It chokes, coughs, snaps. . . . A gentle moan reverberated and then it all gave up.

I leaped down from my chair. I shook the glass doors in exasperation till they rattled as if the clock were starting to strike again, but by now it was too late.

I stepped back into the middle of the room, eyeing the clock in disbelief, in case it shuddered and began to strike as I walked away from it. A feeling of horror suddenly made my blood curdle. I had broken the clock! Broken the clock! I bump into a chair. My heart lurches into my throat. I look around the room. No one about. I listen carefully. Silence. Immense, paralysed, drenched in sunlight. I don't want to believe in this silence. I lift my eyes towards it. Stare at the ceiling. Ornate like the vaulting in a church. Some kind of arabesques: blue, yellow, pink. Exuding tranquillity. Equanimity. The great tiered chandelier hanging in the centre slumbers too, its forest of candles extinct, not stirring at all. What's become of all those explosions? I walk over to the window. But in the window, beyond the languid afternoon hour, the trees quivering in the heat, the faded blue of the sky, there is nothing but desolation. Everywhere desolation. Terrifying desolation.

I am weighed down by my anxiety, by my distrust of this blissful stillness. I move aside a chair, though it doesn't obstruct me. I walk over to the grand piano in the corner. Stroke its back like it were a cow, though I feel like ramming my fist into it as hard as I can. It is all covered in dust. In the sunshine it seems encrusted with verdigris. Whatever do those maids get up to? Always on heat, giggling and gossiping, and the piano stands undusted. They ought to be supervised. Their every movement properly supervised. I write my name in the dust with my finger, Jacob. Then bigger, Jacob. And bigger still, Jacob, Jacob, Jacob. Then I wipe it all away.

It is only now that I notice how many pictures there are on the walls.

One of their lordships, still quite young, though bald as your knee. Erect, proud. In a high collar. A cloak. Top hat in one hand and the other resting on a cane staked beside his leg. He has a sparkle in his eye, you can't tell if he's smiling or laughing at you. And his regard is so immediate, as though he was watching someone standing right in front of the picture. An uncomfortable feeling comes over me. And here's another gentleman. Tall. Tall as the frame itself. Also standing, but with one hand resting on a desk, indistinct in the darkness. This one's gaze is gentle, benign almost, fixed somewhere far away, far away. Wizened, jaundiced, he must surely be sick, his face shrivelled like a small fist, his eyes sunken, and that far-away gaze, as though he'd already caught a glimpse of death. Poor man. Now a child with golden curls astride a grey pony. Further on, a lady. I stand before her picture with my mouth gaping wide, she is that beautiful, like an angel.

Her gaze is clouded by embarrassment. Perhaps she can see me ogling at her bare arms, dazzled by the tiny crucifix which slides around her neck and slips between her half-exposed breasts. Yet it lasts but a moment. Her eyes widen and rest tenderly upon me. I want to tell her how beautiful she is, that she should be hanging in a church alongside the saints. I want to kneel before her, offer up a prayer, tell her some long tale, full of longing, from the depths of my soul, things I would never confide to anyone else. That I once dreamed about her under a juniper tree. May she forgive me. It wasn't out of pride. Or sin. I myself don't know why. But, in fact, it was as though she was dreaming about me. In broad daylight. In the palace. In her wide bed. Between her silk sheets. So I could hardly believe that it was me, that it wasn't someone else instead, that it wasn't his lordship, but me. I recognized myself from the stink of sheep, though I didn't want to. I was afraid I hadn't had a wash or combed my hair. But I couldn't for the life of me remember whether I'd spent the evening by the river, or if it had been raining during the day. And I was so burning with shame that I was unable to open my eyes to look at you, my lady. I just felt myself beside you, but scorched by your body, your bedclothes. I lay there in fear, curled up, and I think I must have even prayed that you wouldn't want anything from me, because I could hear the words inside me, feverish, alarmed. Just caress me at the very most, and let's go to sleep. Say my name, and I'll be satisfied. For how come such a great lady should dream of me, between her sheets, in her bed, in her palace? Me! But what could I do? I feared your dream might be fickle, your dreaming it at all might mean it was morbid, unchaste perhaps. That maybe you were only dreaming of me because you'd had it too good, because you'd grown bored of clothes and rings, fine gentlemen, balls, endless balls, trips abroad, the waters, all that. That there's nothing left for you even to pray to God for. Therefore you desired me. But when you wake up, you'll regret it bitterly, be ashamed of yourself, terrified. You will ask yourself in trepidation, What can it mean, dreaming of a shepherd? But how am I to blame, if I'm somewhere and I don't know that I'm there, when I'm perhaps not even there at all? I was at your mercy, lady. I didn't dare deny, even, that you were dreaming about me. Nor did I dare to rouse myself from your dream. I lay with quivering heart, waiting for you suddenly to burst out laughing and release me from the night of your dream. You'll make fun of me perhaps. Oh, stupid Jacob! And I'll feel relief, as though I'd been restored to a state of grace. I'll open my eyes, see the sun above me, hear the bleating of my sheep nearby, and complete myself the words you were saying to me, so that even the memory of me won't linger. Oh, Jacob, you stupid thing! But worst of all I was afraid I'd never set foot in the palace again, even to ask for pardon. That I'd never be able to look anyone in the face, not even the valets or your maids. I'd even have to avoid myself. For you don't know, my lady, how terribly sinful I felt beside you, as if it were I who had dreamed about you. Though I felt good in your dream, happy. Perhaps I even secretly desired, without admitting it to myself, that your dream would never end. And I saw you so close to me, like now. I saw you through closed eyelids. In the deep wells of my eyes. And I wanted so much to touch your hair at least, to stroke it, to see whether you were only real as a dream, or real as flesh and blood. I could feel my hand swollen with passion for you, but I was afraid that this hair of yours would never be mine. That there, where I could see it, feel it, hear its softness, I would touch nothing but a fathomless void. Not a trace of your hair, not even its sweet fragrance, just a void. But I wanted it so much that I already had my hand full of it, full of its heavy black loam, my hand full of its gentle softness.

Something restrains me. It's the scornful eyes of an old gentleman who sits right beside her, reclining in an easy chair. He looks at me, but it's as though he looks straight through me. I walk up to him. He laughs scornfully. Who is it, then? Maybe her ladyship's father. Maybe her grandfather. Maybe someone from an earlier era. Beneath his bushy eyebrows, in his hawk eyes, there lurks an all-consuming power of penetration which sends a chill running through you. He seems to see right into your innermost self, into your thoughts, desires, hopes. Seems, like a soothsayer, to know all about you, to know more about you than you could possibly know yourself, things you'd never suspect were within you, things of which you have no inkling, so that if it weren't for the fear he arouses in you, you might feel tempted to ask him about your future. He leans slightly forward, his hands resting as if casually on the arms of the chair, but his long dry palms laid out as if for people to kiss. You can tell, besides, from his whole posture that he's not sitting there for the sake of having a rest. Nevertheless I feel sorry for him. Perhaps it's because he's old. Or because now he must sit there in this chair for ever; he can't even feel fed up with it, can't even adjust himself or close his eyes in half-sleep, in half-death, as he could if he were chained to his seat by illness. The only things remaining to him of life are the pleasure of pouring scorn on others and this power of penetration, feverish with envy, in which he finds his only consolation and which gives him his one defence against the living. He was stupid to have himself painted so old. And what's more, with gout. And those eyes so unrelenting.

Oh, if I was a lord like that, I'd summon an artist to me and say, Here, have as much as you want of everything. You shall paint my portrait. Not in the way you want to. But in the way I tell you. You shall sleep in the palace. In your own room. Eat whatever you like. Drink to your heart's content. Even find yourself a girl. One of the maids. From the estate. A lady even. I'll have a frock-coat made up for you. You shall have your own carriage. Four horses. A valet. What else do you require? Tell me. Light? Well, then we'll knock down a wall. But you shall paint me from sunrise to sundown. You shall paint me until there's no more of me to paint. Day after day. So that I'll not only be one lord and master like him up there. But so that I'll be everywhere. Such as only I can be, or even not be. Let there be myriads of me. So that nobody will be able to get away from me. Nobody forget about me. And so that I shall only be just as you paint me. For every day and for evermore, just as you paint me. And so that I shall be more real in every picture than I actually am. More real. Remember. And you shall sign each one at the top, saying it's his lordship. And when I tell you I'm to be fat, then I'm to be fat. Make my double chin spill over my collar. My cheeks as rosy as drops of blood on milk. Both my hands laid in front of me, plump, white. And so that I'm too tight for my chair. So that my horse sags under me. So that when I drive out, the wheels of my carriage cut into the ground as far as the axle. And let people say of me: So well fed, things can't be going badly for him. And so that I shall swell with pride, whenever I look at myself, that this is me. That it's all me. And so that everywhere I've got curly hair. So that people can envy me. Oh, God never gave you riches, Jacob, but he gave you beautiful hair. May the girls ruffle my hair and kindle their fire. And if I am to be painted asleep, then make my dream soar above my head. And in this dream. . . . Well, what in this dream? I think you should paint something pious. It wouldn't do for his lordship to have dirty dreams. I am kneeling perhaps before the high altar like in church. In full view of God, the people, all the saints. And round about me they'll be saying, Such a lord, yet he prays like anyone else. Such a lord, yet his lips never stop reciting prayers. His eyes closed in humility. His soul held in rapt attention. Such a lord, yet he makes the sign of the cross with his hand like an ordinary mortal. And now he leans forward before the elevation of the host. Raises his hands in contrition. Oh, look, he's even beating his breast. Maybe he's confessing his sins. Such a lord.

I feel I need a good laugh. I restrain myself so as not to burst out laughing aloud, but how can I, when laughter is bubbling up inside me? I can hear myself as far away as the next room, through the open door, as if someone sitting at the table had said something that made them all collapse with this laughter and I was just laughing along with them, though I'm the loudest of all. Perhaps it's not the done thing to laugh so sincerely. Perhaps it offends certain ears. I ought at least to stuff my hand in my mouth. Pretend I've got a cough. Apologize for having choked on something. The artist asks me whether he should paint my laughter as well. Paint it. Paint it. And I go on laughing, probably just because of the laughter itself, but I haven't laughed so idiotically, yet so happily, for a long time.

Until I feel more relaxed. Feel like sprawling in my chair. So I sprawl. Stretch my legs in front of me. Fling my arms wide. Press my head and shoulders into the back of the chair so that I can feel its softness somewhere deep inside me. I feel blissfully at peace in body and soul. I feel happy. And not content with sitting here, I even envy myself for sitting here. And it's so soft, so snug around my body that all I want to do is sit in something like this for the rest of my life. And I wouldn't just sit, I'd also dream about myself sitting in an enormous palace, in an easy chair, unaware of either my body or of my very existence, it's so free of care. And I don't even know what I want because there's no longer anything that I could want.

Oh, I could sit from morning till night in something like this. The world would indeed be beautiful if I didn't have to live in it, but needed only to marvel at it from an armchair, contemplate it, be moved by it and by myself. Ailments afflict me one after the other like plagues afflict the earth. One hasn't yet passed, and another is already upon me. I still haven't learned to live with one, before another is hard on its heels. A headache wears off and hot flushes, cold sweats come along. The burning ceases in my gullet, and breathlessness bears down on my chest like a stone. But I'm not complaining. I know it's not to make up for my sins. It's only fate desiring to single me out, and there's now no other way it can. Anyhow, you know it's been like this ever since I was little. The sun always disagreed with me and the shade was always too cool. Or when the limes were in bloom, or when the rains set in. For me there was never a right time. Never a right place. The best place is still here, within these walls, because it's what I know. And so I've become one with my chair. I'd even regret it if I had to get up now. Though all I do is sit and wait for health to come. But what good is it to me?

Suddenly I leap to my feet. Look around. I imagine someone is in the room. As though he'd been here a long time and had been observing me, eavesdropping, laughing into his sleeve at my expense. Perhaps hidden somewhere. Perhaps behind the curtain. I peep behind the curtain. Perhaps concealed by the doors. I peep behind one wing of the dining-room doors, then the other. I do a circuit of the room. I peer underneath the grand piano, under the table. Nowhere a living soul. However, I fail to recover my peace of mind. The fact that I can't find anyone just worsens my torment. I can no longer believe in myself. I don't even want to. I'm not capable of it. I can't tell if it's my own fear scaring me off, or some great longing for something – I don't know what – which gets more and more intense, more and more exacerbated. I feel like saying something, I don't know what, yet more than anything I feel I want to mimic this senseless prattle of mine, and then mimic my own mimicry.

I glance, without meaning to, at the old gentleman in the picture sitting in his chair. He sits, just as before, full of lifeless gravity, his haunted eyes still smouldering with scorn. He sits, yet looks as if he'll come back to life at any moment, screech his senile squeal, rub his hands together in glee, slap his knees.

But I can hear my father's voice as if he were standing right by my ear. Oh, Jacob, if only you'd put your mind to being a valet one day, I'd die peacefully, knowing you'd become a human being at last. Think about it, Jacob. Make an effort, Jacob. Pray, Jacob. Take the young ladies a little bird someday, tell them it's lost its mother, and you'll touch their hearts. Be there to take her ladyship's hand when she needs it, so she may remember you. And if the coach horses should bolt and you happen at that moment to be herding your sheep along the road towards them, then spare neither your legs nor hands, but leap to it, cling to the horses' muzzles with all your might, hands, teeth, whatever you can, and don't let go, don't let go. Remember. Let them even trample you underfoot, it's still better than the life we lead. And if you should save them, then God will have already blessed you with good fortune. For only death befriends those such as we. Not God, nor his lordship, nor our dreams of drudgery, only death and death alone. Don't ever take the name of death in vain, children of mine, nor you either, wife.

And it was that evening that it happened, when we came in as usual from the fields, night-time almost, and we sat around the kitchen like roosting hens. And there were a lot of us, for our parents had spawned children God knows how and when because we were all about the same age. We had nothing to light the room with, but then we didn't need to see each other. Each had his hunger to chew over in the dark. We sat as silent as the grave. Not one of us dared to speak, in case he unintentionally let slip something about food. Then hunger would raise its ugly head within us, irritate, infuriate us, and we, God's little innocents, would leap like wolves at each other's throats. Only Mother wandered around the room pretending she was cooking something, rearranged the saucepans, banged the cupboard doors, washed something up, but we all knew she only did it because she had to. There came a moment when her shadow drew close to Father's. Here you are, eat it. Give them some. There's a lot of them, but only one of you. Here, eat it. I can do without! He stood up. Began to grope around in the dark for his cap. Where are you going? It's night. Time to go to bed. There's somewhere I've got to go. Somewhere I've got to go! I'm going to the palace! I'm going to see his lordship! We heard him hauling his scythe off the wall. The sound of the blade scraping against something rang out like an ill omen. We cringed in horror. Fell silent. Huddled together in the darkness. Mother too was cowering in a corner and wasn't so much crying as stifling her tears inside her. We sat up perhaps until midnight. Suddenly Mother ordered us to kneel and say our prayers after her. At first we said them loudly, vying with one another, then more and more softly, more and more softly. Mother alone offered up the prayer, and we just mumbled till it eventually sent us to sleep. And after us, she too fell asleep. We were woken only by the watchman when day was already breaking. He stole into the room like a ghost and began to shake Mother, shouting, Your man's no more! Your man's no more! Wake up, your man's no more! Lying in the flower-bed in front of the palace! Cut his throat with a scythe. He said he'd bumped into Father in the flower-bed, hadn't recognized him at first and had lain in wait, thinking he was someone come to steal the roses. And he told us we had to collect the body before his lordship woke up.

Oh, if I were the lord and master, then I wouldn't wake up till around midday. And I'd go to bed with the sun. And if the day were overcast or if it were pouring with rain, then I wouldn't get up at all. For the best place is in bed when it's raining outside. Splashing against the window-panes, grey, cold. But you are in bed, in the warm. I'd look out of the window bespattered with rain, and feel pleased that life treated me so well. And I'd even get a perverse satisfaction that it was pouring out there, that out there they were getting soaked to the skin under their sacks, festering in the rain when I was here in my bedchamber, in my palace, in my silks, lace, eiderdowns; that out there they were freezing to death when I was in the warm. And if I got tired of the rain, then I'd order the curtains to be drawn, the lamps to be lit, a sunny day to be created, or a bright evening. And I'd order a fire to be made in the hearth, let them out there get wetter still in this rain, freeze, rot. What do I care? I'd order something to be read to me, for why should such a great lord have to make the effort to read himself? It wouldn't even be the done thing, in front of the servants. At the very most I might get up for a bit in the evening, go for a wander round the palace. But I'd get back into bed for supper. And let them feed me. Let them feed me. And I'd make such a fuss, my God, such a fuss. I'm not eating that because it's too salty, or that, what kind of food do you call this? Let the dogs have it. And that, what on earth's that? That's supposed to be food? What are you feeding me on? You're obviously trying to put me off my food. Or, God forbid, stop me falling asleep. Oh, I know you, you villains! You're stalking my dreams. You want to see me spend the whole night tossing and turning, moaning, groaning, maybe even blathering incredible things, maybe confessing my sins, beseeching someone for forgiveness. You want to eavesdrop, hear the things that torment me. But you'll never have that satisfaction! Get the hell out of here with your filthy tricks! Or you'd like to see me spend the whole night long falling from a great height. That at least might relieve you of some of your resentment. What? Or climbing on to a pebble like an ant, climbing up and flying away. And so on till dawn breaks. Climbing up and flying away. Or walking on and on until I wake up, without progressing a single step forward. Or screaming that I'm being buried alive, and nobody will be able to hear my voice except yourselves. And what fun it would all be for you, oh, what fun! It would be as though God had at last heard your prayers, you idiots. Ha! Ha! Ha!

Or I'll summon a valet and say. Well now, tell me what's been going on in the palace. Only speak slowly and precisely. Since morning. Or no. Go away. Get out. I feel tired. Tell me tomorrow. Just bring me my drops before I go to sleep. And remember, don't overdo them. Or my heart will start pounding later like a hammer. And remind my secretary to write that letter to the Prince at long last. And to write it nicely. Let it begin thus: In the name of the Father, Son and Holy Ghost, Amen. In the opening words of this letter I enquire, Prince, after your health, and whether that mare of yours has foaled yet. No, no, what am I going on about, my God! It's not meant to be like that, but like this: Your Excellency, Honoured Prince and Sire, for a long while I have owed you these several words, but time, please forgive me, which has made us all its subjects, has not permitted me to put pen to paper before now. Or hang on a moment. Perhaps you could go and eavesdrop on what her ladyship is up to. And if you can't hear anything, then peep through the keyhole. I'm sure that priest is with her again. That priest again. But what can I do? When I tell her I've had enough of the parasite, she replies that he's a man of God. Because he's devoted his whole life to spreading the word. That they talk exclusively about God. That he's not interested in anything except her troubled soul. And his effect on her is, apparently, like that of water from a health-giving spring. But what do I care about water from springs? I cringe in my compunction, bitterly regretting that I succumbed so easily to my suspicions. But she still struts about afterwards, offended, haughty, unhappy, won't let herself be placated, shuts herself in her room for whole days and nights on end. I sometimes spend all evening knocking, whimpering, My lady, my own, say something at least. It's me. Don't you know me?

It's me. I can't go on without you. I've come to make peace. Do you hear? Say something. Sigh at least, so I can hear you're still there. But she stays silent beyond the door as if she wasn't there, though I know she is there. I can see her in my mind's eye. I can sense her like a dog.

Well, and so? How was it? Come on, tell me. Is she sitting with the priest? And what else? Are they saying their prayers? Couldn't you hear whether she was laughing or not? And how was he speaking to her? Wasn't he saying, My most marvellous of women, you, your image could be in the church instead of the saints? One could pray to you day and night? Put one's trust in you alone out of all the saints? Accept even non-forgiveness from you? Confess one's sins more sincerely than to God? Wasn't that what he was saying? Oh, because a priest like him knows how to talk. Not like ordinary mortals. I've never been able to talk like that. Even when I work it out beforehand, rehearse it like a prayer, I only have to take one look at her or she raise her eyes to look at me and everything gets distorted, I flounder, awash with my own shame. But I would so much like to tell her beautiful things rather than simply stare at her, pine for her, attend with bated breath her nightly footsteps as they approach my door and pass by, approach and pass by, whilst I remain there tormenting myself that somewhere else she is opening a door, lighting a lamp, now sitting in front of a mirror, brushing her hair. And when I reach the moment when she takes off her clothes, I'm fairly writhing in pain.

For we sleep in separate rooms. As befits gentlefolk. So that one half sleeps here, the other there. So that one half sleeps in one wing of the palace, the other in the other. So the entire expanse of the palace stretches between them. So they only ever meet over supper, over music in the drawing-room, when guests are present. Understand, stupid? Their lordships can't do it in one bed like you lot out there, three, four to a bed, heads together, legs together, parents and children, brothers and sisters. And nothing but sin comes out of that.

And she, when she peels off her finery, she doesn't do it in order to go to sleep, I know very well it's not in order to go to sleep, but just in order to torment me, shame me with her body till it hurts, humiliate me. For she knows, even though I'm in my own room, that I can see her every movement. And it's in front of me she undresses, even though I'm not there beside her. It's in front of me she speaks. Ah, how sleepy I am. How tired. What a long day it's been.

And she peels off her clothes so listlessly, yet so lovingly, as if she were sated feasting on herself. Strokes her own neck, embraces her own arms, takes her breasts in her palms, drawing them into herself, caressing them, even though it's all rightfully mine. She turns on all the lights, illuminating the walls, the ceiling above her, then parades round the room in bright sunlight flaunting her breasts before her own self, her hips, her nakedness, shameless almost, yet so resplendent. She excites herself with her parading around; I count for nothing. Anyway, who knows whether such a great lady isn't sufficient unto herself?

And when at last she sinks into sleep, only then do I begin to dream of going to her. I lie down beside her soundlessly like a cat, beside her body, against her open side, in her warmth, in her heavy slumber. And all night long I simply hold my breath and listen to her breasts, hips, legs, hands, her hair luxuriating above me, her heart beating inside my head. But when I hear that she's dreaming, definitely dreaming, dreaming somewhere miles away from me and in no hurry to return to us, and when there's still a while to go before dawn, then I secretly touch her, unbeknown to her, but so as not to ruffle her dream, touch her as I would a sore place, just for a moment, for the flicker of an eye, for the most fleeting of thoughts. And that satisfies me for my whole night with her, for the whole of my life with her. And when morning comes, I won't let her get up so as to prolong the memory of that night. Won't let her, saying that for her it's still not daybreak, but only first light. Stay awhile. Day has not yet shaken off the night. Chill still pervades the air. Dews have not yet dispelled. The sun only now begins its life anew. Stay awhile, and the day will be shorter. And she replies so sweetly: Oh, my husband, my lord. I am overwhelmed by sadness that you are going off to your rooms and leaving me all alone in my bed. Lie at my feet so we can look at one another.

But when grief wells up in me because of her, then I come to her blind drunk, legless, propping myself up in the doorway, my mouth full of incoherent mumblings. But inside I feel like an injured child.

Full of pain that I can see her, that she's mine, that I'd been coming to her, to her and her alone, singing to her, singing all the way from the tavern, through the dark night, through dogs howling and people roused from their sleep. I haul her out of her murky corner. She lays into me: You're drunk again! So I swipe her across the face. Again and again with both hands. Mercilessly. Throughout the whole house. Oh, I'd like to give her a good hiding, thrash her like the peasants thrash their wives. And I'd neither let her call upon God, nor even breathe a sigh. And as if that wasn't enough, I'd chase her outside with an axe. I'm going to kill you, I'm going to kill you, let's finish it once and for all! She grovels at my feet, clasping her hands together before me, saying never again, never ever again, as her doe eyes sink away into puddles, ponds, lakes, leaving but a glimmer behind. Then I wrench a lamp from the wall, still fully aglow, and hold it up to her face, shining it upon those tears. I grab her madly by the hand. Come on, we're going! I feel her dainty fingers crunch in my palm. Come on, we're going! And I drag her outside. And we fly off into the night, the dark hollow night. Me in front, she following with her hair streaming, her tears, her instincts warning of something bad, but as obedient as a pet animal. Where are we going? Dear God, where are we going? Ah, but I know now, where we're going. To the crossroads, to the wayside cross. There I make her get down on her knees. Swear, you bitch! Then I force her, like a dog, there, in the dew.

And when pain and resentment well up inside me again, then I don't say anything, simply pull her to her feet from under my legs, wind her plait around my fist, and we walk away into the dark deep night, beyond the village, across the fields, towards the river, there to drown the both of us.

I can still hear her terror-crazed voice. My husband, my lord, why do you look at me so distrustfully? I cast my eyes round the room. Not a living soul in sight. I'm surrounded by desolation, and in this desolation everything suddenly seems somehow alien to me. These walls, the portraits, the furniture darkened with age, the enormous grand piano in the corner, the whole of this palace round about me. Though maybe it's disbelief making itself heard inside me, and in moments of disbelief you tend to doubt even yourself; maybe it's just some momentary weakness, maybe exhaustion, maybe fear. But what have I got to be afraid of? Here I am. But where is she? Where is she? How can such a vast palace exist without her? Empty. It simply can't be true that there's nobody here, nobody. Only me on my own. Alone in all this enormity. What would I do all on my own? Sorrow would have devoured me long ago, grief for someone else's shadow, for someone's voice, for the memory of them. And yet here I am. I imagine that in a minute someone somewhere will slam a door, a peal of carefree laughter will ring out, piano playing will reach my ears, that I'll hear someone's footfalls passing on the other side of the wall, someone knocking on my door. Perhaps it'll be my valet. I'd recognize him from his breathing. He always knocks so timidly as if it were the first time, each time as if it were the first time he had to confront me.

I reach for the bell standing on the chest of drawers. I ring. It resounds with a dry rattle. I wait. I ring again, louder this time. Then I ring to all corners of the house. I even find it gratifying. Loud, impatient, almost castigatory. I'm not certain anyone can hear me out there, so I go into the adjoining chamber, too, just to make sure. I go out into the corridor, ringing more and more persistently, letting it echo round the walls, doors, for it's already beginning to annoy me that no one answers. Anger me even, for no doubt the wretch has fallen asleep. Otherwise he'd be coming running at the double, bowing and scraping, chicken-hearted in his eyes, fearful lest I should sack him, begging forgiveness. It's always like that, even when he's just a tiny bit late, when he misses the first bell. Then he stands before me trembling, stooping, so out of breath he can't articulate his words and simply reaches for my hand. I almost tear it away from him, from his shaking bony hands, as if they were claws, from right under his lips almost. For I don't like it when they kiss my hand. They seem to be showing you respect, but they're only trying to ingratiate themselves. Though people say of me, What kind of lord can this be who doesn't allow his hand to kissed? It must be because he's afraid of us; not because he loves us; because he hates us, not because he loves us; his conscience must be eating away at him.

I stare into his scared chicken eyes and feel my anger melt away, yet I'd been intending to give him a good telling off, shout the roof down, blaspheme, even chase him from my chamber. But now I feel sorry for him and try to smile at him indulgently, but he shuts his eyes from me. So I tackle him gently, as best I can:

Don't be afraid, I didn't want anything from you. I simply wanted you to put in an appearance. Because I feel sad, all on my own. I wait in the hope that someone might come, utter a word, console me. But no one does, no one. That you might sniff me out like a dog and come of your own accord, if only to ask if I needed anything. To see if I'd dozed off in my chair, and then you'd put a pillow under my head and straighten my legs. I kept ringing and ringing. I'd already given up hope of your ever coming. I thought you too had abandoned me in my darkest hour. I was already saying to myself, so much for your loyalty. And perhaps you'd robbed me as well, as a parting gesture. You're all the same. The whole lot of you. Obviously you'd imagined I'd taken flight with my frothing horses. That I'd take flight even before this war came upon us. Bearing my terror away with me. Without a word of thanks for your devoted service. Without entrusting all this to you, making you look after it as if it were your own, so that not even a needle would go missing. Is there no one left who'd remain loyal to me, is this the end of loyalty? The palace stands wide open, and everything is yours now. Perhaps you've already buried me and dance on my grave singing Alleluia. Who knows how far you'll go, perhaps you spit on my name already. Come on, let's go on the rampage, his lordship's no more! What's that? Well go on, out with it. You, you! Don't be so scared. Don't shake like that. Oh, evidently you've a guilty conscience. Open those eyes of yours. And have a look. Have a look. Here I am. God has spared me, unscathed, healthy. No dream, no apparition. Me. For it's not so easy to get rid of me. Me. Though you might like to erase me from your memory, I shall live on in your humility, in your unfulfilled desires, in your fear, in your dreams, maybe even in your missing of me. It's only you who believed too readily in your curses, hates, prayers, omens, presentiments, portents. In all their shapes and sizes. And none of them worth a farthing. And you imagined I was no longer here to lord it over you. But I, you see, am still here. Again you've been too smart for your own good, idiots! Now you're simply laughable. Ha! Ha! Ha! Laughable. For where was I supposed to have fled to? Where? And what for? I was only out shooting. You were already imagining God knows what, but I, as you see, am only returning from a shoot. And I'm waiting for someone to pull off my boots, take my coat, bring me a warm drink, and perhaps ask me how it went. Any luck, your lordship? Yes, yes. Though what kind of shooting can you call it nowadays? Bare fields and less and less game. So many fine gentlemen setting out together, my God, so many magnificent horses, with their beaters, with their dogs, every gun more splendid than the next. And after what? Hares! Partridges! Yet when we come across a stag no one can tell who shot it. More bullets in it than there are gunmen. It won't be long before we're going out to hunt ants. For we already have to breed our own pheasants and let them loose in the fields, so they can return to the wild. A sense of shame sweeps over you when you fire at a thing like that, which you can't even see properly, which runs away right under your nose and which you only realize afterwards you were meant to kill. And even when you do kill it, you still don't know for certain whether it fell from your bullet or simply from fear. And there's so much death in it all, it robs you of any joy. Only how can I not go hunting when I'm the lord and master? People will say immediately, It's because of types like you that we're a dying breed. And you yourself? Yes, you yourself? How, at the end of the day, can you know who you are? Supposing you get fed up with one thing, become unaccustomed to another, or your conscience forbids something else? How do you know who you are? Every time I raise my gun to my eye, I resolve only to take aim, lower the barrel, and let whatever it is run away. But I fire nevertheless, because if I don't fire there will always be somebody who'll fire instead of me and who'll also spread the word, that it was he who fired, and then we'll all have to take our caps off to him and listen humbly till he finishes his story. There's never a shortage of types like that.

Oh, but once upon a time hunting expeditions were really something. Once upon a time nature herself cried out to be ravished. She was insatiable. Like an old maid. Oh, those were times long before you can remember. Maybe you used to hear about them. Instead of bedtime stories. For those were the days. Beautiful days. Expedition after expedition. No time of year was the wrong time. Winter or no winter. Harvest or no harvest. And who cared if the peasants came to you later bewailing their trampled fields, plundered homes, violated daughters? Who in those days ever paid them any attention? Idiots. Incapable of comprehending any kind of joy. Virtue, land, grub – that was their Holy Trinity. And I used to scatter it to the four winds.

And such a hunt, my dear, was a real holiday. A holiday, understand? None of your Christmases, Easters, but a genuine holiday, sublime. The huntsmen would assemble at the meet in their hundreds, my God! Princes no less, counts, squires. With their servants, horses, dogs. Swarming like ants in the forecourt. They cheer and fire in the air, dogs bark, horses whinny. Then they all move off into the forest. And the palace ladies wave their handkerchiefs. A great lump lodges in your throat; you imagine you're off to the wars. Into the fierce and bloody fray. You're a knight in armour. A warrior. Burning with ardour, almost, to fall in battle. And may you be slain in the forecourt. So the ladies can see you. Those were the days. Such a hunt would often last a week or more. Not like today. When you set out in the morning and return in the afternoon.

But there's one hunting expedition I don't think I'll ever forget. And before it took place I'd had bad dreams, my horse broke a leg when it was being led out of the stable, and a gun on the wall fired of its own accord even though it was unloaded. Just imagine, unloaded yet it fired! Nobody even touched it. I sensed something was going to happen right from the start. We kept riding on and on. It was already getting on for midday, but the forest was still deserted, silent as the tomb. No sign even of a lone bird or a hare leaping out from nowhere, only the desolation which got denser and denser as though the forest were overgrown with desolation, not trees. No one uttered a word but I could see they were all uneasy. Their faces clouded by uncertainty, perhaps by fear. Many would have liked to turn back. Many would have been prepared to sacrifice their own horses, if only to hear the flapping of wings in the trees and the crash somewhere in the undergrowth. I myself was haunted by a worsening presentiment. Moreover I'd not forgotten my horse, the gun, my dreams. I looked round at the other huntsmen. They were all staring at me. Oh, there's something not right, I thought to myself. Is the forest enchanted or what? I ordered the beaters to scatter amongst the trees and start shrieking as if they were game. And the servants to chase after them. And the bugler to sound the horn till he was winded. They scattered like I'd ordered them. And it was no ordinary shriek they raised, but hell itself, all around us. Bellowing, screaming, howling like wolves. No one spared himself. With their sticks they pummelled the tree trunks, the earth, the brushwood, until in the end they grew so demented they began to sing like drunkards, blaspheme to the whole forest, shout out ominous threats of revenge against all the things they hated, whilst every now and again one of them would burst into laughter or tears, the barking of dogs. The forest filled with alarm. The dogs uttered a squeal and nestled close to the horses. The horses twisted and turned on the spot, lost any sense of direction, wrested their heads free of the reins.

Every so often one or other of the huntsmen rode up to me, pleading. Silence them, your lordship. Our mounts are taking fright. The dogs are scared stiff. Silence them, your lordship, for otherwise you'll never silence them.

But I replied, Let them make the most of it. Let them make the most of it. For anger had already got its grip on me. Anger at the whole situation. Though I sensed that if we failed to catch at least a hare or if some bird didn't flap its wings, something bad would happen. For something had to happen. Some of them were shifting uneasily in their saddles, getting ready to shoot, clutching their guns in their hands. Beneath me my horse too was fractious; it walked like it was dancing, tossed me out of my seat, shook the reins again and again, snorted. What could it all mean? Maybe we'd start arguing or, God forbid, shoot the beaters as if they were wolves, wild boar, stags, hares, wildfowl. Or else we'd start shooting one another. And with good reason. If only due to the fact that it had befallen us to be alive at one and the same time, and all of us equally rich. That we had to put up with each other. And had to be courteous too, though in our hearts we had consigned one another to hell long ago, because there was always some unpleasantness going on between us, not to mention the various minor animosities, petty jealousies, gibes, sly remarks, lost or won.

I watched my neighbour. Yet he was no worse than the rest.

Besides, he was sitting so docile on his horse that the horse seemed to move without him. He once won a village off me at cards. But I later won back two villages plus a stallion. Anyway, he won honestly. Put down his ace on top of my queen, even felt embarrassed, poor fellow, yet he spoke up. Forgive me, my friend, but your card owes me everything. For a fleeting moment I caught a glimpse of his head falling from the smoking barrels of my gun. Of his startled horse tearing itself free in a single bound from under his body, and that body tumbling into the brushwood where dogs laid into it savagely. A shudder passed through me, for my neighbour was staring straight at me as if touched by a premonition.

Oh, something undoubtedly would have happened, for we were already nearing sunset and there was still no sign of any game. Just this deserted forest stretching on and on. Deserted forest. Deserted forest. And ourselves trapped inside it with hell in our hearts, and all around us the beaters collapsing from the strain of their screams. Maybe we were even longing for something to happen, even for the worst.

And then there appeared before our eyes an enormous stag. So enormous it was hard to believe it was a stag and not a phantom. We thought it was perhaps some strange bush in the midst of the clearing, or that we were being charmed by a vision. For the dogs caught no whiff of it, neither did the horses sense it, nor did it alarm the beaters. It was grazing peacefully, quite unconcerned, and didn't even raise its head to look at us, the brute! But after a while everything in our midst began to teem with joy, excitement, cries. The dogs went crazy, the horses started to dance beneath us, the beaters fell on their knees and offered up to Heaven prayers of thanksgiving. But then alarm began to spread among us. How come the stag doesn't run away? Doesn't raise its head even, doesn't take a look at us? Just nibbles the grass. Whatever kind of a stag can it be? Perhaps it's not a stag. Rather too big for a stag.

I don't know what came over me. Perhaps some instinct told me that any moment we'd all make a bolt for it, hot on each other's heels, into the forest, and those of us on horseback would be the first. And imagine what kind of stories the beaters would spread about us then. I proposed, therefore, that we formed a tight ring around the stag and sounded the horn. So the horn was sounded. Sonorous, joyous, soaring to the skies, but so awesome it seemed to be courting death, coaxing death as it approached from out of the trees, guiding it towards us. The sound of the horn sent shivers up my spine. I felt that the sound was bearing me away somewhere along with my horse, into ever-thicker thickets, distancing me from the huntsmen, the dogs, the beaters, the forest clearing with the stag grazing in it. That I could no longer see them even, no longer hear them. That there was nothing but a resounding stillness all around me, a dense green stillness. And that nothing threatened me now in the boundlessness of this stillness, not even the memory of myself. I felt relief seeping into me from out of that sound, from out of the trees, from out of everywhere.

Suddenly I heard the fretful voice of one of the huntsmen right beside me. He almost brushed his horse against mine. What on earth are you thinking of, my lord? Surely you can see it's not going to run away, it's not afraid of the horn or of the dogs' barking. A devil, not a stag.

And a moment later another huntsman. His face dripping with sweat. His voice brimming with alarm. What do you think you're up to, my lord? We're not going to fire, are we, if it doesn't run away?

But what else can we do? I said calmly. We've come here to hunt, my dear fellow. And you will be the first to fire.

Me?

Yes, you.

He fired, but in such earnest the shot landed in the foliage. Those that followed did likewise. With tears in their eyes, they fired and missed, cursing me, swearing. All old shots, yet they missed. Their hands trembled as though they were taking aim for the first time.

Someone rode up and gave me some friendly advice. Let's chase him away a bit, my lord. As you can see, you could reach him with the barrel of your gun. Even if it were just over there, into those bushes. He'd be camouflaged a bit and not so obvious.

After a while someone else was leaning towards me and yelling his head off. Do something, my lord! For God's sake, we can't go on like this! Can't you see what a nerve he's got? He's sniffing us out!

And after him yet another. But I didn't even glance in his direction. You're insulting us, my dear fellow, you're ordering us to fire as if it were a tree trunk, not an animal! It's a disgrace aiming from such close range. What scant regard you must have for our honour, our consciences!

And after him there came another, and another, then a tenth. They rode up at a gallop almost, yelling, seething with indignation. Till my horse took fright and shook so much beneath me I had to shorten the reins with a jerk to make it stand still.

Someone flew past screaming, There's no way out! He's too close! Our hands shake, tears spring to our eyes!

But there was a way out, someone advised, almost whispering in my ear. Let's back off on one side, best of all from the south, and he'll make his own way off.

But I sat there in silence, calm and collected, for I couldn't tell them, after all, that it wasn't them I had it in for but myself. I was moved to pity as I watched them missing, firing into the ground, at the animal's hooves, into the forest, into the air, as though they were doing it on purpose, just to spite me.

At one point I glanced at the Judge. He was standing beside me on his gelding and smiling secretly to himself, as though he found the whole thing highly amusing, most of all because it was I who had caused such havoc among the huntsmen. For I was sure he was passing judgement on my pride. He was startled by my glance, screwed up his eyes, leaned towards me and spoke. I have even better advice, your lordship. Let's give him chase, and his heart will burst of its own accord.

At this precise moment a shot ripped the gun out of somebody's hands and his horse stood stock-still. The beaters collapsed in a great burst of laughter, which travelled through the forest like a wind. My horse reared, thrust back its head, twisted and turned, so that it took all my strength to pin it to the ground. Hand over the rifles to the beaters! I screamed, beside myself with rage. Hand them over, let them rejoice!

But amongst the beaters panic broke out, lamentations. They began to emerge from out of the trees, clamouring all around me, from out of the bushes, from out of the earth, wailing, crowds of them swelling into a heap, a mound almost.

We are but beaters, your lordship. We are here but to frighten the fowl, the game, as you commanded us, heedful of where it moves among the trees and betrays itself by sound or sighting. We are here but to beg the Lord God to grant you good fortune, for your good fortune is ours also. We are here but to scare the game. We are like unto these our rattles, like unto our cries ringing throughout the forest. Like unto our thrashing of the trees, the brushwood, the earth. Like unto our howling in place of the howling game. So what do we want with your holy guns? We no longer feel any feeling in these our hands, whether they be ours or not ours, whether they be moulded of wood or of soil, whether they know pain, how they know pain, whether they know no pain at all. And everything swims, dances before our eyes, tears are shed, yet we see nothing, your lordship. So what do we want with your holy guns? We, whom rivers engulf and hailstorms smash like eggs, whom winters benumb like baby birds, we and our children, whom wars raze and pillage, we, whose wives and daughters they rape and slaughter, inflicting upon us worse punishments still so we might be delivered from our original sin, from the power of Satan and all his enticements which lie in wait for us everywhere. So what do we want with your holy guns? We, who are but fodder for the plagues that sweep over us like tempests, whose lips are but for praying, whose crawling multitude swarms for none but God, yet reaps for death a rich harvest. So what do we want with your holy guns? We, who are all like unto Izdi, your lordship, one of our own, whom you once lost at cards along with his wife, and his children, and his free will, which our Lord God – and yours, and yours, your lordship – had promised unto him, because your card did not look kindly upon our misfortune, on our tears and suffering, though we prayed for you in our homes, because your stable-boy brought us the dread news that a great game was in progress in your palace, oh, a great game where entire fortunes were at stake, consciences, souls. But clearly God chose to ignore us on that occasion. So what do we want with your holy guns? We, the bedrock of all misery and misfortune on this earth, so lowly we know not how to distinguish ourselves from our own beasts. We, whose one solace is that we brought nothing into this world and will leave nothing behind, and perhaps, God willing, some merciful pestilence will come along and release some of us from ourselves even more swiftly. Though the parish priest tries to comfort us at Holy Mass, promising that eternity will not elude the more devout amongst us because we are deserving of it. But in return for what, your lordship, for what? For breeding, as they say, like rabbits, or like a scourge, for what else are we pre-ordained to be if not the scourge of the earth? What do we want with your holy guns? We, who curse our fathers for having given birth to us and our own children for having been born, curse them because children will be born of them also, and children of their children, and of those children more children without end, remembering in so doing, that just as we curse them so they will curse us, for a curse hangs over us, your lordship. We, upon whom your favour smiles, your mercy and compassion, your lordship, when one of our wives or daughters slips into your bed and you endow her with your seed, for then we in our eternal hunger get at least a handful of flour in return, a measure of corn in return, a rabbit's skin, a rag, or even a calf if one of them should satisfy you, our most merciful lord and master. And in return for that your eye rests more kindly upon us. So be of goodwill and give us your consent, for we came here not to kill but to scare the game. Increase our woes threefold, but spare us our consciences.

Enough! Enough! I shut my eyes. I wish neither to see nor hear. Even for a moment. I feel turmoil in my head. Even under my eyelids, in their dark shadows, I wish to see nothing. But I can see them nevertheless, clustered together in a tight crush, barely a few feet away, as if they were waiting in the dining-room doorway for me to open my eyes. But when I do open them, I see round about me nothing but the warm radiance of the afternoon. One of its rays falls on my knee. I feel I want to stroke this radiance as if it were a cat come to sit on my lap. Clasp its tiny purring head and caress it. I even stroke it, my finger held above it, barely touching it, so as not to frighten it away. I want to show it to someone. I look over my shoulder. Ah, it's you! Well then, what was I talking about? Hang on. Hang on. What happened next with that stag? Don't you remember? Well yes, I suppose I fired and killed it. No, it didn't happen quite like that. I'd had a kind of premonition, hadn't I? My horse had broken its leg. My gun had gone off on its own. So it couldn't have been simply one, two, three, and it's all over, You can't pull the wool over my eyes. You want to go already, is that it? Well, just listen a little longer.

So I dismounted. Yes, that's how it was. I remember now. So I dismounted. Walked up to the stag, maybe a pace away, half a pace. But he just went on browsing peacefully. Well, would you believe it, browsing as if nothing was happening! He didn't even want to take a look at me. Did you ever see such a stag? So then I positioned my gun very close to his head, and I don't know how it happened. I swear I didn't shoot. It fired of its own accord, as though on my behalf. I didn't make the slightest movement. I didn't even feel I had the will to do anything. I simply heard the shot and saw the stag suddenly collapse on to its front legs, and then its whole body slump into the green sward. But that was still not the end of his death. Don't imagine that. His eyes clung on to life for a long while yet. He opened them wide to encompass the whole forest and refused to forsake the world. I saw myself in those eyes, the whole length of my body, my gun still smoking under my arm, green with the reflected green of the forest. And beside him I was so small, ridiculous almost. I felt almost disembodied. I didn't feel as though I was there where I stood, but only there in those eyes setting beyond the hills, beyond the forests, brimming with tears and slowly fading away tear by tear. I'd never realized till then that animals cry. Just imagine, they cry. I never realized. Only this crying of theirs is turned towards death. The tears continued to seep from his eyes for some time, though his body had long been motionless. I saw myself in those eyes, rooted to the spot where I stood, vanquished, without a glimmer of will, without a single thought, without any desire for anything. I didn't dare make the slightest movement, not even to lower my gun from view. It was as much as I could do just to see myself there. It seemed to me that I myself was seeing the last vision there would ever be of me, which no one apart from myself would ever see again. That I was seeing my own death in the eyes of the animal. I felt at that moment almost in league with this death, even grateful to it for having imparted to me some of its brilliance, for permitting me to stand and confront myself as if in the last ray of light traversing the forest, in an intimacy so intimate that I felt at one with it.

That death affected everyone present. For when I turned away from the stag's eyes, once they had finally set, I saw they had all dismounted to a man and were standing with their feet in the green sward, their heads bared, the barrels of their guns pointing to the ground. And the beaters as well. The beaters as well.

But why am I bothering to tell you all this? What do you know about death, you fool? Go on, tell me what you know about death. You see, you're gawping at me as though you'd only just found out from me that there's such a thing as death. Well, there is such a thing. And are you afraid of death? What? Oh, death doesn't like it when people are afraid of it. Because they who fear it, revile it, strip it of its majesty. It's a disgrace even to put such people to death, for it's rather like the executioner being entrusted with the killing of mice. And death is at its most merciless towards such as they. It doesn't even let you die at the appointed hour, in the presence of your grieving loved ones, with candles burning at your bedside, in linen especially laundered for its coming. But it spins out your dying for days on end, weeks, years, until it creeps up on you when you're least expecting it, and rather than killing you with its breath it casts you into an abyss, maybe drags you along on a rope, maybe doesn't even let you die, though it no longer allows you to live. And out of revenge it still tramples you into the ground, treading you into the soil. So afterwards no one knows whether death slew you, or whether it was your own fear, whether you died, or whether you simply vanished into thin air.

I am not afraid of death. The only thing I'm afraid of is dying any old how. For afterwards people might have their doubts about who I was, whether it was his lordship who'd died, or his servant. And that would be a fate worse than death. I wouldn't be able to bear it. I'd return, even if it was from the next world, in order to die all over again in a way which befits me. I'd return, even if nothing else was to befall me apart from this death. Even if I had to walk through the whole of the eternity that divides that world from this. The whole of that infinite blackness. Without the sky above me or the earth beneath my feet. Without even knowing which way to go. But merely possessed by my longing. Without bread, water, sleep, air. Through rains, blizzards. On my knees. On all fours. Drained. Wrecked. As though tidings of great import had chosen me as their messenger. I'd return. Even if I had to go through hell to pay for it. I'd return. I'd plead with God, and if not with God then with Satan, to let me return for this death of mine. For that one day, hour, moment. What do you mean? Go on, tell me, what do you mean? Surely they'll let me? So I can see myself die in a way that befits me, and then breathe my last. I'd return. Because a beautiful death is sometimes worth a whole lifetime. Oh, sometimes death is all that remains of your life. Sometimes you have to wait until death to realize you're human. And as for the damned, it's invariably only death that makes them human; it's only in death that they're born, only in death that they're struck by the blinding revelation that they too were people.

No doubt you're having a good laugh there on the side, what? Laugh then, laugh, you fool. For you've got to be equal to death. So laugh, laugh, while you can. Well, whoever bartered an extra day from it, an hour, moment, sigh? Who? So what's the point of being afraid? You just sow fear inside yourself, but the seeds of fear are as prolific as the corncockle. They immediately shoot up rampant inside you, propagate wildly, outgrow all your hopes, joys, desires, entwine your heart, ensnare your mind, take root in your bowels and eat away at you before death draws near. For what is death? Go on, tell me, what is death? You see, all you known about it is that you're afraid of it. Precious little. He! He! He! But just the thought that such great possibilities lie before you, that you could live or not live, is somehow so very soothing. For even if you were to live for ever, how would you ever avenge your life? Well, how? Tell me. Therefore death can sometimes be a great temptation. So you see, you see. Feel any better, what? Oh, sometimes it pays to have a chat with an intelligent man.

And do you know how I'd like to die? I'd like it to be at this time of year. High summer. Would that the day were sunny, just like today, sweltering hot, sultry. And the sunlight glittering like gold. And I am lying in the drawing-room. Right in the middle. Opposite the door. So I can see everything. And would that the room had grown a little melancholy for my death. I am lying on my wide bed. On one of those beds wide enough for four, so that even when you unfurl your arms like wings, you still can't reach the edges. And in bedlinen white as snow, so white you almost want to die in it because you imagine you'll remain for ever in such whiteness. And this will be my death. As though death were nothing more than this white linen caressing me all over my body. And my head propped high on the pillows. An aura of dignity, not of death. My eyes burn with a piercing brilliance. A kind of agonized composure smoulders within them. A kind of bemused stare, gazing into the far, far distance, penetrating people, walls, the world, perhaps already seeing death. And everyone around me shedding tears, aghast, terrified, that I'm such a lord, yet I too have to die. Though deep in their hearts they envy me this death for being so unseemly, too opulent, yet still too humble compared with me. But if only they would deem it to be my sin, not my death; my pride, not my death.

Oh, I know, I know, people nowadays die more and more quietly, more and more modestly. But my death will be a glorious spectacle, like a wedding feast. Like a wild wedding feast. Not like death usually is. For what do you get out of one of those quiet deaths? Nothing, except your own dying. I'll throw my own banquet. Let people remember that when his lordship died, he died absolutely. Died of his heart, his soul, his longing, his pain, and the whole world died with him. Even his canaries died the day after he'd gone. Even his horses began to drop one by one after he'd gone. And even the mice disappeared after he'd gone. And the barns had been full of them. And on that very day, only a year later, the old farm overseer also passed away.

I'd have the drawing-room decked with antlers, guns. Carpets strewn everywhere. Order all my treasures to be brought in. Chests, caskets. And clocks, and have the time stopped inside them. And all my portraits. And have them strung round the walls one after the other. In one his lordship meditating upon the rich tapestry of his life. Sitting in a deep armchair and staring into space, into his own sky. I'd have that one over my bed. In another his lordship in magnanimous mood. And there again, his lordship displaying his lenience. For he's nodding his head to show he understands why they offended. In yet another his lordship striking a dignified pose. His neck imperious, his celestial brow held high, his stare supercilious, stern. And here, on the opposite wall, his lordship in all his splendour. Between his daughters and his lady wife. There again, his lordship meting out justice. Some people before him on their knees, their heads bared, their faces hidden from view. All you can see are their hunched backs, their bare feet. And you can hear them pleading, imploring, pounding their fists against their hollow chests, swearing they never did it. And amongst them, a dog, a calf, as proof they didn't mean to. They were tempted. And there again, his lordship at the top of the picture, his whole palace spread out below. And in yet another, there I am charging on my white steed, across waters, hills, forests. My horse a streaming trail beneath me. Foaming bloodily at the mouth. Its hooves scarcely skimming the ground. And myself bent over him. Snatching at his mane. My eyes flashing. And so I charge on and on. But what am I charging after? Well, what after? Let them all rack their brains over what after. Let them all squabble over what after. And there again, his lordship at war. Mighty lords can't be without their wars. And may their war be a great one. Red with blood. His lordship slipping wounded from his horse. The soldiers stepping aside to form a gap. A cry of despair wresting itself from every chest. God! God! Perhaps they even interrupt the war. Conclude a peace. Kiss. Weep. And I'll have brought to me many, many more portraits of his lordship. As many as there are in the palace. His lordship in high spirits. Even though he's dying. But then he wasn't dying all his life. Surrounded by ladies. His lordship among his hard-working peasants. Dispensing blessings from his carriage. His hand barely raised. Laden with rings. Like a plum tree sagging under its crop. His lordship greeting his guests. His lordship returning from a shoot. No. From abroad. His lordship as a youth. His lordship as an infant. His lordship reading. By the mantelpiece. Fasting for Lent. In the park in pensive mood. Fondling his dogs. Handing out favours. Oh, what a good man his lordship is!

And candles would be burning all around my bed. A forest of candles. And no eye can stand the brightness. Some people almost think it's my light eternal. Waggonettes, carriages, coaches, festive traps, peasant carts, all assemble to see this death. Hordes of people make their way to the palace. And swell, swell, spilling over beyond the forecourt, beyond the park and enclosures. And they all weep, pray, sigh, oh no, no, not from grief, but so they too might die a little along with me. And this death of mine wouldn't last a mere moment, like any ordinary death, but would go on for a day, two days, a week. And the bells would ring out, ring out. His lordship has died. His lordship has died.

Anyway, you can't put death into words. So it's pointless going on about it. You'd do better to tell me what people are saying about me. Nothing? How come, nothing? Aren't they saying they never see me? For they indeed never see me. I never go out. I just sit within these four walls like one bound by a spell, and think, think. No doubt they're saying I've hidden myself in my palace like an animal burrowing in the bushes. That I'm plagued by illness. That I wrangle with God day and night, sensing my end is nigh. And aren't they saying that I'm writing my will, and an enormous one at that? For my riches are enormous too? And it doesn't bother me in the least that they're robbing me left, right and centre, robbing me like dogs? That even my horses no longer bring me pleasure, when I used to love them so much? They're not saying anything, you say, not saying anything? Well, and aren't they saying anything about what my lady wife's doing to me with that young hopeful? That they walk through the avenues hand in hand. And twitter to one another. Like children. And I see it all and suffer. And aren't they saying that I'm miserly, stupid, a cad, a Judas, a villain, a sly fox? Oh, they could well be. I might even forgive them. I'm not that bad. Speak up, speak up, don't be afraid. You're not to blame for what other people say about me. I know what people are like. I know what people are like, my dear. Whenever they say anything, they always say nasty things. They would even kill me with words, torture me with words, if they could. But just wait till the Bishop arrives. Just let him come. I'll order them all to assemble in the yard. All of them. And form two rows. And may he bless them. Too much hatred has already built up in their hearts. What they need is holy water and penance. And aren't they saying I'm a wastrel? Cards, balls, trips abroad? Isn't that what they're saying? So what do they talk about, then?

After all, they must talk about something. After all, they don't continually keep their mouths shut. And when they do talk, it's more about me than about anything else, worse about me than about anything else, about me as though I was a rabid dog. Oh, if only I could find out who it is who's saying it!

Now listen, you. Aren't they saying I have no feeling for people? Oh, you, you! No doubt you say the same about me. Come on, admit it. But even if you don't say it, you still think it. And that's even worse than if you said it. For if you think it but don't say it, then it means you know that your thoughts are sinful, yet despite this you still think them. And worse still, nobody's forcing you, yet you still think them. Think them of your own free will. You don't defend yourself, or even feel sorry. That must give you a lot of pleasure looking back on it. So where's your excuse? Even your human nature can't excuse you, not even the fact that you're a servant, not even the fact that you exist at all. And that's worse than disobedience, that's hatred.

Ah, you fool, you fool, do you really imagine I don't know what people say about me? I even know what they think, what they feel, what they keep quiet about. What you lot in the palace say and what you don't say. I even know what you're afraid to think. Even what you're afraid to feel. Even what you're afraid to be afraid of. But your fear is sufficient for me to know your guilt. For no one is afraid without good reason. Oh, I don't trust anyone. Even myself. That's why I always know best. I know whatever I want to know. And I never listen to what anyone says, but only to what he doesn't want to tell me.

You lie as though you'd been hired to do so, and you think you can deceive me. Because I listen to you. Isn't that so? But do you know why I listen to you? Because you lie like a real servant. Ha! Ha! Ha! Oh, I like it when they lie to me. When they lie, I know that they regard me as their master. When they lie, I am best able to recognize the truth. And whatever truth I want. Such as they'd never admit to even in moments of the greatest sincerity, in pain, in misfortune; truth such as they are only capable of admitting through lies. But when they do tell the truth, what can I do then? Nothing except hear it out. For then there's nothing for me to agree or disagree with.

Well, so tell me now, just between ourselves, aren't they talking about me and, well, you know what? He! He! He! Speak up, speak up, nobody will hear you here. Well no, not every one that comes my way regardless of what she's like, I'm not that desperate. I like them, I like them, I don't deny it, but I know what I like. I'm sure they boast about it themselves. Dream their dreams out loud in front of one another, try to arouse each other's jealousy, as girls do. And all of it on my conscience. Unburden themselves of their secrets, and fantasize, oh, fantasize till they turn themselves on with their fantasies, squeal with delight, so that all their dreams come true in the end. So that as soon as I set eyes upon one of them, I straight away ask her name, then it's my sweetheart, then I give her lighter work, then it's come to my rooms, my darling, my little turtle-dove, his lordship's not really that bad. His lordship knows how to express his gratitude. But the skinny ones are the worst, barren, with no breasts, covered in pock marks, the ones with no glances, no eyes, transparent, scared. Zealous, inviolable virgins. I'm sure they tell the most awful tales about me. But don't you believe them. Don't you believe them. Women such as they have no shame in them, nor any God. They have only their pain.

But there's no dearth of pretty girls around here. Buxom wenches sculpted in clay, not girls. Girls like trees. Like an apple tree laden with crop. You want to harvest her by the handful. Strip her of her leaves. Pluck her till you touch her shame. She walks across the farmyard, weighed down by her pails, but you want to rush over and help her even though you're the lord and master. She walks across the farmyard and takes your breath away. She walks across the farmyard, ashamed in your presence, yet you'd give her anything, everything, an acre of land, a calf, a cow, everything.

Sometimes I go out and watch them dawdling in the yard, clanking their pails, rounding up their animals, singing to themselves, as though I was watching my horses, my chestnuts, my sorrels, my blacks, greys. I forget I've come to hurry them up, scold them, shout at them, put the fear of God into them, for they've got to be afraid of me, after all. I just see myself now with this one, now with that one, with one of them between the sheets, with another in the hay, with yet another on the bare earth, in a cornfield, in a furrow freshly ploughed. I feel myself grow hard. The stable-boy says something to me, complains about something. Another moment and I'll grab hold of him, shake the life out of him, curse him, punch him in the face. Tell him to clear off. Call him a bastard. Like he was a dog.

But what's up with you? Stop shamming, stop shamming. We're all alike. Only don't tell her ladyship. She'd never get over it, poor dear. Though she knows everything. But that's her secret. And because of that she even forgives me. Even feels a certain superiority over me. I know, I know, but you'll let something slip somewhere without thinking, out of foolishness perhaps, in good faith, when you're off your guard, then someone else will repeat it also in good faith, and so it'll get around. Gossip around here becomes hot news immediately; no secret is ever kept, even the most hallowed. You know what it'll be like. Hysterics, fainting fits, banging doors, tearing around the house. And her maids would peck me to death. She'd run straight to the tower, fling herself into the abyss. Or she'd dress up in her mourning clothes and cross herself every time she saw me, like before some great temptation. Or she'd start packing her things at once, begin to take her leave. Let her go, let her go. I'll get the horses ready myself, her carriage. The *grande dame*. Forever indisposed, weary, sleepy. Forever in pain. Or melancholy. Fear almost takes hold of you whenever you try to get close to her. The *grande dame*. She's never even dreamed of doing what even the simplest girls can do.

And they can do it, oh, they can do it all right. They can move heaven and hell. Even when you're not feeling up to it, they know how to relieve you of your impotence. Even when you try and resist it, for you're the lord and master after all, they'll make you forget who you are. But there are those who know how to feel shame too, the occasional one more than madam herself, even though she's no lady. She undresses in front of you, and it's as though every piece of clothing stung her skin. As though she was stripping herself of her flesh, not of her clothes. Taking her time, making it last, shyly cautious like a deer. She'll turn away, nestle into her own embrace, close her eyes before you. Till you're almost writhing. For she's making a sacrifice of herself rather than surrendering to you. But these servant-girls already imagine themselves to be ladies. They're the worst. With them you have to tread carefully. They can be fickle, get too carried away. A girl like that will sigh longingly, but then say you raped her. They need tender words, coaxing, sweet empty promises. And sometimes you come across a girl who won't give herself to you till she's bared her soul, unburdened herself of her whole life, got it all off her chest. The sin will torment her, God's retribution. But all this is just part of the seduction. Take my word for it. She already fancies herself as a chambermaid, because it happened to her once. And I can't even remember whether it was me or not. Who would remember? Starts a bastard with God knows whom, and then comes to you with her grievances. And she won't be content with just anything, but would like a cow, if you please, would like to be taken on as a maid, wants a plot of land, and a farm-hand too as a husband. And he mustn't be stupid either, or old, or crippled, and must have curly hair, for otherwise she won't marry him.

Though worse still are the gigglers. It's as though laughter flowed in their veins, not blood. Before you even bend over to whisper in her ear, she's already giggling. You ask her whether she likes you, caress, embrace her, implore her to undress – you won't do anything to her after all – but she doesn't respond, just giggles. You don't say anything, and still she giggles. You grow sad, she giggles. You get angry, she giggles. In the end you can't tell whether she's leading you on or whether she's making fun of you. It's as though instead of trying to defend herself she simply giggles, so that you throw up your arms in despair. You say you'll give her a calf, but she just giggles. You lose your head, perhaps she's trying to haggle with you because you're the lord and master and yet so mean. You no longer have any idea. In the end you imagine she's only come to mock you, because as far as she's concerned laughter's obviously the answer to everything. A girl like that could even get pregnant from laughing. Who can tell? Her laughter exhausts you as much as making love. Exhausts you, so you no longer want anything other than to fall asleep. So that when she starts to get affectionate, begins to snuggle up to you, grows sad, it's time to turf her out.

I tell you the best ones are the plain ones. The common ones. The ruddy ones. They may be lumps, but the blood sings in their veins. Neither sad nor gay. They need neither words nor promises.

They don't haggle, don't cry. You can satisfy them with a handful of flour, but some won't take even this and will tell you so too. I don't need it, my lord. What's mine is yours. She'll come to the palace without even saying she's coming to take a bath. And she even undresses in front of your valet. Betrays no shame, no regrets. And when you want to stroke her hair at least, encourage her, she slips away from under your hand, for what does she want with your tenderness? And so she undresses till she's completely naked. What more could you want? Then she walks over to the bed of her own accord, lies down, opens her legs, and doesn't even close her eyes before you, before herself, just gazes at the ceiling and waits, without uttering a word, without breathing a sigh. Oh, these girls know their destiny. They know what they were created for, and that it wasn't all in vain.

Though among them you also come across the tough ones. But these, once they mellow, know how to love, I tell you, they know how to love. Only you've got to know how to handle them. It's no good just one, two, three, and it's all over. Like any old peasant who flings a girl on the bed, as long as he's got her underneath him, as long as he can squeeze himself between her legs. Oh, no, no, my dear. First you've got to rouse her from her own body. Make a point of asking her name, and flatter her that it's a beautiful name. Gaze deep into those eyes and tell her they're like cornflowers. And even though she keeps them tightly shut before you, she'll open them, believe me, she'll open them. For whoever told a girl like her she's got eyes? You'll be the first. Then kiss her once on the arm, neck. Best of all on the hand. That's her most sensitive place. The most private. It's as though you were kissing a wound. More intimate than if you were to kneel before her. A thrill shoots through her whole body. A stab of pain. And she's yours. And even if she tries to tear herself away, then kiss her. Even if she tries to defend herself, no, no, my lord, then kiss her. And don't maul her all at once with your great paws, but run the very tips of your fingers over her body, scarcely ruffling her skin, as though you were getting to know her in the dark. So that she herself marvels at her own self under the touch of your fingers. As though you were doing it with her ladyship. Close your eyes and let yourself imagine that she's your lady wife. That you're all coyness and apprehension. That you're praying to her body. That you're dreaming in your thoughts of her desire for you. That you're snuggling into those arms heavy with sleep. And you'll see, although stifled by tears, she'll blossom into tenderness, cocoon you in her warmth like in a soft quilt, gather your head into her breasts, grasp hold of your hair. Ah you, my lord, my lord! Bitter as wormwood, and yet so sweet. With you I don't know whether to laugh or cry. Oh, you know what to do, you know what to do. With you I feel it's not a sin. Come to me, come, come. And if you want to know all there is to know, then I'm telling you it's best to start with her breasts. And if her breasts are as yet unawakened, have never been roused, then it's the only way. Fondle her breasts and she'll be yours. Even though she might have been full of hatred, she'll be yours. Even though she might have been crazed with terror, she'll be yours. She'll let her juices flow, and she'll be yours. She'll gather you into herself, sigh longingly that you're clearly not as bad as people say, but that she'd still forgive you even if you were the worst of the worst. And she'll forget she came because you forced her. Forget that you're the lord and master, and she but a servant from the farm. And you will feel like a child inside her. For when a girl like that makes love, then she loves with her whole body, her whole soul. With all her pain, all her injury. With all her humiliation, all her unfulfilled longings, with all she remembers and doesn't remember. With her breath, with her eyes. So you reach the point when you can't love her any more. So you imagine that you can only hurt her. So you imagine, yet can't imagine. Oh, my God.

But what do you think you're doing here? Where did you spring from? Eavesdropping on your master, what? I know what you're like. Then I'm left wondering how everyone knows all about me. Oh, do excuse me, my dear Count. We can't even have a quiet chat as befits old friends. And there'd be a lot to talk about. Oh yes there would. So much has happened since we last met. Events piling up on us. Catching up with us. It must be a year since we last met. Yes, yes, almost a year. Just think, a whole year has gone by and it seems it was only yesterday I last squeezed your hand. Hang on, where was it? Where was it we saw each other then? Playing cards somewhere? No, it wasn't at cards. You don't play, do you?

Or perhaps you do? I no longer remember. Or maybe it was when we were taking the waters? But then I don't think you were at the waters either. At a ball somewhere? But where? Well, a good memory was never one of my vices. Forgive me, Count. Memory was never my forte. Ha! Ha! Ha! But next time you come, I'll remember. I assure you, I'll remember. Oh, thank you so much for wanting to visit me at this cruel time.

And as for you, I've told you more than once that when someone's with me, you're not to come in unless I summon you. So I don't have to know what's been going on out there. I forbid you, do you understand? Even if the whole place is falling down, burning down. You're not even allowed to know who's with me. Don't make excuses, don't make excuses. Better take a look at the ears you've grown. Well, what, have they grown? You see, they've grown. They're not asses' ears, are they, by any chance? Ha! Ha! Ha! So the Lord God has punished you for eavesdropping on your master. Oh, you, you! How many times have I told you off already? It's a never-ending saga. And I'm supposed to have been ringing for you? Whatever for? You must have got it mixed up. Perhaps it was the church bells that were ringing? I've been playing cards the whole time with the Count. I didn't require you. Lucky for you I'm in a good mood today. Make me something to eat. Do you hear? I'm hungry as a dog. Only get a move on.

I didn't even realize I was that hungry. I'd obviously been hungry for ages, but the Count arrived and what could I do? I had to talk to him. I thought he'd soon be off, but no such luck. I didn't even say very much, nor, God forbid, did I ask him anything. I nodded assent as though I was listening. But he, he rambled on for the both of us, asked questions for the both of us, answered them, referred to this and that, complained, laughed, grew sad for the both of us. Apparently somewhere sometime we'd betted that somebody's horse would outstrip somebody else's, and then they'd finished together. And then he said something about our being related, I can't remember, either through my grandmother's grandfather or through his grandfather's grandmother. Me related to him! Lies! Heinous lies! To such a lowly gentleman. Me related to him. Practically all he's got left of his estate is that manor-house – a hovel, not a manor-house – a couple of servants, a pair of horses and he's supposed to be a count. A count. And I'm meant to be related to someone like that. Let it be through my great-great-grandmother. The poor fellow doesn't even have a decent *britzka*. He's got a hat like an innkeeper. Horses never shod. And I'm supposed to be related to a man like that! What a joke. A count. And then he went on about my having to meet up with him once abroad and how he saved my skin, for I'd lost everything, drunk my way through it, lost it at cards, wasted it on women. And especially on one. She professed to be a countess, but was just a plain hussy. Well, better not listen.

He saved my skin. From what? I couldn't stomach another word. But what could I do? I listen, listen, nod assent, though my tummy is rumbling away, performing somersaults. But I go on listening to the Count, still not suspecting anything. Maybe something's got into him, I think to myself, maybe he's in pain, let him talk for a bit. Words can be a relief when you're in pain. So he rambles on and on. Until it begins to pall. He talks without rhyme or reason. And rather too long. And about everything. It's a shame to waste so many words on such trivialities. His voice grows hoarse, yet he goes on and on. Doesn't even let me get a word in edgeways, just goes on and on and on. But then I guessed his game, smelt a rat, began to suspect he wasn't talking in vain, that he was obviously going to hold out till lunch-time, tea-time, that he was even ready to go on talking till supper, because from time to time he would look sadly towards the door as if listening out for the clatter of plates. I've found you out, Count, you parasite, I think to myself, now you can go on talking to your heart's content. And on top of all this I'm supposed to stuff your paunch. But you'll have to be satisfied with my listening to you. You won't find anything to eat in my house. I won't even give you a drink. If you get dry in the throat then you'll shut up all the quicker. But not on your life. He goes on and on. As though he'd had a second lease of life. Perhaps he's heard the rumbling in my belly, which has raised his hopes. No doubt he's been reckoning he can bore me to death with this talking of his, starve me into submission. I wouldn't hold out, I'd get up, I'd say, We've had a nice long chat, Count, and now luncheon awaits us. But I've become just as obstinate as he. I listen even more eagerly than he talks. Oh, Count, I'll outlast you, you'll never defeat me with your hunger. Hunger is the very essence of soul. You can go on talking till your dying day. Hunger is my element, Count. You don't know me, or what I'm capable of. I can suffer any hunger, even the hunger that bores away at my insides. Hunger, that raves and rages in your belly like a poisonous beast and gnaws at you here, there, as you struggle in vain to squeeze it into your guts. In vain, Count. Even if you were to squat, or bend over to touch your knees, you'd never stifle it inside you.

And do you know that hunger that is nothing but a void inside you? A vast, packed emptiness, which is like a void yet makes you bulge and burst, which can't contain itself within you? And which goes on swelling, pressing against your heart, thrusting itself into your breast, sticking in your throat like a tuberous growth, throttling you, making you feel sick, yet you can't even throw it up because it won't be forced out of you, as though it were clinging on inside you with its claws. You no longer have the strength to shift it, yet you feel as though you'd overeaten.

And do you know, Count, that hunger that tries to ingratiate itself? It seems like a healthy appetite, like a great, unrestrained, impulsive desire. But beware of it, it's the most insidious of hungers. It only seduces you into a kind of illusory satiety. And you surrender to it willingly in the very hope of this satiety, which you crave to experience. And the more you succumb to it, the closer that promised satiety appears to be. You can almost feel it within you, in your throat, lips, teeth. But it sucks you dry from the inside and with this it nourishes you till you begin to feel the wound inside you, feel the raw flesh within yourself. You feed yourself with your own saliva, then when the saliva runs out, with your own bile, with your own parched liver, till little by little you devour your whole self from the inside in order to indulge that satiety promised by your hunger. But that's still not the worst of hungers, Count. A hundred times worse is the hunger that is not only your hunger but the hunger of your starving children, trembling with the fear that this hunger is a punishment that you, as a father, have meted out to them. Your children, who avoid your gaze, who suffer their hunger in silence as though, subjected to your punishment, they silently protest their innocence. What are you punishing them for, Count? What for? And then there's the hunger of your wife, of your old father, though of all hungers that's the least aggravating. Or the hunger of all the starving amassed within you. Though maybe this is still not the worst, for at least it's shared. Maybe there isn't a worst. For you can always placate the worst of hungers with death. As though death were a table spread for a feast.

Ha! Ha! Ha! Well, the Count couldn't hold out. Couldn't hold out. He talked and talked. Then suddenly he ran out of steam. He asked what was new. What the haymaking was like this year. Was the second cutting worse than the first? I knew he was only asking because he'd grown pensive, melancholy. He got to his feet, sluggish and dejected, and said he must be going, time was pressing. The sun was near to setting. The birds were falling silent. They'd be worrying that he hadn't returned. And at dusk the visibility was bad. He must go. He still had to call on the priest. Look in on the cow that was calving. His wife wasn't feeling well. Some people were probably coming round to invite him to a christening. He had to go. Ha! Ha! Ha!

But couldn't you have told him I wasn't at home? That I'd gone into town or that the *Starosta* had invited me over? That he'd put off his birthday till today, so I could come? That a standard was being blessed somewhere, or that I had to be a godfather? Anything would have done. Some judge could have been dying. So his wife came for me along with her daughter and brother. They begged me, implored me to go to him, because there was something he wanted to confess to me. And stay with him until he died, because he was afraid. And not so much of death, no doubt, as of judgement. He knows what to expect. Or the Bishop could have been returning from the holy capital. Wanted to see me before anyone else. Or even the Field Marshal himself. He could also have invited me. Already a venerable old man with one foot in the grave, it wouldn't have done not to turn up. Or the Princess could have been arranging a ball. So what if it's a weekday? Well, what? Do you imagine people never hold balls on a weekday? It's up to the person concerned. Or the fire brigade was organizing a display in my honour. They need money. For a hose. Is that so surprising? Suppose the palace caught fire? Also, I might not have returned from abroad. Or I'm at the races. Or any old rubbish. I'm at the bank. My neighbour shot a wild boar. I went to visit him. Went to confession. Went out to shoot blackcock. Oh, you, you, what a twit you are!

What, do I straight away have to entertain everybody who turns up to see me, feed them, fatten them up? Oh, they're not going to have it so good. Just because I'm rich doesn't mean that they have to eat me out of house and home. That I have to receive them immediately. Welcome them with open arms. And rejoice too because I have a guest in my home, God in my home. Ah, how nice to see you, my dear Count, my Prince, my good friend, my sweet lady. I was thinking you might come. It's so sad in the palace without any guests. Welcome. Welcome. But all they're interested in is scoffing, drinking. And they know how to pay you compliments, flatter you. Ah, how superbly your cook does partridge! Where did you get such wine, my dear? Vintage, sir, is it not? It's only in your house and in your house alone that one still finds such wines. And the hare makes you want to lick your fingers. My cook does hare too, but what's his beside yours? As long as the art still blossoms in one great family, then we'll not perish yet. Here's to you! Long life to us all!

Oh, how it all makes my stomach rumble! Do you hear? So get a move on. Stop hanging about. My mouth tastes as if I've been eating too much sorrel. My teeth have gone all sour, my lips, tongue. Where did I get this taste of sorrel from? Besides, I can't stand sorrel. I spit it out, spit it out, but it doesn't help. How my belly's growling now. Come on, pay attention at last. Oh, you, you! So you don't believe me either? You obviously think I overdid it yesterday, stuffed myself, drank myself stupid, and now it's all crawling out of me. What's the use of talking to you?

And do you know what you can prepare for me? Something so there's a lot of it, a lot of it. Let me really stuff myself. If not with my mouth then at least with my eyes, but let me stuff myself. I want to feel that sensation of satiety within myself, vast, heavy. Let it hurt me even, gnaw away at me, but let me feel that I've gorged myself.

Let me feel silted up with slime, yet I'll stuff myself like a pig. To the very last scrap, as though I was draining a deep well where nothing remains but sorrow, where life has already lost its charm, but I'll stuff myself for the sake of stuffing. Hey! Let me fall from heaven into hell, let my gullet rebel, parched, inflamed, but I'll stuff myself, oh, I'll stuff myself. Hey!

For if only you knew that when a man has a full stomach he no longer desires anything. At the very most that he might belch. Though when he's really gorged himself, he'll be completely squashed by his belly, even his thoughts, his conscience. And mindful of only one thing: whether or not a belch is gathering to relieve him. Whether somewhere inside that inflated belly it's beginning to whine, sing. Then he becomes totally absorbed in himself, in his insides, sucking like a leech at his sodden guts. As though steeped in suffering. Contemplating his own belly. Pining for his own belly. His gaze concentrated on his own belly as it digests its food. Unseeing. Unfeeling. Beyond the world, beyond men. Beyond God. Alone with his belly. The only person around. Like a wounded beast. Perhaps an injured one, too. Waiting only for the moment when he will belch. For that is now the last bit of good fortune that fate can send him. But it's good to feel gorged. Blissful. Warm. Soporific.

Oh, prepare me something to eat so I don't have to get angry with you. And heaps of it. And let it all smell as delicious as possible. And it has to be hot. Remember. Let it almost scald my lips, for that's all there is to the taste. All there is to the taste, like you had a whole mountain of food in front of you and you were so hungry from weeks of fasting you could devour it by the handful, but you can't because it scalds you. A vicious taste. Here on your lips it's as hot as fire. But there inside you wolves are howling. But you can't, only with the tip of your spoon, cooling it with your breath, puffing on it. In tiny bites the size of crumbs. And let it all smell so delicious that not only does my mouth water but my eyes dissolve in tears, remember.

You know what to do after all, you know what to do. And when you drain the potatoes, cover them up so the steam can't escape. And don't stint me with the *skwarki*. Let there be less of the dripping, and more of the *skwarki*. When the *skwarki* crunch in your mouth, it's as if you're eating not simply potatoes but everything you ever fancied, everything you ever dreamed of. You're eating potatoes, yet you can't believe it. Oh, potatoes! He who's never been starved of potatoes doesn't know their taste. Anyway, what am I doing eating potatoes? I don't feel like potatoes any more. Do you hear? I don't want potatoes. Prepare me something that'll make my tongue want to tear itself out of my mouth. *Kluski*? All right, *kluski*. But made just with eggs and flour, no water. And fine as gossamer. Beautifully yellow like sunshine. With bacon. Perhaps with cheese. No. With poppy seed. Or no. With bacon. No. Let them be with poppy seed. And what else can you eat *kluski* with? Go on, tell me. You don't even have to eat them. They themselves eat their own selves inside you. Slide into your mouth of their own accord. Slither through you of their own accord. But wait, perhaps I won't have *kluski* because I'd have to use a fork. And whoever coped with a fork? You gather them on to your fork and they slip through like worms. Whatever you rake up, you rake through. They themselves rebel against such a manner of eating. Sometimes they nearly drive you mad, for they slip away just as you're putting them into your mouth. Now, now, you've got them, you can already feel them on your lips, you even bend your head forward so they haven't far to go, but whoops, not a single one makes it. All you've got left is your fork. Your saliva. Your fury. And such shame you could smash them into your plate with your fists. For even if you're patient, where does it get you? You try once more. Again it's the same. You try again. And again it's the same. And after the umpteenth time you're no longer in control. Crash! Bang! You chuck your fork on to your plate. To hell with them! Or perhaps you won't even get angry. You'll just feel sad. Ashamed to raise your eyes. You'll lay down your fork quietly, so that nobody hears. You'll get up, say nothing, or maybe you'll say, I'm full. Stuffed full as I've never been before in my life. For it won't be your hunger that you'll want to hide – somehow you'll be able to cope with your hunger – but your helplessness, the fact that *kluski*, ordinary *kluski*, have made a complete fool of you.

What are you looking like that for? Don't you know that God gave mankind only the spoon, and a spoon carved of wood at that, and that everything else was invented by man to the detriment of his fellow men. The fork was no doubt invented by someone sated and fat. Someone whose flabby gut already hid his feet from view. Who had to sit on two stools at once. Who could talk exclusively about food from dawn to dusk, and more eloquently than another man could talk about his entire life. Not only could he no longer eat any more, but he couldn't bear to see others go on eating, either. So he invented the fork, so that nobody could ever stuff themselves again. Hence there's so much hunger everywhere. Because you can fiddle around your plate with a fork, but not really eat properly. And knives must have been thought up by the Devil himself. The man who invented them can't have been at all fat or replete. He could well have been some starved wretch. All shrivelled up, with an evil glint in his eye. Only he couldn't have had a stomach, just a sack of bile instead.

But perhaps you could make me some *pierogi*. What? What with? With cheese. With fried sour cream. You at least know how to fry sour cream? There you see, you've been in service all your life and you still don't know. Though you know what to do with cabbage? So do me some cabbage as well. My God, I'd clean forgotten about the meat. Just imagine, forgotten the meat! A veritable sin. Let it be just as it comes. Stewed, fried, roasted. From an ox, ass, pig, whatever it happens to be. Let it be. And lots of it, lots of it. Ha! Ha! Ha! Wring a chicken's neck, kill a duck, goose. What else is there? Guinea-fowl, you say. Fine, kill a guinea-fowl too. Kill one of each. No, kill two of the smaller ones, or three. Poultry like that tastes all right, but take one look at it and you've already gobbled it down. And the meat must have pride of place on the table. For the meat is the mountains, and everything else the valleys in between. For when the table's so full of meat, piled high in front of you, you no longer want anything else. Perhaps the only thing you might want would be for a hungry man to stand and stare at you. Only in meat can you know for sure that you're the lord and master, and not just anyone. There's so much meat, you couldn't be anyone else. You can feel it. Like angels pampering your soul. You don't even have to eat it, it's sufficient for you just to see that it's meat, see the meat spread out before you. You can feast your eyes on that meat and no longer feel so utterly alone in the world. With meat you can even hold a conversation. Have a good laugh with it. It even makes you wistful, makes you wonder, oh, whether insects – ants, let us say – also ascend into heaven. But from time to time you chew at a drumstick, pick at some morsel, in order to be sure that it's really you sitting amongst this meat, you, and not your dream.

Well, and what else might there be? Speak up. What else? Surely you must know what your lord and master might desire? For what more could a man desire? No, not *prażuchy*. Who on earth is capable of eating *prażuchy*? Two, three spoonfuls and you're blocked up like a silted pond. And what kind of happiness d'you call that? Two, three spoonfuls and the happiness is over. You couldn't possibly eat any more, even with your eyes. And what kind of happiness can you call that, either? You still haven't felt it inside you and yet it's already deserting you. Turning sour. And then an even greater hunger remains within you, for it's a hunger that has been whetted, disappointed, cheated. As though you were sated, but sated on emptiness.

Or maybe something else? Have a think. Maybe something that would be almost painful to eat? So that you're hardly able to believe that you're eating it. That you're eating it with these fingers, this mouth, this tongue, these eyes. That you're seeing yourself eat it with your own eyes, not with the diabolical eyes of another which just smile derisively, not with the unseeing eyes of the blind, not with eyes that have been tricked, but seeing it with your own eyes, seeing that it's you who's eating it. You. Nobody else. Not someone alien and indifferent, not the closest of your closest friends. But you. The closest to yourself.

So then I'll know I can eat anything. This or that, and God knows what, I myself don't know what. But what? Well, what? You say that only peasants eat this. Well, of course, I can't eat the same as the peasants. Then again you advise me against something else. That's not for my palate. You laugh, pull a face or keep your mouth shut, so what can I do? Do I still have to think about what I should eat? So why do I keep you on?

And don't you know what that painful food might be? Half yellow like the sun, and half green. Rather like *kluski*, but not *kluski*. Only a fool would imagine they're *kluski*. And garnished with a kind of red ring, like a garland. But they're not rowanberries. No way, they're bigger. Redder. Like black cherries. But they're not cherries either. Because when you eat this food, it's crunchy. And there are no stones to spit out. Word of honour, there's nothing to spit out. Let me drop down dead if there's something to spit out. And the little blobs of fat laugh at the guests as they eat it, oh, how the little blobs of fat laugh at them! They blab away to each other like long lost friends as they eat this thing. Snort, spit, as the fat oozes from their mouths. And the jokes splutter forth of their own accord, as they eat this thing. And how they plot, deceive one another, as they eat it! And swear, oh, if only you could hear their language when they eat that thing. Don't you know what it is? But perhaps you do know what it is? When the servants bring it in it's all ablaze. Then they all get up from their seats, put their hands together as if saying their prayers, stand deep in thought for a moment as if remembering the dead, then explode into cheers and squeals. They laugh, squeeze one another, weep, kiss, as if they were forgiving each other for something, then they all take some of that blazing thing on to their plates and sing as they eat it, but without moving their lips – it just consumes itself inside them. And that's how they eat it. Or how about that food when the servants don't bring anything in? When they don't serve anything. When there's no sign of a valet anywhere. Nor a plate, nor a spoon, nor fork, nor knife. The table's empty, yet not empty. They sit around it without stretching out their hands, for they don't need their hands even. They sit as though they had no eyes, for they have no need of their eyes either. They wait with their faces uplifted, their mouths held wide open, for it to flutter down from on high and alight in their mouths. What is it? What is it? Come on, tell me, what's it called? Perhaps you've seen it. Perhaps you've heard it. You don't know? You don't know anything. But perhaps it's only in front of me that you don't know. Perhaps someone's ordered you not to know anything that could be of use to me. Let that be as it may. Brew me some poor man's soup. And clear off, clear off.

But what's going on now? They're all waiting for me, you say? Who on earth can be waiting for me? What guests? You're right, I'd clean forgotten. I'm just coming. I'm coming.

I enter the dining-room. I feel a bit ashamed that they've been waiting for me in there, and for how long, for how long? I'd clean forgotten. But hold on, I don't see anyone at the table. The table is lavishly spread, but all around it's empty, silent, dead. Yet I could have sworn that only a moment ago it was still full of guests. I could hear them like I hear myself. The hubbub of their conversation, the clinking of knives, forks, the smacking of their lips, their laughter, jokes, toasts, cheers. It was noisy, as though they wanted to drown me. I could even hear them digesting their food, the acid juices hissing inside them, and their bloody bladders like distended stomachs strangling the words in their throats, churning up their senses. Their swollen genitals contorted. I could hear them. But hardly any of them saw anyone else. They didn't even notice when I slipped away, though I'd been sitting in full view of them all. They'd been eating, drinking, so what could they see? Gossiping, yelling, so what could they see? Their eyes clouded by laughter. Not even God would have been in a fit state to appear before them. And that glutton put away more than anyone. That greasy pig. He didn't look at anyone, didn't speak, didn't rejoice, but just kept putting it away. His eyes were almost bulging. He had the air of someone engrossed in prayer, in repentance. My heart bled when he dumped almost an entire hare on his plate. God, I thought, please forgive him, for I never shall. And if only someone had rebuked him with a hostile glance for the wrong he was doing me. Not on your life. It made me so furious I couldn't watch any longer, and I walked out.

I went out into the park to get a breath of fresh air, to soothe my eyes, my heart. The birds were singing in their throngs, so cheerfully. Sunlight glinted among the leaves. A peacock emerged from the bushes and spread its brightly coloured tail so beautifully it brought tears to my eyes. Stone figures of neither men nor women, garlands adorning their heads, rose up naked before me and greeted me with a dignified silence. Somewhere not far away a deer cast its eyes about and vanished. I walked on feeling I was no one in particular. I felt diffused, dissipated in the singing of the birds, in the sunlight, in the peacock's rainbow tail, in the peace, in the verdure, in the intense greenness soaring to the tops of those ancient trees, the oaks, beech, spruce, then descending to the grass and the roots, encompassing that immense infinity enclosed within the park.

I don't know what to say; maybe I've offended them. I feel,

however, it's not the done thing for me to sit here and not say a word. I try to put something on my plate in order to hide the silence. But this seems to make the silence all the more eloquent. So I say whatever comes into my head:

This hare isn't bad at all. If only it were a bit more tender, it would be even better.

And at this very moment I recall the dream I had last night. I seize it as if it were my only salvation. I speak.

D'you know what, Cousin, I dreamed about you last night. But it was so weird and, I would say, rather improper, actually, that I really can't tell it you in front of the ladies. From your point of view it wasn't the best of dreams. I remember I once had a similar dream about my father's uncle. He was a true aristocrat. And a fine man, oh my, what a man he was! The ladies simply went wild over him. And I mean princesses, countesses. One even drowned herself because of him. Another slit her wrists. And d'you know what happened? Just imagine, a plain servant-girl put some curse on him. I don't even know what for. Anyway, about a week later, when he was apparently feeling a bit drowsy, the poor fellow fell off his horse, and the horse trampled on his head with its hoof. His portrait is even hanging in the palace, I'll show it you sometime. He had such a handsome head, but after that he was unrecognizable.

But why are they all looking at me like that? I can feel their eyes upon me. And there's so many of them, the place is swarming with them, and all of them fixed upon me intently, stonily, as though I was guilty of some crime. They castigate me, wonder at me in astonishment, give vent to their scorn, disown me with their curses, and that's not all, that's not all, but I'm afraid to guess at any more. I start to feel awkward and, in my embarrassment, lower my eyes to stare at my plate and don't dare to glance up at them. I try to distract myself by eating, but it's no good. I know I can't get away now with keeping silent, that would be admitting defeat. I have to say something, may they forgive me, may they interpret it as a joke not as an admission of guilt, though I don't feel in the least bit guilty. I really only wanted to cheer them up. But perhaps gaiety only inspires sadness in them, or maybe I no longer know how to cheer people up. I rack my brains for something to say, but the more I persist the greater the void I feel in my head. My silence drags on, becomes more difficult to bear, foolish, frightening. I imagine that by keeping silent in their presence, my flame is being extinguished, that I shall vanish somewhere within my own memories, like the most foolish of thoughts, non-thoughts, mere vestiges of thoughts, that perhaps I am dying even. But here it comes at last, here it comes, it's coming back to me, I can feel it inside me, see it inside me. I raise my head and speak, a little timidly as though apologizing for myself:

And do you know what, my dear ladies and gentlemen? When I was taking the waters last year I had the most hilarious experience. Really hilarious. You'll never believe it. One afternoon I was strolling down the most marvellous avenue – trees as if constructed by human hands, ornamental fountains, little benches, arbours, and peace, above all peace, bluish-green, sublime, angelic. It was very strange that there weren't any people about, as though night-time had descended upon them instead of day. One had the impression they'd all vanished from the face of the earth because of this peace, which aroused in one such a tremendous longing for something, perhaps indeed for death. So there I am strolling along, absorbed in this peace, in the trees, the fountains, the little benches, the arbours. My mind completely blank. When suddenly I see a lady looming up before me, coming towards me. Believe me, she was like an apparition, a miracle in that afternoon desolation. She was beautiful; I still couldn't see her face, but I could sense it; it was as though I'd known for a long time that she couldn't be otherwise. In her long white dress, billowing about the legs it kept concealed, as though borne on a gentle breeze. On her head she wore a white hat, wide-brimmed, all covered in flowers. And in her arms, close to her chest, though I only noticed this at the very last moment, she carried some little creature – I didn't realize at first that it was a lap-dog. And it was indeed a lap-dog. We drew near to one another, and I bowed to her. Oh, whatever made me do it? I didn't know her, I'd never set eyes on her before, yet in that secluded place, at that time of day, I almost regarded it as my duty, especially as she was a lady. She nodded to me without showing any sign of surprise, and I'm sure we would have passed each other by if the dog hadn't suddenly leaped out of her arms and run towards me. I bent over to stroke it in order to please her, for, as you know, I can't stand lap-dogs. But then I saw the dog standing by my left leg and cocking its back paw. Clear off, get lost, I yelled, shocked to the foundations, kicking it aside. Then the lady came running up to me, pleading, Oh, God, let him, let him, whoever you are! Forgive me, my dear lady, I am fascinated by your beauty but I can hardly allow myself to be used as a tree! I beseech you! I detected the pain in her eyes, the tears, so I stood there and let it happen. And when the dog had finished its business, she swept it up in her arms, clasped it to her in a state of frenzied joy, hugged it, whispered to it the tenderest words, completely forgetting about me. Then I hitched up my trouser leg and shyly reminded her of my presence. But what about my trouser leg, dear lady? Just take a look, it's covered in piss. Suddenly, it was as if a bird took flight in her eyes. Yet at the same moment her face lit up and she looked at me, I'd say, irrestibly. But you know, my dear Count, that it wasn't to be. I simply said, But my trousers will dry out, dear lady. And then I bowed and walked away.

A moment of strained silence. But I am eating now. Let them presume the rest themselves, think otherwise. But after a moment I start to speak again:

Oh, this hare could be even better if there was more bayleaf in it. Don't you agree? It excites the palate. And the bouquet doesn't fade so quickly. You could inhale it all day long and still experience that hare-and-bayleaf sweetness, yet not sweetness. Teasing, insinuating, as though all the herbs were mingling together yet each one could still be savoured. For a hare, a properly dressed hare, should reek neither of its guts nor of the open field. A well-dressed hare shouldn't even remind you that it's hare.

But please, please, do eat! It's all gone cold already. Father, Countess, and you, my dear. I beg you with all my heart. And our young lady maybe fancies a nice little piece of pike? I can tell from the look on your face. No? Well, obviously I shall have to ask our priest to keep an eye on you, my love. At your age it's a sin not to eat. Oh, I understand, I understand, at your age you don't even feel like sleeping, but you must eat. Such is the fate that confronts us all. We have to eat, drink, for how else can we know that we exist? Ha! Ha! Ha! Perhaps I'll ask the *Starosta*'s wife to take you under her wing, or maybe your worthy aunt, but I won't excuse you, I won't excuse you. And how are you getting on, Count? Your appetite hasn't deserted you, has it? That's a good one! Listen, everyone, the Count's lost his appetite. His appetite's deserted him. Ha! Ha! Ha! How about that for a first-class joke? The Count, I see, is in an excellent mood. My compliments, my compliments. Well, no, dear Cousin, how can you say such a thing? I shall never agree that rabbit tastes as good as hare. Quite the contrary, though I admit the meat is very subtle. But it smells of rotten leaves. Well, maybe I'm exaggerating. Perhaps I should say, of the soil. It makes you feel as though you've got something growing in your mouth. I can always tell rabbit from the smell, no matter how it's dressed. Oh, I'm not so easily fooled. You say, Cousin, you can smell hare in just the same way. Maybe you've got some growth blocking your nose. Ha! Ha! Ha!

And do you know, my dear ladies and gentlemen, about the fellow I once had working for me here? He was a watchman. One day he was sitting by the gate smoking a cigarette. Perhaps I wouldn't have paid him any attention, except I couldn't help noticing that he exhaled only through one nostril. I stopped beside him, and then he stopped smoking.

What sort of a fellow are you, I says, who can do it with one nostril?

Well, I'm something of an original, your lordship.

Eh, I don't believe you.

So why doesn't his lordship have a bet on it?

But suppose you can't do it? says I.

We shall see, he replies.

So what are your stakes?

Let his lordship name the stakes.

All right, I'll give you a sack of corn if you win.

But he then answered me thus. This is no ordinary art, your lordship, for it to be so undervalued. You have to be born with it. It can't be bought or acquired.

Downright insolence.

So what do you want?

A foal or a calf, if that's not asking too great a favour.

I see that a crowd of people has already gathered around us. They jeer at the watchman, chatter amongst themselves and laugh, but I can feel that in their hearts those traitors are praying either that the watchman will lead me up the garden path, or that I'll lose my nerve. To hell with the calf, I think to myself, though it's a pity, a pity, but I can't let myself down in front of this riff-raff. All right, I say, I'll give you a calf if you win. But if you lose, then watch out.

It must have sounded threatening because the people began to abandon us one by one. We were left alone. Me and the watchman.

Well, just imagine, the scoundrel would have cheated me. But luckily the steward came to my rescue. He appeared beside me out of nowhere and told me what to say. Tell him to exhale through both nostrils, your lordship. Ha! Ha! Ha!

But I can see, Cousin, that nothing will cheer you up. You're as stubborn as a mule, sticking only to your own point of view. It's always the same with people who only really exist when they're eating. One day I'll convince you yet, Cousin. I know how to convince people. How dare you talk such rubbish, Cousin, if I may say so. If I say something is so, then it means it is so. I won't put up with you having your own opinion in my presence. You, Cousin, if you'll forgive my saying so, devour my hare, yet you want to have an opinion of your own. Did you ever hear anything like it? And I'm still supposed to think, am I, that this is an example of your good breeding? That it's even a virtue? One day you'll spit in my face and I'll have to accept that too. Cousin, you're a good-for-nothing. An oaf.

Do excuse me, ladies and gentlemen. Just a family matter. However, why don't we have a drink? And Father Prior, too, along with the rest of us. We implore you. You're fasting, Father? Well, there's nothing simpler than putting off your fast till tomorrow. After all, the Lord God will understand. Especially on a day like today. Today we are free from all sin, all guilt, all censure, from all those things that can never be forgiven, from all humiliation. On a day like today it may in fact be a sin to fast, Father, a sin to remember that it's just an ordinary day and not eternity, let us say. God cannot hold it against man, if from time to time he chooses to free himself from Him. Indeed it was God who first set man free from Himself. He drove him out of paradise, after all.

Condemned him to freedom for not living up to the bondage in which He kept him. And you know, Father, it's very strange that God is meant to be so wise yet He had such a miserable conception of the happiness of man. For paradise turned out to be a virtual cage. The best proof being that, when God became convinced of this, He drove man away from Him so that at least man wouldn't destroy His illusions. And ever since He has kept Himself apart from people, remaining alone with Himself for all time. Now, no doubt, He wanders around His paradise grieving, afraid to admit to Himself that He misses man. I feel sorry for God, Father. Oh, I didn't wish to offend you in any way, God forbid. I really don't have anything against God. I only try to understand Him. Just as a moment ago I was trying to understand my cousin, although I can't stand people who have been badly brought up. But I shall never touch rabbit again. I've been put off it for good. I swear. As I sit here before you. I shall never touch it again.

However, let's have a drink. And perhaps someone will tell us a story, but a jolly one, a jolly one, so we can at least have a bit of a laugh, like at a party when one person says something, somebody else cuts in with a sarcastic remark, then someone slags off someone else, and everybody falls about laughing with tears in their eyes. It doesn't matter if it's untrue as long as it's jolly. Let it be without beginning, without end, but it must be jolly. Indecent, sinful, but jolly. The ladies will forgive us. Anyway, the ladies also like to have a laugh along with us. After all, we're not here just to eat and drink. We need laughter so we know that we exist, that we are alive, that we have not gathered around this table today in vain. For laughter, dear ladies and gentlemen, is as intoxicating as the best liquor. Laughter even softens our memory. Besides, what have we got left now apart from our laughter? We can no longer get by without our laughter. Time was, time was, when we used to laugh, make merry, and heigh ho, that was that! Where have they gone, those wonderful times? So let us have a laugh today, too, if only for a little. On this day that we share together. Laughter is our last hope, and who knows whether it's not also the only thing we can still be proud of? Even though our laughter might be as empty as our hearts.

No, no, things aren't that bad with us. But it always pays to have a laugh. For we'll start yawning soon. The Count, if you please, is already yawning like a dragon. Ha! Ha! Ha! As for me, only laughter will save me now, for it all bores me so. I'm sick to death of cards. Well, I wouldn't say no if I could find someone who'd stake his whole fortune, his soul. And as for women, they're all as alike as one day is to the next. So I only speak to men, to men. Women don't listen. Ha! Ha! Ha! I'm simply gripped by fear sometimes, it even hurts me, when some woman undresses in front of me. When I see her exposing her banality, that flower she fancies is so rare. Feeling ashamed as well. I simply feel sorry for her. I don't know whether I should hate her or forgive her. But if I forgive her, believe me, I feel as though I'd done nothing but humiliate her and myself too, as though all I'd done was take pity on us both. No, no, my dear priest, it's not what you think. There's no need to cross yourself. There's only ever been that first one, the one and only one, who once revealed herself to me for real and for ever. She was above and beyond my wildest dreams, above and beyond my desire. Maybe it was even I who revealed her to my own self, and so vividly, my good priest, that I burned myself out inside her. I can't even remember her, for my memory was burned out inside her, too. And now it seems to me that all the others that have come after her – if I desire them at all – just retrace the form of her body, her shame, even her ecstasy. There is something false in their eyes, in their hair, in their nakedness, in everything about them. Also, they sigh, gasp. Ugh, it's terrible to hear. You imagine you must be ill-treating them. They're not even capable of holding their peace, not just in front of me, but in front of themselves. Hunting bores me, too. It's always the same thing. Partridges, ducks, hares, sometimes a pheasant. And that's your lot. Nowadays there aren't even any wild boar. You set out as though on some great expedition. Like in the old days. Dogs, horses, huntsmen, beaters. And what are you off to hunt for, my love? Those partridges, ducks, hares. Oh, if only we'd come across a bear one day or some other wild animal, then at least we'd still have something to make us tremble. Remember, Count? You from behind the beech tree, me from behind the oak. We fire, we fire, whilst it roars and roars, tearing apart the sky above, bringing the trees crashing down. And what about nowadays?

Everything's more timid than man himself. And, believe me, I'm already overcome by despair when I get undressed for bed and think that in the morning I shall have to get dressed again, and undress yet again in the evening, dress in the morning, undress in the evening, dress, undress, so that sometimes I don't want to live to see the end of the day. It's just as well my valet's there to help me, because on my own I wouldn't even have the strength.

How boring this life is! But what will become of it all? What will become of it all? Surely the only person here who feels happy at this moment is our good priest, for having put his trust in God. And man will never get bored with God. Yes, yes, it's true. But our good priest hasn't anticipated that God might get bored with him. Ha! Ha! Ha! But it's just the same, my dear priest. Just the same thing. For whoever bores God, abuses His indulgence towards us, His kindness, His patience. Thereby reveals himself to be unworthy of His trust. Unworthy even of His grace. Therefore he lives in sin. And maybe in the gravest of sin, as well, for it was not committed of his own free will. And those are the gravest sins, or so we are taught by original sin. And quite right too. Why should God have to be bored by you, my dear priest? Well, yes, I was expecting you'd be surprised. You really are like a child. Though no, no. It's beautiful even, because of that heartfelt pain which lies at the root of your insecurity. Only who can tell, I ask you, my good priest? Who can tell? After all, His thoughts are impenetrable. And an impenetrable thought is an infinity, it is in itself the explanation of every doubt, the justification and cause of every thing, or, if you like, the demystification of the mystery. Maybe He's bored for no reason, and that's the most honest of reasons, believe me. Just as without reason He bestows happiness on some of us and suffering on others. Or perhaps it's because you're so loyal to Him, humble to the point of helplessness. So He no longer expects anything from you, not even the adoration of Himself – for that adoration is only His own adoration, which merely finds its reflection in you, the priest, and then returns to Him. But God is only one of us, my dear priest. He even has the same desires as one of us. If loyalty and humility were therefore all He wanted, He would have created a world that was loyal to Him, and humble. Yet what kind of a world did He create? A world of which He Himself could never be sure. It is said that there will be greater joy in heaven over one sinner who repents than over ninety-nine just men who do not need to repent. God seeks joy, just like man. Just like man, He is tormented by His unsatisfied desires, by His insecurity, but meanwhile our priest is merely one of those ninety-nine just men. So what does it matter, I beg you, my good priest, what does it matter that you might bore God not of your own free will? You seem to overestimate man's free will, or you understand it, if you'll pardon the expression, somewhat parochially. Oh, no, my dear priest, I cannot agree. We should go on arguing for a long while yet, but I'm afraid that everyone would get bored, including ourselves.

And so, my dear ladies and gentlemen, we can't allow you to get bored in our company, can we? Long life to us all! Ladies, ladies, here's to you, long life, and may you grow even more beautiful! That's right! Even more beautiful! And maybe someone will show us how they used to drink in the old days. By the quart, my darlings! Down the hatch in one! So, who'll try a quart, then? Hey, bring in a quart. So, who's it going to be? Who'll be the one? Is there such a man among us? Have we already sunk so low that no one will dare to do it even for the sake of our honour? Not even for the sake of our honour, no one? I'll give a greyhound if someone's prepared to save our honour. The fastest greyhound in my kennels. It's no longer just a matter of drinking, gentlemen. Remember that. If a greyhound's not enough, then I'll give a horse. The very best in my stables. Of the purest blood. A storm of a horse. A ball of flames. Arrogance personified. I'll give two horses. I'll give two horses with a carriage. With a coachman. With a coachman who's strong and obedient. Who never opens his mouth, just bows and scrapes. I'll give an acre of land. So, who's it going to be? I'll give ten acres! A wood! I'll give a meadow! How about you, Count? I'll give you my canaries. All of them. All of them. So, who then? I'll give the prettiest girl on the estate. I'll give a virgin. A saint. Plaits like braids around the wheatsheaves. Eyes like two plums plucked from a young graft, still coated with their snowy powder. Neck erect as a poplar, and slender. So it's unimaginable that one day her skin will be chapped and that her old woman's craw will mar her beauty. Breasts unsullied by a man's hand. Unable to accept one another, each goes on growing to spite the other. The lucky man who rests his hands upon them will feel them growing throughout his whole body. The pits of her arms like the nests of tiny birds. Woven wreaths of warm convolvulus. When she raises her arms it's as if she opens up her body. And her white belly like a sculptured loaf. And her shame almost too painful to bear. But I'll give her away, I'll give her away. So, who's it going to be? Who? No one? Oh, you...? Well, I'll do it myself then.

I stand up, raise the goblet high, way above my eyes. The red glow of the sun catches fire in the vodka. I feel a sense of my own nobility as I stand over the table with my goblet raised high. I can almost see myself standing there with this red goblet, see myself with everyone else's eyes, watching warily to see what toast I'll propose. But I prolong my standing, prolong their fearful watching. The red goblet is no longer a goblet, but a candle ablaze in my hand. I can see how beautiful I look, above this table, above their silence, above their insecurity, so beautiful I almost regret I'll have to lose sight of myself. A kind of liberating sweetness envelops me. I imagine that, if I wanted to stretch out my hand, I could reach the ceiling. But what's happening now? The vodka is beginning to rise in my goblet, overflow, run down my hands in bloody streaks. I shout, transported by my own excitement. Cheers! Long life to us all! And knock it back in one.

Suddenly I'm overwhelmed by tiredness. All my joy deserts me in an instant. I no longer see myself, feel myself. I sit down, desiring nothing. Nothing. Nothing. Not even to look. Not even to think. But here comes that fear that they might notice my weakness. And then the exchange of glances will begin, the smirks, the tacit understandings full of conspiratorial sympathy, behind my back, over my head, like a verdict passed against me, like their pity. This fear brings me to my feet again. I bang my fist on the table. I don't know why. But I regain my faith in myself when I hear how my fist makes the plates resound, the glasses, knives, forks, the whole table.

How good of you all to come! It's so nice to be together. To sit for a while, have a chat, reminisce about old times, even have a drink together. It's not the same when you're on your own. Oh, it's so nice, so nice, to be together.

Yet this attempt to ingratiate myself seems somehow false, sneering. As though I was trying to hide something, and against my will even. I don't know. I don't know. I sit down again. Smile genially, expansively.

I have to tell you that I do enjoy a drink. Sometimes one glass is sufficient, or two, and everything starts to mellow. Even I start to mellow. Believe me. If I have three, four, then everything seems clear and simple. Even the thoughts inside me seem to think of their own accord, all I have to do is give them my consent. And if I drink any more, then I almost feel happy. I feel like a tamed beast. Nothing affords me any pain, I long for nothing, nothing surprises me. I feel I want to forgive people. And I do forgive them. I'm keen to pardon them all. And I do pardon them. And when I really knock it back, I turn into a real St Francis. Then I even want to make people happy. But only when I'm drunk. Besides, the moment quickly passes. But perhaps, my dears, we ought not to despise these fleeting moments, for who knows, maybe it's precisely these moments that arc the eternal thing in man. Sometimes I even resolve to give everything away to other people, and then to set forth into the world with only my beggar's staff. Stand outside the church. If I smile at myself afterwards, then I smile at myself afterwards. But when I'm drunk, my mind is made up. To give away all my earthly possessions. Perhaps to those who have never enjoyed my bounty, never heard a word from me, never been spared one of my thoughts. I will give them all my lands, even the ones I've never known. All my forests along with their game. My pastures, my countless herds of cattle, my boundless flocks of sheep. My horses, dogs, canaries. I'll give them all away. All my servants, chambermaids, valets. All my carriages, coaches. All the trees in the park with the birds singing in them. All these rooms. This entire palace. I'll give it all away! Give it all away!

Or I dream that there will come a time when the people themselves will force their way in here, make themselves at home, throw riotous parties, lay their hands on all these sacred treasures, on all this inviolable universe. May it all be dismantled, and may everyone take away a token in memory of me. How many tokens there would be just from that one mirror, if someone were to smash it! From everything else too. From the stoves if they were split into tiles, from the carpets if they were reduced to strips, to shreds, from the ceilings, from the paintings, from everything. How many tokens of remembrance! How many salvations! How many moments of happiness! I feel almost green with envy. I'd like to be able to experience their happiness with them. The very thought of it fills me with joy, excites me, liberates me. Why? I myself have no idea why. Because of something dreadful, incomprehensible. I'd like to experience this happiness, which I see, which I sometimes dream about at night, as one of them, as one of that great throng possessed by hatred and joy, one of that great throng of women, men, children, old men, which forces its way in here, breaking down the doors and windows. Oh, don't worry, Cousin, it's only a dream. At least suffer the dream as a gentleman! I would like to experience it as one of them, as any one of them, as long as it was one of them, someone quite ordinary, someone in the crowd, someone driven neither by hatred nor by joy, but just someone making up the crowd. Perhaps as the unbeliever willing to be scared by his own flush of courage, as the youth who simply ran after his parents when word got around that everyone was heading for the palace; or as the lame old man with one good leg and one wooden leg, who simply got swept off his feet by the crowd and brought here, to the Rooms. Or perhaps even as their Christ figure. For at a moment like this someone ought to hand himself over to be crucified, so that the moment can become an eternity. So that when they burst in here, they won't suddenly be frightened by these rooms, by this luxury, by these sacred treasures, so that their faith won't desert them, so that they won't renounce their joy and their hatred and suddenly strike the bell of reason, themselves struck down by great sobs of submission. So that they might feel worthy not of that moment, but of eternity.

Imagine them, Count, kneeling here and weeping, they, the triumphant ones. I think even you would be moved by it. That even you would be inclined to offer yourself up to them at such a moment. If you weren't prepared to do it for them, then you'd do it to capture that fleeting breath of eternity, that glimpse of sublimity, which barely has a chance to ignite before it's extinguished, as though it sparked and died within yourself. For what kind of salvation can there be without Christ? Come on, you tell us, my dear priest, you know best. What kind of salvation? Shake your head at least, if you're afraid of the question. Ha! Ha! Ha! And without His thieves too. Yes, yes, without His thieves too. What kind of salvation? And don't imagine I'm drunk. I was only mucking about with you. Anyway, think what you like, but I'm telling you I've never been as sober as I am now sitting amongst you. Hence without His thieves too. What kind of salvation? For without the thieves salvation can't be the same as it was. For in salvation there is, after all, just as much sin as saintliness. Thus someone has to take the sins upon himself, so that someone else can take the saintliness. So they, the thieves, hate instead of Him, curse and swear instead of Him, but they do not forgive their torturers instead of Him, so that He can forgive them. Maybe they also bear His humiliation, His crown of thorns, His side pierced by the sword, the nails in His hands and legs, maybe even the bitterness of the gall He was given to drink, His whole cross, and that's why they were hung on crosses just like Him. Made to bear all human pain instead of Him. They even doubt instead of Him, and thus He's so sure of His own ascent into heaven. Perhaps they are even afraid instead of Him. So that He wouldn't be able to commit any sin as an ordinary human being. Thus He has them to thank for His being God, for without them He wouldn't even be able to bear His own humanity. And therefore they, dying alongside Him, aren't even people, but thieves. And I shall choose some of you to be the thieves. Perhaps you, Cousin, and you, Count. But you don't have to start worrying yet. I still don't know whether you're up to the part. I don't know if I can trust you, if you're deserving. I need volunteers. Those who've been forced into it easily back out. Perhaps you'll begin to regret it, resist it, dissolve into floods of tears, promise mountains of gold when you've no longer got anything to promise. And they'll only poke fun at you, mock you, and me as well along with you. And we won't even earn their forgiveness.

Oh, look, there, in the doorway. A shriek of joy bears them hither. A tide of fever. As they bear one another along. The place is full of them. And I now descend the marble stairs to meet them, dressed in my best frock-coat, which I have never worn before, which I was keeping for some great occasion, should it ever occur, and if not, then for when I die. Dressed in my snow-white gloves. My shiny new boots. These are the first steps I've ever taken in them. And every step creaks as though the marble were creaking beneath my feet. They turn to watch me and fall silent. And I address them. Welcome to my home. Do what your consciences command. Here I am. Bind my hands, my legs, tie me to a chair, and you'll feel less constrained. And your joy will be even greater. Somehow they bind me up, tie me to a chair. Slap me on the back like a brother. Stare long and curiously into my eyes as though they can't quite believe that I'm here among them. Poke fun at me as though I were some freak hatched out of their chaos. Where is my power, they ask, where is my inviolability, if I can't reach my face with my hands to wipe away the dribble, or can't shift my legs from under their callused feet, which trample all over me as they go on asking derisively, where is my power? Where is your power, your lordship? One of us will have to take pity on you and chase the fly from your forehead, so that it doesn't suck its way into your brain. I'm not feeling too sad, am I? they ask. If so, then they'll tickle me. Is death rocking me to sleep? Then they'll wake me up. Or maybe I'd like to say my prayers, in which case they'll hear me out. Or perhaps I long to confess; if so, they'll remind me of my sins. And they confess all my sins for me, one after the other, becoming bolder and bolder. More and more of them press close around me. But a wave of joy sweeps over me, that they've come to my aid like brothers, that I'm able to rejoice with them as though with my own joy. And I rejoice. And I laugh with their laughter. Cheer, as they bring down the mirrors from the rooms and smash them in front of me. When they sing, I sing along with them. And feel no remorse at their curses, when they curse me. And none of it causes me any pain. None of it causes me any pain. Believe me.

They're running riot throughout the palace. I can hear endless doors slamming, the almost musical effect of window-panes shattering to smithereens, the stairs pounding drumlike. I can hear yells of desperation, quarrels, women's squeals – I can't tell whether of joy or terror, for it all drowns itself out many times over. It seems to me that it's not the palace that resounds so thunderously, but some enormous organ which the people play as they run all over it, going down on their knees, beating it with their fists, like choirs of fallen angels released from the bonds of heaven. Yet I feel, as I listen intently to this echoing palace, swelling with sound, that I am experiencing one of the most sublime moments of my life.

Suddenly, in the doorway leading to the corridor, there appears some miserable specimen of a man. More or less your height, Count, but only half the man you are. Embarrassed, he looks sheepishly around the drawing-room. Crushes his cap in his hands. Bows to me once, and then again. A moronic smile on his face. He doesn't know where to begin. He bows to me again. I see I'm late, he says in a sorrowful voice. But I've not come for anything, your lordship. I don't want anything. Let them all enjoy themselves, let them scratch you to bits, but I shall simply take a look round your palace and go my own way. You were an evil man, your lordship. Hell will swallow you up, no doubt about it, but we shall all miss you once you've gone.

And over there some lout is hauling Grandmother's portrait along on his shoulders. Vast as a nuptial bed. From the days of her youth. From the days when she was still a beautiful woman. From the days when she was high and mighty. Her bare arms, her neck, her breasts gleaming with an astounding whiteness. I want to shut my eyes for shame. But this fellow chucks the painting down on the parquet, kneels beside it, bends right over Grandmother's beautiful, astonished face and just gazes, gazes into those enormous eyes. Then he begins to trace his great callused paw timidly over her hair, smiling more and more tenderly, more and more sweetly, as though imploring her, his eyes burning feverishly. Ah, you, my lady. He touches her white forehead nervously, strokes her face, fondles her bare arms. Then he covers her eyes with his paw and draws his massive kneeling body closer to her, as something inside him begins to tremble. Suddenly he lays his head on the painting and kisses Grandmother's hands as they lie crossed on her lap, in the folds of her dress. Nestles his flaxen head into her half-exposed breasts. Presses those great paws into her shoulders till it's painful to behold. And then he drops his great dead weight on to her body, his passion spent, or maybe simply regretting it.

Ah, what a delight it is to see you, my lord! I hear her trembling voice. I don't know her, don't recognize her, but nor does my intuition let me down. It's her. She comes prancing towards me with a gait I can't quite describe – dancing, flirtatious, drunken. She laughs, but her laugh is bitter, fierce, though rather gushing. A frail wisp of a woman, her hair straggling and dishevelled, her ashen face faintly luminous, her flowery dress too baggy, her feet bare. Yet she walks as though she wants to show me she's a princess. Perhaps she's drunk, perhaps consumed by some fever, perhaps she's just trying to deceive me with this smile, with her haughty, dancing approach. It doesn't suit her. What suits her is piety, quietude, humility, work, something in which she would lose herself so completely she would no longer exist, so that not even God would notice her. For even being a woman doesn't suit her.

Ah, what a delight it is to see you, my lord, in such a sorry state. What a delight to be able to feel compassion for you too. To be able to see you at such close quarters, to see you to my heart's content, without any shame, without having to be submissive or afraid. What a delight. To be able to soak myself in your nearness so intensely, till my thirst is quenched. To be able to stroke your hair, as you stroke someone's hair when you long to bring them comfort. To be able to touch your face with impunity and even feel its warmth in the palm of my hand. To be able to force your eyes to look. Your thoughts to remember. To be able to say to you whatever I like, whatever can be put into words, whatever hurts you and whatever rejoices within you, whatever memory recalls and hope inspires, and you won't even have the strength not to hear. To be able to feel neither guilty nor submissive in your presence. Accursed in your presence. Non-existent in your presence. To be able to miss you, even, without the foreboding that I was bringing unhappiness upon myself. To be able to disbelieve all the things people say about you.

You weren't expecting me, my lord. You weren't even aware of my existence. But it's so easy to perish in the abundance of your riches that I am not the first to perish. I am not the only one to have thrown in her lot with you in the sole hope that one day you'll cast me a kindly glance. Perhaps you'll even ask who my parents are. What's my name? And you'll say what a pretty name. Perhaps you'll even tell me to come to the Rooms, to sweep away the dust, clear up after your guests, do something to help before Christmas, before the spring, it doesn't matter what, it needn't be anything, as long as I'm closer to you. Though you'll attach no special meaning to your words, unaware that I shall take them to heart. And when I come, perhaps you won't even recognize me as the girl you once told to come to the palace, on a generous impulse, for your own solace, in a moment of carelessness. For why should you recognize me, you, who recognize no one in this world apart from yourself? Why should you recognize me among so many, among so many who are so alike? But perhaps my desire for you will single me out from amongst everything else. And maybe you'll succumb to my presence alone, for you have no idea how all-consuming presence in itself can be. You don't know when, but it'll force itself into your eyes, into your thoughts, into your memory, into your anxiety, into your words. You'll surrender perhaps to my bustling about in front of your eyes, though you'll surrender out of boredom, out of indifference, like you surrender out of boredom to staring at an empty wall, at flies crawling over crumbs of bread, or out of a window when you can't even see whether anything lies beyond it or whether that glass boundary is simply the end of the world. Maybe you'll think to yourself, when you no longer feel like thinking about anything in particular, how clean and tidy I am, how quiet, so quiet, that I'm here and yet you can't hear me, that I'm submissive, made for work, for housework, as though I was of service only to my own hands. But you'll think it. And I shall be that thought of yours, the least burdensome of all your thoughts. And maybe I'll arouse your interest just because I am. Why yes, just because I am at all. And then maybe because I am a woman. Because I'm ugly, thin, consumptive, as though that wasn't enough to put you off, but also because I am a woman. As inconspicuous as a mouse, yet a woman. You won't be able to distinguish my lips from my pallor, my eyes from my sadness, my desire from my fever, yet I'm still a woman. My body's nothing to speak of, my breasts almost shaming, yet I'm a woman. And furthermore a woman swallowed up by sweeping the dust in your chambers, visible only as that sweeping of dust, as though vanishing along with that dust, swept away by her own hands. Yet still a woman. Almost deserving of pity for being a woman. And so I shall take shape from out of your boredom, my lord. But maybe because of this I shall appear to you other than I am, for I won't arise out of your desire – maybe I'll be even richer because of your compassion for me, your pity. Perhaps in me you'll even discover for the first time that you've been yearning for ages to feel compassion for someone, to take pity on someone. And maybe because of this I shall seem different from the roses that bloom for you every night, whose bodies are the only pleasure they can give you. Upon whom you can bestow nothing of yourself, for their bodies require nothing from you in order for you to desire them. Whose deformities you can't even forgive, for they know no deformities. They are born of crystal, of light, of flowers, of sweet fragrances, but not of flesh, which would be nothing but eternal anguish if no one ever forbore its inadequacies, which must go through the hell of fear and doubt before it surrenders itself to pleasure. They, I'm sure, never hide their shame before you, never cower in your arms, in the palms of your hands, never shudder when you take them, for none of them ever suffers at the sight of nakedness. They simply blossom forth in front of you, vibrant and sublime. They recline on the bedding all the better to be seen, as though they were reclining in heaven, as though they were reclining only for themselves, for they are surely sufficient unto themselves both for their own pleasure and for yours, my lord. Roses, which you have to want only for their bodies, for that's all you can do with them. Which will allow you only as much as they themselves desire, and they desire very little, for they have no need to desire anything more.

Perhaps I shall discover that emptiness within you, my lord, when you've already cooled towards one and haven't yet begun to want the next. Perhaps I shall discover that emptiness and fill it up, without your even wishing me to, without your longing for me – your emptiness itself will draw me in as the only presence round about you, and I shall become the only presence within you.

All you will be able to do is fear this emptiness inside you, feel yourself suddenly alone and all the more solitary because you're a great lord, feel yourself abandoned by everyone, by everyone, and you won't even have the courage to ring for a valet, so you won't have to hear that he too has abandoned you. Perhaps you'll even sense death within you, for you're as unaccustomed to emptiness inside you as summer is unaccustomed to snow, and then you will surrender to me and to me alone, like you'd surrender to any other woman at such a moment, like you'd surrender to God, even if you'd never known Him. I shall be the only one who'll discover that fleeting emptiness inside you, like the lucky man who discovers a blossoming fern on midsummer's night. And you will spot me, shower me with emotion because you yourself will long for emotion; you'll understand me as you understand yourself, not me, and perhaps you will say, Come closer. Come on, come closer. Don't be afraid.

I longed for you, my lord, but you never saw me. You saw only the prettier ones. I yearned for you across mountains and seas, throughout all the time we never spent together, throughout your absence in this world, throughout the cruel fate that took you from me, throughout the furthermost distance, as only I knew how, but you were still further away, as far as the span between heaven and hell. I prayed for you to get well, though you were never sick, for you to return unscathed from the war, though there was never a war, for you to be happy with me, though you were never with me. And I prayed not to God, but directly to you, and I was never afraid that I passed Him by between us. And I even put on my mourning clothes, for you weren't enough for me, I wanted to experience your absence too, so that your entirety would be complete inside me. Oh, but to imagine you, my lord, that was too easy, too meagre, too happy – I wanted it to hurt as well. So I stole up to the palace when there was a ball on and imagined that it was our ball, that we were dancing together through the rooms and chambers, that somewhere I could hear my own laughter and your laughter alongside mine, that there was nobody there except us, the music and my happiness. And it so happened that the watchman found me asleep, frozen to death, wet with dew, and sent me running back home.

I walked right before your eyes, my lord, yet you were blind to my presence. Once I even spilled the milk in front of you, as I carried it from milking, so that you would be mightily angry with me. And with good reason, so much milk gone to waste. So that you would swear at me, attack me with your fists, grab hold of my hair and rub my nose in that spilled milk. Perhaps you'd even banish me from the estate. So that you might just notice me, so that at least in that short moment of anger you might become full of me. But unfortunately for me you were in a kind mood that day. And all you said was, Oh, clumsy girl! And you glanced at the pool of milk as if it were a puddle left by the rain. And you spoke so graciously that someone else must have been speaking instead of you, for you were far removed from the both of us. Not even for a moment did I tear you away from your thoughts. Though the people who saw it said afterwards that I'd been very lucky. And they talked about my good fortune for a long time to come, even today they still go on about it. But I wept at that good fortune, envying your dogs, which can fondle your hands with their coats, or your horses, in which you find so much consolation.

You don't even know, my lord, that it happened, but you were mine once. Only for one night, but you were mine. You came to me at midnight, when sinful souls seek each other out. I was ashamed that my bed had nothing but a rough canvas covering, that I hadn't made it up with sheets for your coming, that I had no case for my pillow, that the inner slip was threadbare and you'd get feathers in your hair. I was ashamed. That maybe the fleas would settle all over you, that you weren't used to my younger sister at your feet (I didn't know how to hide her), that there were so many of us in the one room; then there were the hens on the stove ledge clucking in their sleep, the pig in the corner behind the partition, and the cow down the end who likes to shake her chain in the middle of the night. And it was so stuffy, reeking of bodies, animals, breath. I was ashamed. For a moment I hoped that maybe it wasn't you. For it was beyond my belief, beyond my understanding. I don't know, but I was afraid of something. Maybe I was afraid of you. Your hands were so awkward, not like those of a gentleman, and your breath was so bitter, urgent, as though you'd fled from somewhere and come running to me to hide yourself in my body.

As though you sought tenderness only from me; you, who are so great in yourself, sought tenderness from me, wanted someone to feel sorry for you, and so you nestled into me like an injured child nestling into its mother, into my body splayed out for you. Then we sunk into one another. The room was airless, stuffy. But you were gentle, my lord, with the gentleness of sheep. I could feel that gentleness in your hands as you stumbled shyly over my body. I could feel it when you took my breast in your lips and listened to my heart as it raced towards you, as though you were trying to guess from its beat just how much I wanted you. So perhaps I was afraid lest you didn't want anything from me, only that I should desire you. And when I awoke in the morning, all wet because of you, you were already gone from my side. You'd vanished without even waking me. Only the hot, crumpled bed and my body full of you were witness to our having enjoyed each other that night. And I knew I'd conceived, my lord. I didn't feel like getting up, though the sun was already high in the sky; I'd forgotten I had to rush to the estate to milk the cows, I'd forgotten everything apart from that night.

Oh, look what a belly I've grown! My body's about to split open. My legs sprawl all over the place with my every step. I can't cope with carrying him any more. How long has it been now, how long? I should have given birth a long time ago, but I'm afraid to. He's already big; he runs, kicks, as though he was trying to cross a river inside me. He's already so big that it seems to me it's not him who's growing inside me, but me inside him. In his burgeoning body, in the shadow of his limbs, swaddled entirely in his body as though swathed in a vine, wrapped in his warm, wet body, permeated by his body, pinned down as by a fallen tree, so that I no longer feel my own body, only his body, huge, hard as stone, trembling with my trembling, thirsting with my thirst, shamed by the sin I committed with you, my lord. At night I can feel how he lies down inside me, and how, if I can't sleep, he too lies wide awake for hours, tormented by my thoughts, tossing from side to side, jostling me with his elbows, stretching his arms and legs, or even tickling me with his long lashes as he stares fixedly at some point in the darkness. Tell me it's a good thing that he doesn't want to be born. Tell me. For what would he do in this world? He's branded by sin, after all; sin would be his destiny. And perhaps he'd long to return to me, finding no joy for himself elsewhere, perhaps pining for me day after day, but what good would I be? I couldn't even be a mother to him any more. For once I part with him, it'll be for ever. And in parting with him, my lord, I'll be parting with you too for ever. Thus I walk around constantly heavy with child, constantly brimming with benignity, with anticipation. Oh, if only you would just glance at me now and say, Come on, come closer. Come closer.

No, I don't want anything from you. Just let the people gather, oh, let the people gather, and I'll tell them how you dishonoured me, my lord. In floods of tears I shall swear before God how you dishonoured me. I shall rend my garments, lay bare my body, and let them look, let them feel ashamed at how you dishonoured me. Let them see my belly full of you. And these long scars like snakes left by your hands. Let them see it all. Oh, let them see the fullness of your lips still upon me, let them see your hair, my breasts shrivelled after you'd sucked them dry, let them see how you dishonoured me, my own lord and master. And in return you didn't even give me a cow like you gave other girls, not even a heifer, though you gave one to others, with pasture too sometimes, with a watering-hole, with the right to trespass on your land, but I didn't even get a calf. That's how much you dishonoured me. You didn't even give me a day off work, not even that one night we spent together; you ordered me to make up the time. Swear, that you came to me that night. Swear, before people begin to gather here from out of the chambers, that you will notice me again one day and ask me my name, and that you'll say I have a pretty name, and that you'll ask me to come to the Rooms, and that you'll remember that puddle of milk, which I spilled at your feet. And that there, beside that puddle, from which people fled so as not to see what would happen to me, you will gently take my chin in your white hand with all its rings, and raise my eyes, panic-stricken, red with tears, to meet your eyes, and say to me, Don't cry. I don't want anything more from you, just those words, Don't cry. Swear, and I'll cut loose the ties. Can't you hear the people coming? Swear before they gather. For only with my help will you be able to get out of here, as though I'd seized you for myself just as they are seizing your riches. Can't you hear them?

Too late. Too late. People are already descending upon us from every direction. Squeezing through all the doors. On tiptoe. Lurking in secret corners. Some of them hovering in the drawing-room doorway, glancing around before crossing the threshold, as though they bore fear along with them. And from the more distant rooms come their shrieks, barks, howls. They're after the game! It can't be anything else, they're after the game. That's the dogs! The pointers, greyhounds. But they fall silent as they sweep into the drawing-room. They go berserk as if they'd lost the scent. And after them come the beaters. You can hear them lamenting. Thrashing the furniture with their sticks, battering the walls, splintering the mirrors. Someone somewhere strikes the piano. And plays. Plays to the whole house, echoing through all the rooms. Bringing the walls tumbling down. Playing to the very skies. Your heart stands still in panic. Your heart swells to fill your very throat. You want to shove your fists in your ears and smash your head to smithereens. Suffocate yourself. Trample on yourself. And after the beaters come the gunmen. Some with their guns at the ready. Peacock feathers in their hats. I'm suddenly seized by a wild, uncontrollable laughter. For they're all in fancy dress, in my frock-coats, in my dressing-gowns, in my shirts. They look like guests from a ball the morning after, abandoning themselves to eccentricity so as not to fall sad. I rock with laughter. And the dogs, great God, have mercy on the dogs! Dogs in dresses, in shirts on top of dresses, festooned in dresses. And in every kind of dress imaginable – morning dresses, day dresses, evening dresses, ball dresses. Dresses so long you can't see their paws underneath, can't see their claws, or so short they don't even reach the knees of the smallest. You can't tell a dog from a bitch, a pointer from a dachshund. The dogs themselves have vanished into thin air. All you can do is laugh at them. Weep for them.

People, what's got into you?! I speak. Shout. Feel myself shouting, feel my throat stinging from my shouting. I'm ripping my mouth apart, yet they don't hear me. I can tell from their expressions, from the look in their eyes, from their sneering, sinister smiles, from the silence which they spread all around me. Perhaps they're praying for me, perhaps deciding what they think of me, perhaps weighing up their verdicts. People, what's got into you? Look how I'm rejoicing with you! Listen how glad I am to be with you! Ha! Ha! Ha! Nothing can harm me now! It's all yours! Take the lot! Distribute it amongst yourselves! It's all yours! I'm one of you!

No, your lordship, you cannot be one of us. It's not enough for you to be one of us just this once. In order to be truly one of us, you would have to be with us for a long time, suffer patiently, live without hope. In order to be one of us, you'd have to live to regret the day you were born, not the day you must die. So how can you be one of us, such a noble lord? We've decided to organize a hunt for ourselves. A magnificent hunting expedition. With dogs. With huntsmen. With real game. With horns sounding. We've been poaching in this world quite long enough. Tortured enough poor creatures with our snares, decoys, traps, pits, pummelled them to death with our sticks, strangled them with our hands, heedless of whether it was a doe-hare heavy with young, or whether we were wresting a mother from its babes, for our own children always brought us much more pain than those of the hare. Oh, we've been poaching quite long enough. Now we want to kill like noblemen. But we don't know how, and that is our weakness. Perhaps we need a horn to lead the way. Here, take the horn and play, for none of us will do it right. And in return we'll let you be a stag rather than a hare when we make you run away. Play, play a refrain that will strike a chord in the hearts of the game, for how else shall we know that the hunt's begun? Play to us, and let the dogs move off into the forest, let the beaters move off too, let's all be on our way. Play, and let it ring out throughout the forest. A refrain that is long drawn out, auguring ill, full of rejoicing, but full of bitterness too. Perhaps the refrain will embolden us. For the refrain paves our way. The refrain proclaims that we come not in stealth or as cowards. That we lie not in ambush, but challenge the game to come forth and meet us. Here, take the horn and play! And we'll find you a horse for this refrain so that, when you play, you won't have to stand there like a condemned man, but will tower above us. Hey, you there, come here a moment. You can be the horse that will bear his lordship! The horse that will bear our refrain! Just get that dress off you and put on a saddle-cloth.

And don't get any funny ideas about being a stallion, because it won't get you anywhere. You'll be a mare. And don't stand there so stiffly, but lightly, on your pussy paws. And don't let your back sag. Hey, you there! I'm talking to you, yes, you, stop playing at being a greyhound!

You're laughing, Cousin, no doubt wondering where they'll get their game. But we, Cousin, we are their game. We'd forgotten about ourselves. We'll give them their game. Ha! Ha! Ha! Real, live game too, timid, helpless. All we can do is give them their wildfowl, hares, stags. For all we're good for now is fear. There's no life in us any more, only fear. Even what you imagine to be our dignity, Cousin, is also nothing but fear. You've not actually said so, I know, but that's what you think. We're already scared of each other, my dear. Fear is our love, our hatred, our conscience. Fear is the only thing now that binds us together. And it might not even be such a sad thing. It's all the same in the end, whatever keeps us going. The only trouble is, we haven't got anywhere to run to. The best we can do is to flee from room to room.

Oh, I can already see you there, my dear, standing on your hind legs, ears pricked up. It's not the wind, not the wind, that you can hear. It's people, though they're still a long way off. But what's this, Count? Go on, have a good snort, snort away. I see you'd like to be a wild boar. I understand. The Count fancies himself as big game. Well there's enough of you to make two wild boar. I'd advise you, however, to think again. The death of such a boar is not a thing to be envied. It doesn't die so easily, my dear, as for instance a hare. A hare staggers a bit and then it's all over. Sometimes a single shot is enough, and not a very accurate one either. Sometimes just the report is enough. Enough that he's frightened, and it's all over. A boar on the other hand, my dear Count, oh, he requires a bullet that is well-aimed, deep-seated, sincerely meant. And how difficult that sometimes is even for the best gunmen. It can happen that the boar will rise again to face a second bullet, a third, a tenth. For there's so much rage inside him that it won't let him give up the ghost even if he wanted to, as though it were in league with the gunman. Half dead already, he'll still drag himself off into the bushes, though he's no longer fighting for his life but for his death. And how much pain must he shed, how much blood, how much sorrow, before he finally gives up the ghost – what am I saying, gives up the ghost? – before he makes his peace with death. But such a death is not worth living for. I wouldn't advise you, Count, to be a wild boar. You must choose the nature of your death, not the nature of your skin. I'd advise a more trusting beast, which would display more consideration for the gunman, for the beaters, for the dogs, than for itself. Which would come up to the gun of its own accord, peer right into the barrel, courting the bullet as though nuzzling a loving palm. With such consideration you can even conquer death within you. Oh, even if you were a stag. For a stag, my dear, somehow trusts death. Maybe his instincts tell him that some kind of eternity will remain when he is gone. Those antlers, those horns, are always some kind of eternity. But as for you, Cousin, I'd advise you to remain yourself. That's too much for you as it is. Besides, I'm sure they won't recognize you.

For what can we do, my dears, now that the shooting season has opened for us? A cruel and unforgiving season. We'll never find anywhere to shelter from it. But the worst thing is that we don't have anyone to curse, nor do we know whom we might hate, whom we might weep for. Oh, tears would relieve our feelings, a driving, torrential rain of tears, our river of tears, our deluge of tears. But our eyes are dry, our eyes are unseeing. Even your lovely eyes, dear lady, are dry, unseeing. Those two precious stones, how could you ever cry with them? Though it seems to you, no doubt, that the world takes shape from out of your eyes, from out of your cornflower gaze, that the sun radiates from out of your eyes, that its gracious warmth is a reflection of your own gracious warmth. Do you really not want to hear that the hunt is drawing nigh? A magnificent hunt? How can I share my hearing of it with you? Perhaps, Cousin, you could put your ear to mine, and you'll hear the barking of the dogs approaching, furious, though still a long way off, as though they're on to the scent, on to the trail of blood. Can you hear them? And can you hear the beaters? And the huntsmen? How can I share my hearing of it with you? Does no one among you really want to know what is happening to us? We are alive. That's the truth. The honest truth. But what of it? Are we even aware of the fact that we're alive? Or have we just got used to being alive? But perhaps that's already more than we can take? Perhaps our having got used to it is also beyond us now? Perhaps we have merely surrendered to it, believing it'll shelter us from the world? Perhaps, therefore, we only feign to be alive? Feign this great life of ours. Our life of plenty, gay and tranquil. Life, our colourful life, a jewel among the peacocks! But are we at least aware of one thing, of this one thing: that we can never know less about ourselves than when we're seized by true gaiety, when we're shaken by empty laughter? For only when we know this can we really begin to live. Know that we can't forget about ourselves even for a moment, nor drift away into dreams for a moment, nor deceive ourselves, nor console ourselves. Know to the point of distrust of ourselves, hatred of ourselves, compassion for ourselves, fear of ourselves. Know though we may know nothing else. But that's how it is. Though we may shield ourselves from ourselves behind a shroud of darkness. Though we may be inaccessible even to our own intuitions. Though we may never do anything but suffer. For perhaps suffering is in fact the richest source of knowledge we can have, the source of both our wisdom and our need. And real knowledge consists not merely of wisdom, but of need at the same time. Such wisdom may be humble, bitter, boding no good, but only in this kind of wisdom can we understand ourselves as we can in no other, even though that other might be the wisest of wisdoms, the most perfect, omnipotent, awesome, like the wisdom of God, the wisdom of His heaven and hell, even though it may be full of goodwill towards us, like the unconscious wisdom of the birds, the wisdom of day and night, of the earth, of the waves. Oh, we know almost too much if we suffer. Know all there is to know – from hatred through to love. We ourselves are wisdom unto our own selves.

But what am I going on about? All one can do with you lot is eat, drink. So let's drink, eat! Let's laugh! Let's drink! Let's eat! It's so pleasant, after all, joyful, easy, uplifting, intense. Like nothing else in the world. Nothing. Nothing. You can really feel it inside yourself. You can immerse yourself body and soul in your eating, drinking. Look around you without seeing, hear without hearing, think without thinking. For when you're eating even time stands still. Take a look, my dears, my treasures, at the mountains of food in front of us, at the meats, sauces, and loads more besides, loads more besides. But sadness has dropped a damper on us like sparrow shit. Drowsiness is creeping up on us. Perhaps we'll start to cry. Cry, us? Oh, no. Never. We're in high spirits. I, for instance, have a baby bird breaking out of my soul. But what's up with you, Cousin? You do have some sort of a soul, don't you? It's abandoned you, you say? That's terrible! Your poor soul. But perhaps that unfortunate hare is hopping about somewhere inside you. Or, no, no. The rabbit. Ha! Ha! Ha! But I'd sing, you see, if you'd only let me. I'd drink to every one of you. Embrace every one of you, my spirit is so expansive today. I feel simply brimming with elation. With my nobility. Like a bird on the wing. I feel so high. My God, what high spirits I'm in! Hey, let everything around me rejoice with rejoicing! Let rejoicing flow from rejoicing! Hey! For when I'm in high spirits, then everyone else must be in high spirits too. Everyone! Even you, my jewel. And you, my good Father, so stop fretting about eternity. And you, my dear Countess. And you. And you. All of you. Eat! Drink! Sing! No, no, my dear Cousin, you haven't had enough at all. Obviously you've no idea what your limit is. You see, I told you, you didn't know anything about yourself. Your gullet, you say, is burning? Praise be to your gullet. Your liver's playing up? Let's drink to your liver. But eat, eat, or I'll order the valets to force-feed you. Then you'll have to eat even if you haven't got room. I won't spare you even if you begged me, even if you cried, it wouldn't help. Even God won't help you now. You always used to be such a glutton, Cousin. I used to recount, where and when I could, how proud I was of my cousin. On one occasion you just came over and cleaned me out, stripped me bare like ants stripping a corpse. You left empty larders in your wake, cooks steeped in mourning. What do you mean, it was all a long time ago? Those days were different? People used to eat differently? As far as I'm concerned then and now is all one and the same. All one long today. All an everlasting today. How could you ever dare to say such a thing, Cousin? I assure you it's not so. But perhaps you wish to be absolved of your sins already? What? Find yourself in hell already, so you can have it all over and done with. What? Eh, Cousin, stop trying to be so clever-clever. This gaiety of yours is somewhat dark. You'd have been a church beggar. A church beggar. It was me who got you out of your debts. Me. Just remember that. Your children would have been running around barefoot, covered in snot; you wouldn't have been able to tell them from peasants' children. But who bought you out? The Lord God, perhaps? What, it's not the done thing to talk about it in the family? Oh, there's many more things besides which I could go on about, but to hell with it. Let's drink up! To the very last drop! No, no, my good Father. When it's been decreed to the very last drop, then it has to be to the very last drop. Like in Holy Writ: It has been decreed, Amen. Like you were my brother, best man, go-between, it's been decreed to the very last drop, so to the very last drop it shall be. If God won't absolve you of your sins, then I shall. You will come to me and I shall give you absolution. God damn it. From everything. From anything you want. From all your christenings, funerals, from all your doubts. I'll give you absolution. From your housekeeper. I'll give you absolution. Don't worry. You won't even have to say very much, yet I'll give you absolution. For with me you'll find as much understanding as you could possibly want. With me you'll find heart enough for the whole world. The very essence of a forgiving heart. So drink up. Wherever you place your ear, there will be my heart. And here. And here too. In my hands, in my head, all around me, like this whole drawing-room. What am I saying, drawing-room? Like this whole palace. And so soft and pliant. Like wax. So drink. Drink, Father, drink. Sometimes I don't even have to tell it, and it starts to snivel. Sometimes I laugh, and it suddenly gets cold feet. Sometimes I feel like hanging one of my peasants, stringing him up on a branch. Believe me. But my heart forgives him. I've got a bell, not a heart. Listen. Here. Is it ringing? It's ringing. And is it ringing here? It's ringing. Well, and what about here? You see, it's still ringing. Oh, my heart, which never lets me down. I have as much heart as you could want. You don't believe me? So have a drink. But what do you lot care about my heart? What can one ever do with you lot? Nothing. Nothing. A day hasn't gone by yet in your company, and I already feel tired of life. You corpses! Corpses! Oh, I'd be better off listening to my canaries. My little birds. My singing. I get up and go. I'm going.

I don't even care to look at them as I take my leave. I don't even feel any resentment towards them. I can hardly lift my body, my legs are like clay, I feel sick, sad. Though my head feels clear, almost lucid. Fortunately here's my chair already. My dear kind chair, my loyal friend.

Oh, how good it feels! I look out of the window. The light is already fading. Doubtless the sun will soon begin to set. Silence descends on me. Peace.

Ah, Bishop, it's you. Do come in, do come in. Welcome to my humble abode. But why so late? I've been waiting and waiting here for you. I've been waiting for ages. I'd already given up hope of your ever coming. And there's so much I wanted to say to you. Please, sit down at least, and listen with me to my canaries. I was just sitting here immersed in their song, and it seemed to me that I was no longer in this world, but somewhere beyond it, somewhere beyond it. Perhaps you know where, Bishop? Oh, listen. Do you hear? Sublime, isn't it? I'd even say angelic, if it weren't for my respect for your divine person. Forgive me, but it's such a long time since I last listened to them, what with all my daily worries, troubles, thoughts. And now their song sounds to me almost uncanny. But it's more beautiful than it used to be. More noble than it used to be. More manifold. More pure. Not so precious. Do you hear? That's the one with the silver feathers, there above the piano. And now do you hear? Do you hear? Wait, don't say anything. Listen carefully. Well it's true, isn't it, that there's no comparison between them and the nightingales or the blackbirds? It's the essence of pure song. Not even birdsong any more, but disembodied song, simply song itself. Above and beyond all the birds, as it were. So how are your blackbirds coming along? Have you still got them? You say they sing to you like angels. Then blackbirds must be enough to satisfy you. Anyway, they're nice birds. Not quite the same as canaries, but blackbirds will do. Oh, listen how they're competing with one another to impress me, to see which one can sing the most beautifully. As soon as one starts up, the others don't give him a chance. They're nothing but sycophants. They know me, they know that their singing can make me melt like wax. Nothing can disarm me as much as their singing. Neither tears, nor pleas, nor fear, nor the wrath of God, only them and their singing. For when someone cries in front of me, when someone begs for my favour, when someone threatens me with hell, then he makes me hate myself. And when I hate myself, I hate others too. Also I feel at my most intimate with them when I listen to their singing. You can't even know how much I like to feel myself totally absorbed. It's the one and only thing I'd willingly choose to take with me from this life – my total absorption in their song. I could listen to it from dawn till dusk. Listen and listen, nothing else, just listen.

Do you hear? That's the one over there by the window just starting to sing so sublimely. He's obviously cross with me for not noticing him first. Poor little thing. But don't strain your little throat, my darling, for then what would I have left after you'd gone, and what would you have left of yourself? That's how one of them died on me last year. Simply sung himself to death. He wanted to cheer me up because I'd been wandering around sad for days on end, but he paid for it with his life. It was about this time of year he died. First he stopped singing, then eating, then drinking, and then ... better not recall that dark hour. He must be in heaven now. But what good is that to me? It's consolation only for heaven, no consolation for me. Tell me, was he saved at least? You don't know. And I gave him such a send-off. Such a beautiful funeral. And was it all to no avail? I invited lots of people. All the gentlemen from the neighbourhood and from further afield. I never invite so many people even for my birthday. Oh, it was a riotous funeral. It was a pity you weren't able to come. And afterwards they all had to be fed and watered. I even ordered the old women to be brought from the village so that he'd have someone to cry for him, for no one can cry quite so poignantly as they. It's as if they already know death somehow, as if they'd already experienced it. And in return for their crying I also had to give all of them a sack of flour. And even that good-for-nothing, my nephew, came. And he, after all, no longer believes in anything. I wrote to him nevertheless: come, if you feel close to my pain. And he came. Oh, I know him inside out now. Yet he was the saddest of us all. But he also cost me a small fortune, oh, a small fortune.

We walked round the park three times carrying the cages of

canaries. And I ordered the cages to be put down over the grave in the flower-bed, among the red roses planted especially for that day. And thus we bade him farewell, listening to the singing of the birds and the crying of the old women. Sometimes he appears to me in my dreams, and that's all that's left of him. Sometimes, just for a moment, I imagine I can pick him out somewhere among the others, and that's all that's left of him.

And for that one, oh, there above the mirror, I gave a hundred acres, would you believe it? One hundred acres of good arable land. One hundred acres, not of woodland, not of meadow, but of good wheat-growing soil. And it was worth two hundred. For that's no ordinary canary, as you might think. It's a canary of ancient lineage. A bird of the blood. No trace in him even of the nightingale, let alone the sparrow. He's no longer a canary even, but song itself. A great and mighty canary. His lordship, the canary. He wouldn't be able to support himself in the air even if he tried, poor creature. His wings are merely for adornment. The leaves on the trees would be too sharp for him. The ground too jagged.

Or that one there. Look. No price could ever be put on that one's head. A prince among canaries. It's my love, Bishop. My pain, all of my joy. And to think some tax collector once had him. He used to come to the palace, and I used to tell them to say I wasn't at home. I used to send him to the steward. But he would always insist he wanted to see me. So one day I received him at long last. He says he has a canary. So what, I think to myself, a canary's a common enough thing. But next time he came with the cage. I saw, I listened, and my heart almost stood still. It was that one over there. I thought, you've no idea what you've got, my good tax collector. But he knew, he knew. He even came to me with that canary to prove he was my equal.

Sell it to me, I said.

No, he said. This canary is all I have, my lord.

Then sell it, I said. You'll become rich.

I'll become poorer than I am, your lordship.

I'll give you so much you'll be able to put your feet up for the rest of your life.

But what would be left of me then? I am only myself when I

listen to his song, and I'm only a tax collector because it's my fate to be one.

I'd already given up hope of ever getting the canary. Till one day I was having another go at him and, just imagine, in walks my wife. He took one look at her and blushed. I watched her. She gave him a rather odd smile and then left immediately. It was as if someone had thrust a dagger into my heart. So that's it, you traitors, I think to myself. You'll pay me back dearly for this. But I give nothing away so as not to frighten them. Oh, I'll find enough patience in me for the both of you. I'll wait, I'll wait, I think to myself, until you draw closer together, become infatuated, long for each other until it hurts, draws blood. Then I'll let you loose on one another, let you loose. But before I let you loose, your hearts will really be aching. You'll scare yourselves, torment yourselves so much that you'd sooner go to your deaths together than go to bed. I shall haunt you, intrude upon you, roam around day and night, catch your whispers, vows, confessions, pretending I know nothing, know nothing. Though I shall suffer between you just as much as you suffer, but in return the canary will be mine. Mine, you scoundrel of a tax collector, mine, you unfaithful wife! You're in my hands now. The canary is mine. You Judases, desecrators, wretches. And when the decisive moment comes, I know what I shall do. I shall go away, set out on a long journey, for a long time. And you will get into bed together beside yourselves with passion, but then I shall suddenly return, in a raging fury, driving my carriage at breakneck speed right into the palace almost. I shall sweep into your love-nest and jeer at you. So what are we up to here, my dear tax collector? Then the canary is mine! Ha! Ha! Ha! The canary is mine! Mine! Mine!

Can you hear it, Bishop? It's that one there. Now he's stopped. Drowned already by the others. He's so refined, believe me, that he never likes to sing along with the others. He immediately falls silent, becomes anxious. Oh, how they've all started to sing! Like cascades of tiny bells. Perhaps this is what the dew sounds like slipping from the leaves, if you could but hear it. So what does it remind you of? Cherubs ringing the peal for the Annunciation? It makes me think of a sleigh in the distance. The sun at high noon spilling its rays upon the earth. Besides, you can't put it into words. Try to lose yourself in this song! Really lose yourself. So you can't hear anything beyond it. Meditate upon this song, even if it's only for a moment, as though you were meditating upon God. And you surely know how to meditate upon God. And best shut your eyes. I won't distract you. Like I've shut mine. Look. I can't see anything. Even here, behind my eyelids, I can't see anything. I see only their song. All around me their song. I see a singing darkness in my unseeing eyes. Of neither water, nor earth, nor night. It quivers, densens, then explodes in black. Then it falls away in strings of rippling beads. And again it quivers, densens. Can you hear it? They've all started to sing now. Their special hour is approaching. They know me, they know I always come at this hour to listen to them. Then they start singing at their most beautiful. I sit myself down here, in my armchair, and shut my eyes so as not to see them, so as not to marvel, so as not to judge, but simply to hear them. Believe me, it's the only way in which I myself can become their song. I nestle into this celestial song, hide myself away in it, and only then do I really feel I have a soul. Only then do I feel I have a soul inside me, when I listen to their song. Only then, for otherwise I can't even tell whether I have a soul or not. Come now, don't get angry. I had only myself in mind, nothing more than that. Because I, you see, need a soul only from time to time. Like now, when I sit here listening to my canaries. Beyond that, what do I need a soul for, even if I had one? It would just add to my worries, my troubles, and I've got enough of those as it is. The only moments when I feel free from myself are when I'm listening to this song. Then it's as if I'd been swallowed up by this song, as if I'd become nothing but the reflection of this song, no longer myself. Nothing but the quivering of a myriad tiny throats. Beyond this I cease to exist. I am, as long as their song rings out above me, as long as they don't wilt in their cages, as long as they don't stop, as long as they're not tempted by a mouthful of seed. This song of theirs, believe me, renders me scarcely a moment, a frail fragile thing, and so intense, so moving, that I experience every tiny part of that moment as joy in myself and as pain at my passing, as my eternity and as my transience, at one and the same time. And yet it's so fleeting, as though I didn't exist but simply put in an appearance and then vanished again along with that appearance, as though I just appeared and disappeared without any sense of time, as though I didn't exist in time but only as an instant. Besides, what's the point of going on living, my dear, if an instant cannot stand for the whole of your life? This great life of yours. Which couldn't be any greater if you lived it a hundred times over. Though to tell you the truth, I don't even know if I'm aware of anything apart from my hearing when I sit here engrossed in their song. Of anything apart from this sublime – yet at the same time tormenting – hearing of their song within myself, within every moment of the non-existence of my existence. Perhaps this state of hearing is yet one more state of the human condition, along with living, sleeping, dying.

Yes, yes, it's inconceivable. But now you understand how hard it is for me to love anything else after hearing that song. Everything you look at seems to be sickliness, hypocrisy, delusion. It's hard even to understand anything any more, harder still to forgive. It all fills you with disgust. You feel as though everything around you has been downgraded. All you have left is your own revulsion towards all the things that sully with their mediocrity that song echoing inside you, that nobility. Towards everything that has the audacity to exist alongside that song. Towards everything. For it's all lying in wait for you. Plaguing you. Making a slave of you. Therefore you must defend yourself if you want to save within yourself that moment of nobility inspired by the song of your canaries. But how can you defend yourself? When the one thing you can't find is tolerance of all the vulgar things around you. For what is vulgar, is sinful. That nobility, once attained, becomes the measure of all else. Oh, I don't deny it's a severe one, but it's the only just one.

But maybe all this is a sin. Perhaps we're not meant to yearn for nobility. For even if we have attained it just for a moment, then we'll never be able to be humble again, not even towards ourselves. We'll simply turn into a constant longing for this nobility. Its slave. Its blind fanaticism. Though God too is nobility. So how is that so, Bishop? Is it still possible for a man to love anything outside himself once he has felt that nobility within? Even if it's only for a moment, like in the singing of the canaries? For how, how can you, if you feel that everything else strips you, robs you of that beautiful moment, that all vulgarity, all sordidness, has conspired against you and against you alone? That its very existence is against you, even though it's an affront to real existence, that even its silence is against you, that even its dying is against you. And just think – all because you became immersed in the song of the canaries and the song lived on inside you.

How can I feel noble, my dear, when they come here day after day? And if only it was for something worthwhile, but all they're ever after is my pity, my favour, my mercy, because one of their houses has burned down or another's children are starving to death. Besides, I can hardly say, Go away, because just now I'm filled with nobility. Could they ever understand anything like that? All they understand is pity, favour, mercy. As though nothing else existed in this world apart from pity, favour, mercy. And they would strip me of this song, of my complete immersion in it, and thus leave me deprived of any emotion. Of that emotion that is so refined, fragile, fearful inside you, the slightest doubt would frighten it away, and what would you do then with all their favours, pities, mercies, weighing you down like millstones round your neck?

Besides, do you imagine they really come here for favours, for pity, for mercy? No! No! Don't ever trust their humility, the Judases. They come, but they destroy me, eat away at me, scratch bits off me, so that afterwards I feel an abomination in my own eyes. I feel as though I no longer have anything human left in me. I feel abused, defiled. Full of sin. A worm. Not even a ladybird, an ant. Not even a spider. Ashes. Dust swept up from a country road. And I'm meant to show them compassion?

Oh, you don't know them, Bishop, you don't know them. Perhaps they're humbler on your estates. But you've got God on your side. You can leave the worst things to Him, and be left in peace. But I have to cope with it all on my own. And if I don't want to receive them, or I've got a headache, or I'm away somewhere, then they sit down in the forecourt and make themselves at home, and wait till my headache wears off or until I return. It may be a day, two days, a week, they wait as long as they have to. They sleep on the bare earth beneath the trees, they eat or they don't eat, yet they wait. In foul weather, in the scorching heat, yet they wait. And when evening draws in, you can hear them praying for my head to stop aching or for my safe and speedy return. Except that's not quite true, for they're really praying in order to torment me. If only you could hear them just once, Bishop, murmuring their prayers out there, steeped in the darkness. Midnight. You imagine they'll stop at last, that sleep must overpower them, when suddenly, quite unexpectedly, they start to intone a rousing chant. From every throat. A blazing conflagration rather than a chant. Impossible to bear. And why so loud? But then they don't care if God can hear them or not, only that their prayers should reach me in here, reach inside the palace, and if I'm asleep, that they should force their way into my dreams and wreck them. The park and the darkness separate you from them, but you can hear them as though they were singing right here, on the other side of the door. My head could split from the pain of it. They sit out my greatest pain. I may not be at home. They sit out my absence. They'd be prepared to sit me out to the bitter end, provided I allowed them somewhere to sleep, allowed them to eat or not eat, and, well, allowed them to recite their prayers in the evening.

Believe me, I never sleep when they're waiting out there. I pace up and down the room, afraid to go anywhere near the window, though I can't see them in the darkness. Did you ever hear anything like it, Bishop? They're only waiting for me, yet I, their lord and master, in my palace, within these thick walls, I am afraid of them. Yes, I'm afraid of them. Though I don't know why. After all, they're only asking for pity, favour, mercy.

I know I could give the order to break them up. Yet I can't, however. I usually don't have the courage to say simply, Break them up. I pace up and down the room and listen to those prayers outside the windows, in the darkness, as though it was only the wind rustling in the branches, the rain falling. And when they don't sleep, I don't sleep either. That's all I can do. Sometimes I walk over to the window, quaking with fear, and stare, stare into the darkness where they are praying for me, as though I wanted to drive them from that place with my stare, maybe placate them. And I become filled even more with the nearness of their praying. Perhaps I even pray with them, even though I don't know I'm doing it. Perhaps I'm standing watch over them so they can purge themselves of all their prayers, and all of them to no avail.

Sometimes, however, I can't go on, I can't go on. Something starts to happen to me and I run away from them into the rooms, into the chambers, into the depths of the palace. But their prayers are everywhere, penetrating the enormity of the palace. You can hear them everywhere. Prayers praying everywhere of their own accord. In here the walls, the furniture, the night, all repeat their prayers, whilst out there they're already asleep under the trees, exhausted. Sometimes I run to the tower, the servants rushing after me. What's got into you, your lordship? Shall we break them up? They're ruining your peace and quiet. And I feel I want to say, Yes, break them up. Perhaps I even pronounce those bitter words full of pain, but I don't hear myself, and neither does anyone else.

Oh, sometimes I wish I had my whole life over and done with. My own self over and done with. Yes. Yes. That self that sits here in its deep armchair, in this chamber still full of light yet full too of impending night, and opens its soul before you. That's me, Bishop. I, who torment myself here and everywhere throughout this palace, in my own memory even. I, who know myself less and less, I, who find it more and more difficult to live with myself. Maybe it's even my own self that I hear as though it were them, for how could their prayers ever pass through these thick walls, these closed windows? Maybe it's my own self I'm running away from when I can't bear to hear them? Maybe I'm tired of myself, moody with myself? Maybe my life has gone on too long? Just think how long I've already been living. How intensely. Already my memory can no longer encompass it. Already I'm getting lost in it. And when I stop and think what a long time I still have to live, it sends shivers up my spine. If only it were possible to get through that immense stretch of time – which would otherwise drag on and on – in the course of a single day, a single moment even, and thus spare myself this agonizing slowness, this existence no longer split up into years, months, days, but into moments. And you'd experience yourself in every one of those moments as if it were the whole of your life, from the moment you are born through to the moment you die, and maybe earlier too, and maybe further on. And how many of these moments are there inside you? As many as there are stars in the sky. But sometimes I would really like to be old already and to be able to look back on it all, just look back on this great life of mine, which has already passed by. Thoughts such as these occur to me more and more often, my dear. I'd even say it brings me a strange kind of relief – seeing myself as an old man. I even feel affected by it, almost moved by a tenderness towards myself. His lordship as an old man. What a great life he had! Raised so high he was almost larger than life, and now he just looks down on it. Then I feel even more affected by myself. For there at the very end I am filled with peace, filled with forgiveness towards myself. Perhaps I've become eccentric. But so be it. I'd bear my eccentricity too with dignity. It's only a peasant, my dear, whom they say has gone round the bend when he turns eccentric. They'd say of me that my eccentricity was wiser than my reason. That I was wise, oh, wise in my eccentricity. Who knows, anyway, what it means to be eccentric? And I would wander from chamber to chamber as though I was looking for something, inspiring fear in the valets, in the maids, in all the cousins, relatives, aunts, who have occupied this palace like lice infesting a tree, and who are now trying to devour me. They will have to puzzle me out, and I won't give away the slightest clue to put them on the right track. I shall laugh within myself, pour scorn on them as I watch them tormenting themselves, trying to understand me, trying to understand anything at all about me, trying to catch a smile at least, an intimate glance, a friendly word. And I shall never show I recognize any of them. Any of them. Only my daughters will be allowed access to me, so I won't be entirely alone in my eccentricity. They will be with me, and I with them. And that will be the sum total of my world.

No, no, they won't abandon me now. I shan't let them, even if they try to tear themselves away from me, implore me, curse me. I'll deceive them if I have to. I'll deceive myself if I can't do otherwise, but I shan't let them. What would I do without them? They are, after all, part of myself. My life. It's not they who were born of me, but I of them. Every day I am born of them, every hour. From out of their laughter, their banter, their little bursts of enthusiasm, from out of their words, their dreams, their anxiety. Just listen how the place is full of them. What wonderful creatures they are! Once upon a time I used to think there were no creatures better than horses. But that was a long time ago, a long time ago. That was before they came along. Now I'm ashamed I ever thought like that. Such thoughts are even painful. I feel as though I'd committed some terrible sin, though truly it was before they came along. But maybe my feeling of guilt is my love for them. Or maybe my love has merely found itself something to feel guilty about so it has something to grow on. Though sometimes I shudder at the thought of them ever finding me out, for what would I say to them then?

Listen to them. They're singing. It's not the canaries. It's them. My daughters. Can you hear them laughing? Perhaps they'll come running in here. Only, I beg you, don't tell them how much I worry about them. They've run off somewhere else. Somewhere else. How dainty they are! Their footsteps scarcely rustle as they slip by. Scarcely rustle. Perhaps they've run off to the flower-bed to pick some roses. God, God, if anything should ever happen to them!

And do you know what, my dear? Take a good look at the roses sometime. But not in the way you'd normally look at them. I'm not sure how myself. Have the courage, perhaps, to be suspicious. If you were the gardener and had planted them yourself, forgive me for saying so, but if you were the gardener, I'd recommend you to creep into the rose-bed at night like a thief and steal them, desecrate them. Do something like that, do something that wouldn't normally enter your head, something that would even be against your nature, and perhaps you'll catch a glimpse of them as they really are. Just ordinary roses. You'd never have suspected it. I once saw them in that way when they, my daughters, brought me a rose each, brought me their joy, brought me their eagerness, but for me those roses just went dull in their hands, dazzled me with their blinding redness. And do you know the sun, Bishop? Yes, yes, our own sun. The sun that we all share every day. It was they who first showed me that it doesn't only shine, but that it plays as well. Every one of its rays is made up of strings. Even that one falling in here. You can place your hands over one of those rays and pick out the notes with your fingers, and it will play, it will really play. I've heard it.

I even tried it out when they weren't watching. Yet that music doesn't depend on your fingers, but perhaps on your innocence, on your having no premonition of anything to come. Sometimes the three of us go for a walk round the park and gather the most beautiful leaves from amongst the autumn decay. And then we argue over one leaf after another, get angry over one leaf after another, become sulky, jealous.

Mine's the prettiest.

No, it isn't. Mine is.

It's not true. Mine's the prettiest.

Do you know what each one of those leaves means to me? Every one of those ordinary, russet autumn leaves? No, they can't abandon me. It's not true. Don't torment me, Bishop. After all, they're my daughters. I'd have to stay on all alone after they'd gone. So what use are they to me? What use is this palace? What use am I to myself? And I already suffer quite enough, watching them grow up. And I already miss them quite enough, remembering them as they once were. Sometimes I simply can't believe that they're them, that they're the same as yesterday, the day before yesterday, scarcely any time ago. That they're still them. There's been so many of them already, yet they're still them. Besides, those former selves never died, but still exist, live on, I can see them, hear them. Yet should I still expect them to be the same? But what am I supposed to do? I pretend that I know nothing, that I suspect nothing. I hide it from them, from myself. And they themselves, God willing, suspect nothing of what is in store for them. Though sometimes I'm gripped by the sudden fear that they might appear in front of me one day, brazenly stripped naked, smiling ingenuously, chirruping away as though they'd come to lure me into the park to look for leaves. Daddy, come and play with us. Or what shall I say to them when death stares them in the eye, and they ask me, Daddy, we still haven't grown up, and yet we're dying already?

The one thing that can free me from all this, is old age. Only old age. I find in my very longing for it, believe me, a kind of peculiar yet perhaps cruel satisfaction, which soothes my everyday life. If only your life consisted just of your own! But it's an enormous dumping ground. Therefore perhaps my nostalgia for old age merely proves that I've been old for a long time already, that I'm the old age of the whole human race. Perhaps when I entered the world, I was already an old man, but in the form of a child. For perhaps no one, Bishop, ever begins his life anew, but just goes on living, and hence no one ever begins to suffer out of his own self, but just carries the suffering further. Therefore, is it so surprising that I feel so close to my old age? That I put all my faith in it, just as the earth puts its faith in the sun, as desire puts its faith in its gratification, as though old age was the only aim in my life, the only safe haven on this earth, the only relief that remains when life is done? They speak, after all, of the landing stage where you, tired of life, drift in to moor. Tired of life. How soothing that sounds. Don't you feel almost seduced by the very words themselves? They release a kind of hope, like the hope of hunger for satiety, of tiredness for sleep, of darkness for light. You have no idea how much I'd give to feel that blessed indifference within me at last, that indifference towards the world, towards myself, to feel the blood slackening its pace in my veins and my heart slowly distancing itself, further and further away, quieter and quieter, to feel within me at last the gelling of the day before evening. I am ready to bear that indifference without a word of complaint, without a sigh, with humility, my one consolation being to have my life over and done with, my great, long, terrifyingly long life over and done with at last. To have that most certain of certainties, that this life no longer threatens me. Here I am, his lordship, the old gentleman, having brought my rich destiny to a close like an ordinary day, and now only sleep awaits me. Is that not a relief, Bishop? To have that destiny lying like a dead stag at my feet. For maybe that's the one joy that remains from life, that life is behind you at last. That your own self is over and done with at last. For a man, take my word for it, is more painfully condemned to himself than to anything else. No one affords him so much anguish as he himself. He can't even forget about himself for a moment. Can't even get through a single night without dreaming about himself. He must be himself continually, even though he's had enough of himself. And everything that he experiences, he experiences only as his own self. Every other human being as his own self. Every thing as his own self. Every time, even the most far-removed, be it beyond his memory, be it beyond his intuition, only as his own self. So each one of us almost becomes the whole of humanity. And as such he is almost too vast for himself, too immense for his own frailty and imperfection. Maybe he's even his own sun, but like the sun he can encompass only one half of his earth, casting over the rest the eternal shadow of doubt and insecurity. And he doesn't want to suppose even, suspect even, that he's there too, in that eternal shadow. I often get the painful feeling that we ought to confess to something in front of our own selves, because we always seem to be covering something up. I myself am not sure what we should confess to. After all, we don't know ourselves, we only sense ourselves instinctively. However, I know from my own experience that no one can ever be at peace with his own existence until it's gone full circle, until it's burned itself out utterly, turned to ashes, to oblivion, even passed beyond the grave. This perpetual fear, which continually throbs inside me, which tortures me, which violates my sleep, which impels me to strain my ears, to peer into the darkness, which distrusts the silence - this fear is no empty figment of my imagination. Perhaps it's even what's meant by human nature. Perhaps it's what keeps watch over us. Leading us astray like blind men, though it's so full of spite it manages to turn our lives into hell. So full of spite, you sometimes wish your life was already over and done with. For only in your old age, when you feel yourself liberated from the desires that often wrought more havoc in your soul than hatred, when you're able to recall things of your own volition, with impunity, because they've all withered away behind you, only then can you afford to be indulgent towards yourself, kind towards yourself, show yourself a little affection - for without that affection your life would be cold as stone, as anyone's would. Then you can even afford to be understanding towards others, for you're indifferent now to them as well.

Sometimes I even see myself sitting here in this same chair, steeped in my weariness yet still dignified. I see my own face, placid and benign, and I smile through my misted eyes at other people's smiles, at everyone whose eyes meet mine, at the park beyond the window, at the sky, at my life, at my memories smoothed and polished like pebbles in a river, and I feel nothing but relief, nothing but great relief. And I smile. How profuse my life seems from there! How happy, how serene, how different to how it is now. From there. Seeing myself like that I almost envy myself my old age. I seem so serene I am almost beautiful. Almost as beautiful as if I'd died a painless death. His lordship, the old gentleman, his eyes still twinkling to this day with their old irrepressible desire to be perverse.

The only answer you have to all this, Bishop, is God. Here I am baring my soul before you, and all you can do is tell me to submit to His will. If I'd always relied like that on His will, I wouldn't be who I am today. When did He ever help me in all this? Did He ever help me at all? Was He at least aware that I existed in this world which He Himself created? Was He at least moved by me, just once, oh, quite ordinarily, like you're moved by some worthless little creature, like wisdom is moved by worthlessness? Was He at least moved, if there was nothing else He could do to help me? But He couldn't. He couldn't. He could at least have appeared to me in a dream and told me that He was just as helpless as I was but that it was His fate to be God. And it would all have been so much easier for me, knowing that He too was only fulfilling His destiny. Or did I ever once enjoy, I won't say His favour, but His justice? And He is just, is He not? He is justice. You even once said so yourself, yes, you. I can remember it as if it were today. It was afternoon; there were several of us, and we were sitting in the drawing-room drinking wine and discussing this and that. That someone had returned from abroad and was outraged at what shameless dresses the ladies were wearing nowadays, that some epidemic was wiping out the foxes, that somehow you never see any partridges any more, that someone we knew was on his last legs, that it was bound to be a hard winter. But we also spoke about justice. And you said then, Bishop, that there is only one kind of justice that is fair to all: God's. That it weighs up and counts all our sins, regardless of whether you're a beggar or a gentleman. You spoke wisely but, if you'll pardon me, such justice inspires no confidence in me. For, you see, beggars usually have more sins on their consciences than gentlemen. Beggars are condemned to sin, but gentlemen sin of their own free will. Beggars sin because they have to, but gentlemen sin because they choose to. That's the difference, my dear. Therefore one lot of sins cannot be equal to another. So why should they be weighed up against each other on the scales, if I may put it that way? In judging a man you must weigh up his suffering as well as his sins. For otherwise justice merely becomes the meting out of punishment. And so in fact God doesn't judge, Bishop, God punishes. He is above justice. For justice, when it passes judgement, is itself judged.

So don't pray for me. It's too soon. Too soon. You ask whether I believe in God at least. Ha! That's a good one! No, I don't believe in Him, but I'm afraid of Him. And what am I supposed to confess to? And what for? To what end? Forgive me, my dear, but you're talking to me as though I was some shepherd come to confide his fear to you. I shall forgive myself my own sins, Bishop, and if not now then sometime else, though others may wish to weave a web of them in order to trap me now. But I'll cope with God somehow. He's not so unrelenting. I'll put up some wayside shrine and we'll come to some agreement. My grandfather put up a shrine, and all anybody remembers about him now is that he was a God-fearing man, albeit a great one. Yet was he really so God-fearing? I can remember him, after all. I was only a child, but I can remember. He taught me to ride. Taught me to fire a gun. If he had a soul at all, then it was already in the pay of the Devil, I can assure you. And if a wayside shrine is too little, then I'll put up a church. And if a church is too little, then I'll put up a cathedral. What's a cathedral to me! And such a cathedral that people will gaze, gaze upwards but never see the top, for the top will merge into the sun. And the birds will crash into it in their flocks, and the clouds will part before it in humility. I will erect it on the highest mountain. And when the bells begin to peal, they'll be heard in the furthermost corners of the earth. They'll be heard in people's souls, in their consciences. Perhaps even God will hear them one day. And it won't be joy that will flow from them, nor hope, nor comfort, but terror, such terror that not only mankind but all creation will fall down on its knees – horses, cows, sheep, dogs, cats, mice, every kind of reptile and vermin, everything that is capable of humility, everything that is sinful, and everything is sinful. Everything that moves on the face of the earth, that bears fruit, that refuses to submit to death. Perhaps stones too, rivers, forests, fields. God, after all, needs such terror. And the bells will ring, ring, ring. And there will be prayers in this cathedral day and night till people's tongues drop out, till their mouths dry up like meadow springs in time of drought, until their thoughts are scorched, till their raised palms, their bended knees, are turned to stone. Until their eyes no longer stare in vain, no longer weep in vain. And there will be the eternal murmur of confession, for not only will their sins themselves be sins but their hopes too, their longings, their sufferings, their hungers and loves, everything touched or heard, everything smelled or seen, so that the husband will become the sin of the wife and the wife the sin of the husband, the fathers the sin of the children and the children the sin of the fathers, and all together they'll become the sin of God above them, the sin of sins, which surpasses all other sin. And the penance will be the severest that people can impose upon people. Yet perhaps there won't even be any people in this cathedral, only their prayers, only their sins, only their penance, and that will be enough in itself to fill the cathedral to the skies. Enough to bolster the greatest pride. And above it all there will be the eternal playing of the organ, and their singing, as resonant, expansive, celestial as the walls and vaults. And God in this cathedral will be enormous, so vast that no one will able to encompass Him with his gaze, so vast that all eyes gazing at once won't be able to encompass Him. There won't be room enough for Him in any mind, in any heart. And He won't be hanging on a cross, for how could a God who was too weak to help Himself ever inspire hope in others? He'll just sit sprawling on His golden throne. The hairs on His head will be like willow branches. His great eyes will be boulders, so nobody will be able to tell whether He's staring at them or staring into Himself. Every toe and finger will be a spiry fir tree, and His big toes will be twisted oaks, so stunted they could never reach the sun. And His belly button will be a tree trunk one hundred years old. And the veins coursing through Him will be like the paths that weave across the meadows. And the wound in His side will be hacked out with axes. And watering-cans will be hung in His eyes like two huge tears, for what sort of God would He be if He wasn't a little bit human? And the people will flock to His legs like ants, crawling all over His feet and begging for His favour, His pity, His mercy, but no one will get higher than His ankles, not even those who have made it up the slippery poplars to the crows' nests – not even they will get further than His ankles. For when they start to make Him itch, all He has to do is stamp His feet and send them all tumbling to the depths of hell. Ha! Ha! Ha!

You see, even you, his servant, are gripped by fear at the thought of Him. So you're saying that all I've got to do is not forget and put something in the collection plate sometimes? Ha! Ha! Ha!

Well, what is it this time? Can't you see, you blockhead, that I'm not alone. The Bishop's with me. Kneel and kiss his hand! And you forgive him, Bishop. He's an honest soul but, if you'll pardon me for saying so, a bit simple. Well, speak up. Speak up. I'm listening.

I stand by the window, fold my hands behind my back, and pretend to be staring at something out there in the park, at the sky, at the weather, as I always do when they come to me with some problem.

Well, say something. Speak up. I'm listening after all.

Such is the habit I've adopted. It somehow enables me to accept the worst with dignity. It somehow places me above the thing that I'm about to find out about. Above my own feelings of embarrassment, dismay, fear, compassion. For every nonentity of a valet who comes to me with some piece of news is only on the look-out for some such reaction in me, so that he can feel closer to me. A complete nonentity, yet he wants to bring me right down to his level. But I know how to defend myself against them. All I need to do is stand up, clear my throat, walk up and down the room a couple of times, then stand by the window deep in thought, and immediately I sense that piece of news shrinking away from me behind my back along with its bearer, aghast, veiled in nothingness, in absurdity, so that it would dearly love to flee from the room. For whenever I feel my hands locked together behind my back, I am ready to take anything, even the death of my dearest horse.

I see the daylight is fading for good. The sun still shines with a brilliant radiance, but that radiance is already feeble, dulled. And the park too has lost the bright verdancy of the afternoon and turned a more shadowy shade of green. A sad tranquillity emanates from it.

Come on, stop shaking. Speak up. Who is it at this time of day? Ah, him again, the one who's been seeking justice. Well, hasn't he found it yet? Couldn't you have told him that I've got a headache? The stupid fool wants justice at this hour. He must be mad. Or that I'm not at home? And I'm supposed to waste my time on his sort, am I? And when of all times? Right now. Anyway the *Starosta* is due any moment. And our neighbour, the Squire, will no doubt be coming over as well. Perhaps the parish priest too. And it's not as though it's the first time. It's not as though he was the victim of real misfortunes. He's nothing but a rebel. Yes. A rebel. If only he was a thief at least, a loafer, an idiot, a drunkard. But no. A rebel. You'll never bump into him either in church or in the tavern. And if someone doesn't believe in God, then he ought at least to be a drinker. There's no two ways about it. It's human nature. And if you're neither one thing nor the other, then you're a rebel, no doubt about it.

Once, his horse reared. I don't know, I think it was when it was loaded up with corn. Well, I understand, it happens sometimes. But anyone else would have grabbed the horse's bridle, tried to lead it on a bit, would have waited a little, coaxed it, and maybe it would have calmed down. At the very worst they'd have whipped it across the back, belly, fetlocks, muzzle, till they drew blood. So be it. I would have forgiven them. Forgiven many a one, though to me a horse is a sacred thing. But at least I'd have known they could drive a cart. But he did nothing of the sort. He flew into a temper. Seized the horse by the scruff of the neck and threw it to the ground. Well, so wouldn't you call him a rebel? And still he threatens to bring me to justice. Even if he has to travel the whole wide world for it, he'll find it. So go, you fool, go, even if you have to go to God Himself! Go with God beside you. Only where will you go? Where will you go? You don't even know the way. Do you know at least the points of the compass? Do you know in which quarter the world ends, and in which it begins? Do you even know on which side of the trees the moss grows? But when did a fool like you ever reach anywhere following the moss from tree to tree? Ha! Ha! Ha! But go! Go! Oh, you'll walk out of the village and find yourself on the edge of the world already. You'll stand on the brink of the precipice. You'll see all eternity in front of you. You'll fall on your knees before God, so He might at least light a little star to guide you on your way, a fire somewhere in the marshes, so he might arouse in you at least some vague premonition. But before you finish praying the wolves will tear you apart, half-way through the Ave Maria. But go, go, you poor, barefoot fool. And bring me this justice when you find it. I'd like to see it. Only don't get it wrong. For you could always bring me a cow and say, Here it is, your justice. To hell with you! Oh, what a joker you are, what a joker! And who'd have thought there was so much humour in a man like you? And first-rate humour too, one has to admit. A cow as justice. A just cow. Bovine justice. Ha! Ha! Ha! You'd do much better to go to the tavern, drink well, sleep well, dream well, and you'll forget what it was you wanted. Go, go, get lost to the ends of the earth! I have no wish to punish you. You can punish yourself! You'll punish yourself much worse when you punish yourself of your own free will, when you punish yourself with your own stupid hopes. And so you'll return to me. If not for justice, then for pity, but you'll return. You won't have anywhere to go, and so you'll return. For you'll have to return somewhere. You'll understand and you'll return.

And so he returned. Oh, I'm not just playing with words. He was nothing but skin and bones, but he returned. Legs worn out, eyes wild as wolves', wits deranged, but he returned. I even felt sorry for him. I'd even forgotten how he'd offended. I ask him, So tell me, what was it like out there, then? You must have been walking and walking, you poor thing, dragging yourself on and on. And don't worry about the other thing, I've forgiven you.

Then he says to me, You're a hard taskmaster, your lordship, but you're poor. Poorer than my poverty, poorer than my misery. Than my baseness. And what's more, you don't understand anything. You are great, powerful, but the most you can understand is that it's enough for you to forgive me for justice to have been done. No, your lordship, I don't want forgiveness, even if it came from your heart, I don't want it. Judge me. Judge unjustly, vengefully, but judge me. For what have you got to forgive me for? I haven't returned here for justice. I've returned to ease your pain, your lordship, for you are poor indeed.

But now I know why he's returned. He's returned in order to torment me. Also because he failed to perish in the wilderness. The wolves ought to have devoured him. I'd even forgotten about him. So what am I supposed to do with someone like him?

But now he's gone and chopped off his hand. Can you imagine it, my dear, chopped off his hand? Well, chopped it off, simply chopped it off. And not out of despair, but out of hatred. The scoundrel was bored with his work. Rose in violence against his work, not against his hand. But it's you who should be sorting out his type, not me. That's what you're here for – to maintain order. And don't give me any Yes sir, Yes sir. Just get on with it, otherwise I'll complain to the *Starosta*. I think you know what should be done with him. He rose in violence against God, my good sir, Who gave man work for his salvation. He wanted to show me that he could get by without working. That it's not so omnipotent as I think it is. That it'll be neither his fate nor his faith. That he himself will choose his own destiny. He'll choose it himself. The fool. Just let him try. He wanted to show me that it's not worth him wasting his time on it in return for such a dog's pittance, in return for nothing but hunger. Just let him try. To show me that he'll at least get his revenge on it in return for its own vengefulness. That he'll liberate himself from it. So, what have you got to say to that? What have you got to say to that? Don't forget that he decided on this infernal game just to get at me. I know now that it was to get at me. He hates my guts. He's ready to burn my house down. That's why I ordered them to summon you. But now he's gone too far, the fool. He doesn't realize that work and man are one and the same thing. As if a bird could liberate itself from its flight, or a fish liberate itself from water, or from what else, well, from what else, don't you remember? It doesn't matter. As though there existed any way of coping with work other than submission. As many people as I lay off, as many come begging at my gates. He sees, after all, what goes on at the gates. They'd work for nothing, as long as they could just work, for even destitution causes them less pain than idleness. He should pray. Pray. But he goes and chops his hand off. And wouldn't it have been better if he'd drowned himself? He'd have left me in peace at last. But would he ever really leave me in peace? His is a horned, unbending soul. Perhaps in the pay of the Devil? Who knows?

And which one did he chop off? The left one, you say. Are you sure you mean the left one? How could he ever dream of such a thing. Well, didn't I tell you he returned with his wits deranged? The intention alone would have been enough. He didn't have to chop it off at all. Yes, yes, the intention alone. The very fact he wanted to harm himself. That he stood over that hand with an axe and said to himself, Eh! You! That in itself would have been enough. Then he might even have even burst out laughing. And what followed wouldn't have counted any more. Then no amount of laughter could have made a mockery of such a moment. It would have remained as it was, noble, painful. Perhaps he might have understood something of what he was doing, even if he'd got cold feet. Now he'll never understand anything. It's too late and it hurts him far too much. Now he has to maintain his loyalty to that hacked-off hand. His loyalty to himself. Oh, he feels the pain of that hacked-off hand inside him as though he had a hundred of them. He doesn't exist any more, doesn't exist. That hand exists instead of him. So he defends it, demands redress for it, seeks justice for that hand, not for himself.

I feel sorry for him. I really feel sorry for him. I don't like such terrible things. And to think that if it wasn't for all this, I wouldn't have to pity him now. I wouldn't have to know him. Or know anything about him. Or have to try and guess who he is, or whether someone like him exists at all. And because of a man like him, I too become helpless. I become, as it were, a little part of his helplessness. And in this shared state of helplessness I come across some fool, an unhappy fool, but a fool nevertheless. For what can I do for him? I can sympathize with him. So I sympathize. I can forgive him. So I forgive him. I can be unable to come to terms with it. So I don't come to terms with it. But none of this helps him. True, I still feel sorry for him. He's an unhappy man, yet he doesn't even realize just how unhappy. Though maybe it's a good thing he doesn't realize. The only happiness the unhappy fellow can hope for. Perhaps you, Father, could do something to help him. Perhaps you could hear him out at least. Commend him to God. Or to some saint, perhaps, if God is too busy. Yet a kind word might be enough. He needs a kind word. A kind word more than anything else. He's persuaded himself that it's justice he's after. But he doesn't even know what justice is. He's never come across it, so how can he know? What he's really after is pity. I assure you, Father. They always get them mixed up. So if you can, help him out, comfort him, hear his confession, explain things to him. Tell him to take his time. One day he'll get what he wants on the other side of life. Or take him on as your resident beggar. He can ring the church bell for you. He can manage it with one hand. Of course he can. It isn't a very big bell.

But you, hang on a moment. You said it was the left hand. Are you sure it was the left? Ah, he's a crafty devil nevertheless! Well, just stop and think what a crafty devil he is. He chopped it off, and yet it's as though he didn't chop it off. He's not such a fool as I thought. A fox, maybe. A philosopher. The sort that sells himself to the Devil, but then it transpires that he bought him. He chopped it off, but that doesn't necessarily mean he really did chop it off. As though he didn't want to chop it off, but chopped it off. Chopped it off, yet didn't chop it off. Oh, you see. Do you understand anything of what I'm saying? Yes, exactly. Though I feel better that it was the left. So you tell me why you think it was the left and not the right? Yes, you tell me. Let me have your considered opinion. You don't know? So you see, you don't know. Well, tell me in that case which hand is more important? You've got two hands. Show me. Here's the left and there's the right. Which of them is the more important? Well, to you. Which one? How come you're taking so long to decide, as if it wasn't obvious? You're hesitating? There's no need. Nature has already chosen for you. It's not a question of I think so. It's the right hand. You see? But what does he do? If he'd really wanted to get his revenge on himself from the depths of his soul, from the depths of his bitterness, from the depths of his hatred, he would have chosen the very worst option. Or rather he wouldn't have chosen it. It would have chosen itself. Oh, he's cunning. All right, let him be, he didn't drown himself. Perhaps death was too little for him. Agreed. But once he'd decided to do violence to his hand, then he should have chosen the more important one. The right hand. The right. The only important thing now is that there should be no suggestion of falsehood. But the pain, the pain. Unadulterated. Festering. So that the pain would be above and beyond him. I'd be afraid of him then, I'd dream of him, I'd not sleep because of him. He wouldn't have to keep coming to me then, making demands. It would be enough that he was in this world for me never, never ever to know peace again. That hand of his would cause me such pain, flare up on rainy days, itch on sunny days. I'd feel it creep all over my body. I'd be afraid to touch anything, even my own face. Maybe I'd stick it in the door jamb in order to stifle the pain. And so, you see, I still can't protect myself from him. Because there's too much cunning in this hand for it to be merely madness.

I can even imagine him standing there above the tree stump in the middle of the night, with his axe, with his tears, not knowing whether to chop it off or not to chop it off. He doesn't know which one. He lays down one, then the other, transfers the axe from one to the other. When he lays down the left, he feels sorry for the left. When he lays down the right, he feels sorry for the right. Vengefulness boils and then cools within him. In the end he doesn't know any more whom he's meant to be getting at by chopping off that hand. He already feels the fresh chill of the evening. The world around him seems too still. It distresses him that not even a cow starts to low nor a child to cry, that people aren't arguing somewhere, that the dogs have fallen silent. For even when some useless horse is about to break its leg, the dogs are already howling like maniacs three days in advance. And then everyone knows that something is about to happen, that something is about to happen, that something must happen. He knows less and less which hand. Now he even has to add fuel to that vengefulness within him instead of it fuelling him. Just a little bit more and he'll throw aside the axe, snatch his hand from the tree stump and start to run away into the night, wherever his legs will carry him, bearing away that hand like a stolen piece of bread, pressing it to his face, to his lips, to his other hand. Oh, the sky has been studded with stars for some time, as though blemished with thousands of tiny pimples. And only when the moon rose and illuminated the hand on the tree stump did it happen. But no, still not the thing that he intended. Only the thought suddenly occurred to him of how he'd get by without his right hand.

And here he betrayed himself. Here he gave in to falsehood. Yet perhaps it wasn't here, perhaps it was earlier, perhaps later. But here he warded off his own self, humbled himself, grew crafty. He decided to do something else. Now he could no longer not chop it off. He'd let slip his opportunity. Condemned himself only to pity, to compassion. Even the idea had lost its sway inside him. Yes, yes, it was a weak idea born of a weak will. The fox in him awoke and took a bite out of the man. Though in his own eyes he was obviously cunning, perhaps he was even pleased with himself. You fool, you fool, you'll chop off your right hand, and then how will you cope with only your left? How will you cope with a hand that you had more to complete the pair than to help you in life? How will you cope? Such a hand will only be a burden to you. Even more of a burden than if you didn't have it at all. You don't know what it's like because you've got them both, because you've got the right hand, which stands in for the other as well as for itself. But let the left remain your one and only hand, and you'll see it'll become your hell not your helper. It'll no longer be your lot to contend with fate, but with your own left hand, suddenly all alone, born again, clumsy, useless, unable even to button up your collar. You will have to teach it everything all over again like you were a little boy, patiently, over the years, spoiling it, comforting it. And how with a hand like that will you ever scoop up the water from the spring out in the fields and bring it to your parched lips? Before you reach them, the drops will slip through your fingers. And how will you eat, how will you eat with such a hand? Before you get your spoon anywhere near your mouth, you'll be driven mad by hunger, the beast will rear up inside you, you'll slam down the spoon in your bowl and walk away. But you need to eat, you must eat, even if you have nothing to eat. And how, with such a clumsy hand, will you ever threaten anybody when you feel full of bitterness? Even if it's only God. Not to mention the lord and master. But God? And it's easier to threaten God than anyone else. Will you be able to stretch up a hand like that towards heaven? And supposing some grand-dad shouts at you from across the road, Hey you, whatever's that you're threatening me with? Ha! Ha! Ha!

Even if you were to steal eggs from the estate with such a hand, would you ever get them home in one piece? Or could you untie a knot in a rope? It'd be quicker with your teeth. Or just suppose the carriage horses take fright sometime. Just suppose they fly into a rage and bolt, and you're there on the road to face them. Perhaps God will even send you those horses so you'll be able to stop them and make up for your miserable life. What a stroke of luck, just think, the horses charging full pelt towards you, and in the carriage her ladyship and the young ladies fainting with fear. The coachman has slipped from his box. The horses are charging along out of control. Charging straight towards you. They know that you are there to stop them. A cry rings out in their wake, a cry to you. And you're already rushing to help, you can already see yourself leaping at their foaming mouths. You're hanging on. Pulling them to the ground. The horses calm down. Stand still. You've already managed to calculate what you can now expect, a heifer at the very least, perhaps a cow, perhaps a living. Happiness has already taken possession of you. You're burning for it. The horses are right on top of you, right on top of you. But how will you stop them, you fool? With that left hand? Do you think you can stop those horses, dizzy with speed, with that clumsy left hand? Oh, you poor fool. One of them has only to snort and it'll be all over for you. So you'll have no alternative but to throw your whole body under the horses. But your body's afraid to do it. For just let them trample you underfoot, mow you down, and then what good will even a living be to you? And so you'll step aside, bowing to the carriage as it hurtles past. You'll fly into a temper, burst into tears, spit at your own feet.

Hang on a minute though. Did you say the left? Are you sure you meant the left?

But perhaps he's left-handed. You don't know? Ha! Ha! Ha!

I don't feel like laughing at all, yet I laugh. I feel that my laughter is false, yet I laugh. It even gives me pain, fills me with disgust, yet I laugh. I laugh. As though I wanted to savour the fact that I am here in this room, in this palace. I stand in the window, and I see it all. The park rising up before my eyes, the sky, the red glow of the setting sun. I see it all, not only out there, beyond the window, I see it within myself. Even so my insecurity gnaws away at me. I try to remember. Have I really been standing here by the window all this time? Or perhaps I've only been standing here since then. Since when? I don't know. In this window, in the park, in the sky, in the daylight setting within me. Wasn't I still walking round the room just a moment ago? Now angry, now full of resentment. And in the doorway wasn't there some cringing valet with hanging head repeating his thoughts out loud, like *Kyrie eleison*, your lordship? Isn't that now all part of oblivion, and isn't memory only the fact that I'm standing here by the window? I stand in the window, in the park, in the sky, in the setting sun. Silence descends upon me. Whence such silence? I turn away from the window. Besides, it wasn't so long ago that there was the murmur of voices all around me, footsteps pacing on the other side of the wall, resounding with a hollow ring on the stairs; not so long ago that I could hear conversations, quarrels, someone laughing even, and so loudly, piercingly, that it made me angry. I was already on my way to inform them sharply that this is a palace, not a stable. And now suddenly this silence. Visible, tangible, you could take it in your hands and pour it through your fingers like sand. You could pluck it like apples dangling above your head, shake it like a tree. Even the furniture seems to be intimidated by the silence. Even the piano breathes this silence like a bloated animal. The walls. The clock. I feel myself silenced almost to the point of insecurity. Is this really me? But this silence is blissful. I sit down in an armchair. How blissful this silence is after all that. But maybe it's not silence, but death? I leap to my feet. I glance fearfully round the room. No, no, it's only the silence. I sit down relieved. I'm still saying something, but only for the sake of saying it. Tell him that, tell him. I close my eyes. I don't see anything, even beneath my eyelids. I don't want to see anything. I can't see whether the sun has set further, or whether, like me, it's stopped setting half-way. Suddenly I sense that someone is appearing beside me. Someone has entered the room, no doubt about it, for they've stumbled into this silence as if they'd bumped into a chair in the darkness. It's started to vibrate. I hesitate for a moment. I don't know whether to open my eyes. I open them. I don't look at the room, however. It seems to me that my slightest movement will deprive me of something. Perhaps of the certainty that I'm sitting in my chair, perhaps of the hope that has suddenly unfolded inside me. I enquire shyly, trembling:

Who's there? Who is it now? Who? Am I imagining things? But perhaps it is you? Perhaps it's you? You? So come closer, come closer. Don't be shy. His lordship isn't as bad as they say. His lordship won't do you any harm. So you've come? You've come? How good it is that you've come. I had faith that you'd come. That you wouldn't forget your lord and master when bad times came upon him. I had faith. I even dreamed of you today, and a dream is almost like faith. I dreamed that you'd come. So here I am, sitting and waiting for you. Expecting that when I'm with you a mellowness will flow into my heart, peace into my thoughts, forgetfulness into my memory. You alone can bring me solace, for here they all deceive me, torment me, intrude upon me, as if I'd been imprisoned by them in this chamber, in this palace. I've had enough of them. Enough. I've ordered all the doors to be locked. I won't let anyone in. I am not here. I am here only for you. So come closer, come closer. Let me at least have a look at you. Let me have a good look at your youth. For there's no doubt that you're young. You must be young. Otherwise I wouldn't have longed for you so much. So intensely. As though we were kept apart by your pride and my humility. I want you to be young. Don't hide yourself away. I can hear you after all. I can see you. I can see you as if in the pool of a mountain spring. Almost transparently. I can see you undressing in it. All you've got on is that one dress, yet it takes you ages and ages. Ages of fear and longing. Ages of uncertainty. And there is so much shame inside you that, having uncovered your nakedness, you still defend yourself from yourself, still cower in your nakedness, still wrap your arms around yourself. You let your hair drop over your eyes, your eyes drop over your feet. You cry. Ever so quietly, like a light rain. You can't deceive me. After all, I can hear you crying. I can hear. For you yourself don't know what to do next with this nakedness of yours, as though all you were made for is crying. Though you're so young. So young, it almost hurts. It might seem that you belong to yourself. But you are yourself only when you cry like this. Beyond that you already belong to the idea of you, to the desire for you, to the longing for you, to the emotion aroused by your body, to submission, to pride before you. To all those things that even your youth cannot be. For it's in this crying that your vulnerability has its beginning. Your sudden vulnerability, which perhaps you don't even suspect in your own body, nor in your breasts, nor in your arms, nor in your hips, nor in the meadow where you lie. But don't be afraid, I am watching you from out of the depths of this pool, beside which you sank in your sorrow. Maybe you've noticed me too, for you dip your hand tentatively in the water and ruffle its transparency. And when it becomes clear, you ruffle it again, muddy the surface. And only when you are invisible in it do you gradually draw back your hair, unbind yourself from your arms, release your breasts like white rabbits from a cage, rise from your crouching position, from your shame, and stand wide open, opening your frightened eyes to look at yourself. But the water recovers its tranquillity. The water congeals, swallows you up. The water becomes filled with you as with silvery fish. The water glistens with your radiance. The water is transformed into your naked body. And when you stand like that, calm beside that water, waiting for it to tell you your fortune, I throw a pebble into your reflection from the other bank. Panic envelops your body in there. I throw another pebble. You begin to tremble. But your confusion is not enough for me. It seems to me that you still don't feel anything. I put my hands in the water and rock you to and fro. Gently at first, so you don't run away, so you're drawn into this rocking, into its blissful sweetness. But then I toss you on the waves. Then I brush you, rake you aside. Muddy you. Destroy you. And then, I don't know whether from fear or fury, I begin to bail you out from this water in handfuls. But for every handful of you I bail out, another handful appears from somewhere.

Don't cry, don't cry. You've only come to sweep away the dust. Tell them all whatever you like. You were only here to clear up after the guests. And be pleased, be pleased, that you roused his lordship from his torpor. You'll be consoled for a day, then again you'll be sad, again you'll start to torment yourself, again you'll be swallowed up by your destiny, and you'll only ever be as much of yourself as you yourself dream up from time to time – on your way to church, beside the cows, behind the geese, when you can't get to sleep. For do you even know how much suffering there is in you? Perhaps as much as there is longing for you in me. Perhaps our suffering is one and the same, and we don't know it. Perhaps it's you who are my memory and my forgetfulness, and everything that I feel because of you. Everything that I feel at all.

I could reward you lavishly in return, if only you wanted me to. I am powerful. I could dress you in gold, if only you wanted me to. I could make a real lady of you. You wouldn't have to milk the cows any more, others would do it for you. You wouldn't even know how to milk. Your body would be liberated from the smell of milk, your hands healed of the udders, your back cured of its pain, your legs of the earth, your eyes of their tears. You would sit in front of mirrors, tending your youth, your eyes, eyebrows, hair, mouth, your long neck. You would change your dress from morning till evening, and pull faces, oh, pull faces till your maids collapsed at your feet from exhaustion, whispered prayers, implored your dresses to have mercy on them. Look how many dresses there are here. They're all yours. You could go on changing your dress to the end of your days. You could even not get up, but just lie in those bedclothes whiter than clouds. You could even not eat, though food would be brought to your bedside on silver platters with flaming candles. I would buy you earrings of pure gold. I would adorn your fingers with rings, so that your old hands would never ache again. In church you would raise them high, to God Himself, though you don't know how easy it is to placate God with hands like that. And you would laugh, laugh, until you'd laughed away the whole of your old life. And I would buy you teeth entirely of gold. And teeth like that laugh in your mouth of their own accord. With teeth like that not only silence is golden, but every word you utter. And you'd wear slippers smaller than children's feet. You'd be recognized just by your legs. People would say of you that you're unaccustomed even to walking. But why should you walk when you have carriages, breaks, coaches? Your shoulders and neck I'd leave uncovered, though. For what adornment could there be better than gold and rings, if not your own young body? What could be richer than your own young body. Oh, let them torment me, that bare neck and shoulders. Let them tempt my eyes towards you, my hands, my thoughts. Let me feel pain that anyone else who chooses may look at your bare neck and shoulders, and assume whatever he will for himself. For how more intensely than through my own pain could I know that you're the one for me? It's as much as I can do to hang round your neck a little crucifix on a gossamer chain, like a tiny drop of blood. May God too understand how it feels in the soft seclusion of your breasts.

And if you were to die, I'd arrange a funeral cortège. Four funeral horses would carry you step by step in a slow march, though not straight to the cemetery but throughout the whole wide world. The Bishop would walk in front with twelve priests. And I'd hire people in their swarms to wail their despair for you, for my own pain wouldn't be enough for me. I'd hire people as though for the harvest. I'd hire so many that they'd still be walking behind you singing your praises, remembering what a great lady you'd been, long after you'd already entered eternity. Oh, what a great lady you were! What am I beside you? I have remained behind in my great sin, with my guilty conscience. You used to console yourself by helping the poor, in order to make up for me. You used to pray, to suffer, because throughout all your life your lord and husband ran after other women. And if only it had at least been ladies. At least ladies. But he brought in servant-girls, ordinary servant-girls. He filched the prettiest of your maids. Spared neither the lame nor the blind, mothers nor virgins. And he sired more children here than all the peasants put together. And he didn't even know that he had them. Couldn't even remember with whom. Whenever a girl came to him, he would first of all order her to strip naked, stark naked as the Lord God created her, then to walk in front of him, and he would laugh like the Devil if her breasts wobbled. And he'd become vicious as a dog if one of them burst into tears. And as if that wasn't enough for him, he'd summon his valet and ask him if she wasn't too skinny. And sometimes it was worse still, for he'd order her to get dressed and then chase her out. Oh, his wishes had to be properly indulged for him to give a girl something in return, even if it was only a bag of flour, of millet, of peas. For mostly he would fall asleep before the girl left. He was Satan himself, not a human being.

Oh, you, you! I'm the one who's spinning incredible make-believe. I'm the one who's whining and imploring. As if I wasn't his lordship, and as if you were a great lady. I sit here squeezing my knees together whilst you strut like a peacock in front of me. You don't smile, you don't look sad, just sweep away the dust. Flaunt your naked body like that peacock. And if only you knew that it's naked, stark naked. Nothing can hide you from my sight. You are full of your body as the earth is full of earth. Everywhere here is full of you, in this chamber. And I am full of you as though trapped in a prison between helplessness and desire. Perhaps you're pleased that you've infected me with yourself, that I'm dying, trembling for you. The lord and master, yet behaving like a farm-hand. The lord and master, yet it's so easy to get your revenge on me. You don't even burst out laughing. Perhaps you are laughing, but laughing inside yourself, deep down, and you laugh at me, at me, you she-devil. I won't give you anything. I won't even give you an old rag. And I would have given you a calf. Would have given you a cow. An acre of land. But I won't give you anything. I'll let you go empty-handed. I'll let you go in shame, stained with tears. With a bastard conceived inside you. And I won't even recognize it, not even in secret. And don't come here expecting me to give you something for toffees, for a dress, because it's my son. I shall make fun of you. At the very most he'll be one of my shepherds when he grows up. Sheep will be his life. He'll take after the sheep, not after me. Ha! Ha! Ha! I'll let you go without your reason, laughing when you should be crying, crying when your breast is brimming with laughter. You'll be afraid to walk out of here into the world, because you'll no longer be the same once you've had it off with his lordship, you'll no longer be the same. You'll never be the same again. Because there's nothing now you can do except run straight from here to the river, to the brink of the deep water, and fling yourself into the darkness.

Here I am looking at you, and I don't want to believe that you're bustling about in this chamber. Perhaps you don't even know how young you are. I feel confused by this youth of yours. I feel ashamed perhaps that I exist in its presence, as though any joy in my own presence were impossible when I look at you, as though only you had a right to joy, and only I had a right to sorrow, bitterness. For there's so much youth in you that it's difficult to bear you almost. Don't tempt me, don't tempt me. Have mercy on me. If only you could see yourself. That there's no blemish in you even, that you are, that you are so young. Or maybe you are not, but this youth exists instead of you. No doubt you still don't know what it means to desire something, to suffer, and what for? For why, why should you know? You don't even know this, either – that somewhere inside you there is weeping, not the ordinary weeping from your eyes, but the weeping without tears, the secret weeping, to yourself, for yourself. For you are still the pride and not the humility of existence. Oh, how inhuman is this youth of yours, how cruel, uncomprehending, though it's innocence itself.

Here I am looking at you, but I don't trust you. Perhaps you've come here for nothing. Perhaps just to get your revenge on me. And that's why you've come so young. The only thing you want is that I should desire you in vain, that I should never tire of enjoying you, but in vain. And you no longer want anything in return, no land, cow, heifer, not even my emotion for you, which would have been a small part of myself within you, my completion – but you do not yet have any need for completion. And I want you, I want you. Be glad, laugh, poke fun at me. My only consolation is that I want much more than you can give, for I want not only your body, but your suffering as well, your suffering which would then become my suffering, for you don't even know that this is the only way we can truly experience ourselves.

I wanted you once before in just the same way, with just the same bitterness, with such terrifying bitterness that it was no longer desire but rather vindictiveness, my vicious, agonized, tortured vindictiveness. You were young, you were already so young, yet still you hadn't shaken off your childhood. From that youth concealed within you, lying in wait, impatient, you had already crossed into a youth which was visible, brilliant, like the dawn light brightening into morning. Still ashamed of your body, which took you so by surprise, you were full of fear that you'd sow seeds of disgrace all around you. Still unused to your swollen breasts, you tried to tuck them away inside yourself, hide them from human eyes. When you went to bed, you would slap your bulging hips so they'd stop growing. Still you didn't know whether grace had befallen you, or penance, whether you were destined for joy or for ridicule. And when fear came upon you, you'd rush off there, to the wayside shrine, renouncing your own body before God. Begging Him to preserve only your hands, legs, back, as little as was necessary for life and its tribulations. But then, seduced by your own conscience, you would walk amongst the glowing corn, where even the skylark would never spy you with its song. There you undressed and caressed your naked breasts, whispering words of mercy, conciliation, entreaty, squeezing them in the palms of your hands until the pain made them ooze with their first milk. You would clasp yourself with your hands, the whole of you, your joy, your fear, until the warm trembling of the corn began to wind itself around you, so that you had to run out of that corn away from your own body. And you were still so savage, so unaware of yourself, that you didn't even know how to open your legs. But until you came to accept it, it was I who was taming your body. Until that moment I groped my way over you, with hands trembling because of your trembling, stumbling into your secluded places, recesses, secret refuges, until I had liberated you from your fear and you were smitten with the knowledge of your destiny and realized the joy of submission. Then you arose from out of my hands. With them I drew your outline, like in the sun-baked sand beside the river, and I forgot neither your belly button, nor your nipples like tiny pebbles, nor your little mound covered in wild herbs. You arose from out of my eyes, which searched for you until they wept. From out of my thoughts, such as I was ever able to muster about you. From out of my burning heat.

And you don't even want to hear me. You don't care that I pray to you. You sweep away the dust. Sweep away the dust. So, come closer, come closer. I can already feel you throughout my whole self, in my hands, in my legs, in the small of my back, in the whole of this vast chamber. You drive me to distraction. I can't stand the pain of you any longer. Already the sap is trickling from me like resin from a scored pine. Show me your breasts at least. Set them free. Can't you feel how they strain towards me? How they rebel inside you? Do you feel it? How they bite you till they draw blood, pain, seeking a way to get out of you? Do you feel it? They'd flutter their wings and fly away, if only you'd let them. Leap out of you. Let me take them in my hands and wrest them from you, and you'll see how light you'll feel, how joyous. I shall pick them up from underneath like timid pigeons and remove them from you as though from a nest. I won't even hurt their feelings. You won't even feel ashamed. And if you should be seized by trembling, don't be afraid, it'll only be my hands trembling because they don't yet know your body. And if a chill should run through you, and with that chill perhaps fear, don't be afraid, I will breathe on you gently, bury my head in you, and you'll feel brave again. And your body will lose all its shame, and only one fear will remain to disturb your peace – whether I shall be well pleased with you, whether I shall feel myself graciously received inside your body.

Say something, let me at least hear your voice. Say, I've come to serve you, my lord. For perhaps you're here on your own, all alone in this great palace, and that must hurt you more than it does any ordinary mortal, for you're a great lord. Or say, Perhaps you're all full of anguish, my lord, all full of hatred towards yourself. Though I don't know what I could ever be to you, but just let me be anything you want me to be.

And I shall say, Come here, for you are my only hope apart from death. I shall say, Don't be sad, it's only your destiny, and mine. I shall say, Let us take pity on ourselves.

Ha! Ha! Ha! Ha! Ha! Ha! Ah, you, Count, Count! By all that's holy! Wherever did you get this divine gift of fun? You're inexhaustible, Count. I envy you, I really envy you. But I, my dear, have to know what I want. I can't accept that my nature should do my wanting for me. I'd be afraid of being deceived, of not experiencing everything I could experience, of some part of the pleasure, as you put it, remaining outside my reach. Of not being worthy of this pleasure or of the pleasure not being worthy of me. You say a woman's role is to give us pleasure. I agree. Besides, I think the Baron agrees with us too. Isn't that so, Baron? But pleasure for me, my dear, is not unambiguous. I would say that in the thing that you have in mind, real pleasure hasn't yet been exploited. I would even say it's the most banal part of the pleasure that a woman can give a man, the meanest and, moreover, the most tedious. It's nothing but the surrendering of yourself to greed almost, rather like the greed of getting rich. It's nothing but the joy of persecuting each other, destroying each other, lying to each other. It's already hideous. I suppose it's still all right for inexperienced youths. For what kind of pleasure is it, if it's not capable of outlasting itself? What kind of pleasure is it, when all that remains in you afterwards is emptiness, shame, not to mention the sense of ridiculousness, disgust almost? What kind of pleasure is it, after which you feel as though you'd been cheated, after which you want to rip out that moment from your memory, for even the memory of it – the one thing that remains each time – has begun to cloy? Don't deny it, Count, don't deny it. That's exactly how it is. Think about it sometime. It's not enough, my dear, to lust after women – no matter how ardently you might do so – in order to know them as they really are. Besides, don't you feel that lusting after women is like giving in to the worst of your weaknesses, that it degrades you, even makes you look a fool? Has it never occurred to you how much you deny of yourself when you lust after a woman? Lust maybe even prevents real pleasure. For real pleasure should be the liberation of self, not the loss of self.

I am looking for something more noble in a woman. Well, not love. Forgive me, but love is inadequate by its very nature. You've got to have a good deal of unadulterated faith in it, I would say simple-minded faith, like faith in God, in order for it not to seem ludicrous. Only those who can't help themselves have any use for it. For who amongst us gathered here today would know how to confess to it without feeling that he was telling a lie? Who amongst us would have the conscience? For love is a question of conscience, not of feelings. Yes, yes, conscience. I at least, gentlemen, can no longer afford to love. I couldn't even say whether I still love myself, let alone anyone else. So maybe it's beauty I'm looking for? Oh, no, no, not what you two are thinking. For I see the Baron too seems to be sizing me up with a derisive look. Beautiful bodies, nice figures, youth, you think. But my answer to that is that it's all too banal, vague, fictitious. Beauty, my dears, must hurt in order for it to be real. It must be imperfect, defective, suffering, in order for it to be able to be beautiful. There must be hidden inside it, if I may put it this way, some feeling of shame at itself, uncertainty of itself, perhaps even helplessness, perhaps fear. You will recognize it especially by its dependence on your favour, on your understanding, even on your forgiveness, and therefore on your pact with it. So in fact it's not you who recognize it, but it that recognizes you, recognizes whether you are worthy of it, whether it can trust you, open itself to you, lay itself bare without any shame, expose its lameness, its suffering. And if you are not to be spurned, you must show it trust in equal measure and own up to what you yourself are in front of it. You must understand that you are just as much its reflection, and then you will become one with it. Beauty cannot be pride. Its measure cannot be the measure of our admiration. That would be dishonest, that would be making a lie out of it and out of ourselves, that would indeed create a chasm between beauty and mankind, and one so deep as only the chasm between pride and humility could be. Beauty would then be something inhuman in relation to mankind. It would be just like God, death, fate. We would then be merely its subjects. We would therefore be condemned to the desire to liberate ourselves from it in the name of regaining our humanity. Meanwhile we need beauty. But true beauty also needs us, needs us from the very depths of its being, utterly and completely, greedily, like – well, how do I know? – almost like a child needs its mother, or perhaps it's out of place to speak with such sentiment. It's not capable of getting by on its own; it cannot exist either outside people or beyond people. It simply becomes helpless, deserving only of compassion. So what then can be its measure, you ask? Maybe precisely this: whether and to what extent it allows us to share its suffering, whether we feel ourselves to be necessary to it, whether it longs at least for our understanding.

But getting back to women, the most exciting thing to me is not a woman's body but her nudity. No, no, it's not the same thing, gentlemen. You could say that the body is simply the outward form of nudity, just as a sunbeam is a form of light, or our passing through the world but a form of time. And so on, and so on. If a woman's body is her strength, then her nudity is her weakness. So remember, Count, that a woman isn't ashamed of her body in front of you, she's ashamed of her nudity. Well, my dear, I also know something about women. A woman's body doesn't need to defend itself against you, it is the one that makes you its slave, it is the one that has the advantage because of its very nature. From the very fact that you must desire it – for you are condemned to desire – it derives its superiority over you. On the other hand, nudity is vulnerable, it depends not on itself but on you. It is trust in relation to you, uncertain, fearful trust. It's the woman becoming herself within you, in your eyes, in your desire, for nudity doesn't exist of itself, it exists only in relation to you. You only expose this nudity in a woman. It's as though it were the revelation of some pain, of some unique and unrepeatable secret, which then entrusts itself to you, dependent on your favour, on your understanding, on your emotion for it, on your becoming one with it. You feel yourself to be its complement. And that is indeed beautiful, that is the true pleasure that a woman can bestow upon you. But you'd never suspect how easy it is to wound that nudity within her.

Only the more beautiful her body, the less naked it is. And there are women so beautiful that they're completely devoid of nudity. And because of that, to be quite frank, I don't like beautiful women. Above all because of that. Don't laugh, don't laugh so mockingly. I'm saying it in all seriousness. There is something in a beautiful woman that always fills me with humility, almost makes me feel guilty towards her. There is something so inhuman that when I watch her undressing in front of me, I regret I told her to come. I want to run away from her, want not to see her, not to know her. And instead of trembling more and more passionately at the thought of her, I feel myself being extinguished, feel myself becoming superfluous in relation to her, unnecessary to her. I simply don't understand what she still wants from me, this beauty, this perfection that is worthy only of itself, created only for itself, that undresses after all only in front of itself and only for itself. She doesn't undress, but flaunts her every movement, glance, smile, even her shame. I always have the impression that the only thing a beautiful woman needs from me is my admiration, yet if that admiration could exist of its own accord, then she wouldn't need me at all. As though she needed me just so she could see herself reflected in me, experience herself in me. Her beauty needs nothing from me, neither my understanding, nor my emotion, not even my desire, nothing. Such beauty diminishes me in every way.

And that's why a beautiful woman is not beautiful to me, and even if she is, then it's a banal, self-seeking beauty. Such beauty satisfies at the most what we've come to expect to be beauty, but not our craving for beauty, not our age-old longing for it. You could say, therefore, that a beautiful woman is the deformation of beauty, but not beauty, the whim of beauty, but not beauty, the immaturity of beauty, but never ever beauty.

Oh yes, Count, I concede that beautiful women should adorn our parks, palaces, drawing-rooms, even our churches, I concede that much, but never people. True beauty is not the adornment of the world, my dear, true beauty is its suffering. Anyway, don't you feel, you, the seducer, the old hand, the man of the world, the connoisseur, that there's something alien in a beautiful woman, something illusory, something false? Don't you sense in her beauty something akin to abuse of yourself, of people, of the world? Something inappropriate in relation to yourself, to people, to the world? And have you never felt inside you, when you lust after a beautiful woman, a kind of secret desire for revenge? Maybe you've even had your revenge sometimes, only you didn't realize it.

Oh, I tired long ago of all these beautiful women, of all these ladies, hinds, angels, flowers, stars, doves. When I really crave for it, I get myself a common girl from the estate. And at least I have the certainty that she won't cheat me. She'll scarcely have appeared in the doorway, scared stiff, frightened, saying she'd been ordered to come, when I already feel full of her, feel a kind of gratitude that she has come to entrust her secret to me, her most secret of secrets, that she has come to confide in me. And I am overwhelmed by such emotion that I cease to be the lord and master, I am nobody, and to me she is no longer a common girl.

And I ordered her to come straight from the church, straight from the marriage ceremony. So that she wouldn't even enter her house – let the reception wait – but so that she'd come straight to me. For a woman scarcely crosses the threshold of her house and she becomes melancholy for the rest of her life. But I wanted her to come whilst she was still full of the church, full of her happiness. Whilst she was still full of the prayers, of the organ, of the singing. Carrying God within her like a candle in the wind, for God is always the first thing to be extinguished, almost on the road between church and home. So that she'd come to me smelling of incense, blossom, candles. Innocent almost, absolved of the sin of her body this one and only time in her life, this one and only time released from the curse of every kind of suffering, this one and only time almost a saint. Before they dance her body to death at the wedding feast so that not even her white dress remains of her, before they defile her, exhaust her, before every one of them approaches her and drinks her health, before they rape her in their thoughts, in their beds, in the barns, in the orchards, in the corn, on the boundary strips, under the fences, wherever their lust drives them when they've been dancing with her. Before they breathe their vodka into her, their tobacco, their rotten teeth. Before they break her with the cares that await her, so that not even her shame remains from her time of innocence. Therefore I wanted her to come straight from the church. And so she came, all clad in her veil white as snow, in her garland of flowers, shedding tears like a dripping candle, but she came. She was brought by the groom. A peasant without much sense, but honest. He bowed, asked for my blessing, then spoke:

I've brought her to you myself, your lordship, in case she ran off on the way, for you never can tell with a woman. Here she is, may she serve you well. I'm handing her over with an aching heart, for although she's mine, yours is the right. And if you be merciful, let me at least wait for her, for how will it look if I were to return to my wedding without my wife?

But my answer to this, because I wanted to get rid of him, was that he'd have to wait a long time. He'd be better off going to the wedding feast, having a good time. Then the time would pass quicker and he'd forget about his distress.

And he answered, As is your wish, your lordship. Only let me wait.

I told him this was no laughing matter.

He said with forbearance, Take your time, your lordship.

I said that I wouldn't let her go before morning.

He said, I'll wait till eternity if I have to. There's nothing a man adjusts to more quickly than having to wait.

And then I told him – because my anger had already got a grip on me – that he could do as he liked, he could wait outside the door or remain in the room, squat somewhere in a corner, he wouldn't be getting in my way. Ha! Ha! Ha!

But he answered me calmly as though it didn't concern him any more. I no longer know, your lordship, how I'm supposed not to know, yet you are asking me to humiliate her even more.

And then I told him in a superior way that I'd take her from him, if I took a fancy to her.

And then he said he'd wait till whenever it was I got bored, and I doubtless would get bored.

But my answer to this was almost a kind one, for I no longer felt the anger inside me, only a kind of rankling remorse, a kind of wounded helplessness that I was about to humiliate her in his eyes, humiliate her in such a way that nothing of her would be left over for him except pain and guilt, that I was about to make her sad for the rest of her life, that she would be afraid to step outdoors, except perhaps at night, that she would yearn for death and not for him, crave only death and not him, that she would go crazy and awaken abruptly from her dreams thinking of me, not of him. That neither God nor man would ever forgive her.

Then he replied, But I shall forgive her, my lord.

And then I asked him, almost with concern, So what will you do when she brings home a bastard? What will you do then?

I shall accept it as a human being, your lordship, for it too will be a man.

Well then go, go, and wait, you fool, if you really must wait. But I felt sorry for him. I ordered them to take him to the servants' quarters. Ordered them to give him some meat stew and beer, so at least he could eat to his heart's content. Perhaps the waiting wouldn't hurt so much if he had a bowl of stew in front of him, a jug of beer. Perhaps he'd stuff himself with stew, wash it down with beer, and forget.

And he stuffed himself, drank the whole night long, till all the servants rushed to watch him stuffing and drinking so much that he couldn't utter a word, such a hunger had awoken within him, such greed. But some of them almost made fun of him, saying he wasn't eating out of hunger but out of vindictiveness, and others that his bride wasn't even worth the amount he ate and drank on her behalf. But let him eat, let him drink, and good health to him.

Far better that he should eat, drink, than weep. Let him eat, drink, till he can eat no more, more than his strength, his mind can digest. Let him eat, drink, so long as he doesn't lapse into thought, for then his thoughts would confound him. Don't let him pause for breath even. Let him eat, drink. Whatever he eats, drinks during this long eternal night, will be as much as he'll ever get. For he'll never have the chance again to eat, drink more than he can, more than he might desire, more than if he were starving. And meat stew and beer too. Everyone thought that this stew and beer had conquered the pain inside him, for he'd had so much to eat and drink he couldn't possibly feel any pain. They thought that he no longer had any room to remember anything, that another two or three mouthfuls, another two or three gulps, and he'd fall asleep still dreaming about that beer and stew.

But how amazed everyone was in the morning, when he was found hanging from a tree in the yard. And to think he'd gorged himself and then hanged himself. And moreover at the very top of the tree. So that the people who had gathered round the tree were less amazed by his having hanged himself than by his having climbed so high, and whatever for? Whatever for? After all, he could have done it just above the ground, on the first branch. At least then people wouldn't have been so surprised by the height as by his death. But he wanted them to be amazed by that death, oh, he wanted them to be amazed all right. Otherwise they'd have had nothing to be amazed by apart from the death itself; they wouldn't have been able to study him so calmly. At worst they'd have had to cry. That height distanced him from people, distanced him perhaps from his own death. Don't you think so? If a man has already chosen death, why does he choose it so high above the ground? Tell me, why?

And what's more, he hanged himself in such a strange way it was difficult to believe at first that he was no longer alive and not sitting in the tree watching the dawn after that long night, that he hadn't climbed up there because he was scared of the dogs and then couldn't get down. For, just imagine, he was sitting astride the branch, his neck tied to the trunk, leaning forward over the heads of the people who were standing under the tree and wondering up at him. Some of them even said he was still shaking with the terror that had gripped him before he died. Perhaps it's out of place to speak in this way about death, but he really looked very funny. As though he'd been trying to fly up into the sky and had got caught in the branches. So funny that if he'd known he'd look like that, he'd never have attempted that death, or he'd have hanged himself nearer the ground so it wouldn't have been so obvious. For up there, in the tree-top, all he did was unmask it, expose it to ridicule, put it to shame. Besides, don't you think that if a man can't handle death, then at least he shouldn't make it look ridiculous? We can make life look ridiculous, but when faced with death we should aim for nobility, for it's the last opportunity we have to salvage our lives as well.

Don't imagine I don't know why he acted as he did. It was to get at me, to get at me that he hanged himself so high up, so high it couldn't have been higher, couldn't have been more obvious, more blatant. He wanted everyone to see that it was I who was guilty of that death. And he made extra trouble for me too, because then I had to find a husband for his woman, and I didn't have anyone who'd do. In the end I took aside my farm-hand and ordered him to marry her. He was a half-wit, deaf, an idler, yet just imagine, when it came to the point he demanded an acre of land, a cow, a bit of pasture to go with it, a hare after every hunt, two sheepskins and shoes for the wedding, for otherwise he wasn't going through with it, she being a hanged man's widow.

But I confess to you that this death has never left me either, even though I paid out so much because of it. Sometimes I feel something tickling me around my neck. I finger it, and it's a noose, a rope as thick as my hand. It makes me itch, and because of the itching I start to feel short of breath, but the itching gets worse and worse, somewhere deep inside me, as though I had itchy saliva, as though the air, for which I'm barely gasping, was also making me itch, and yet I can't not breathe it in. Then I find myself sailing on high on a branch. I laugh for joy, shout to the people below so they can see how high up I am, up above everything, above the park, the palace, the village, like a bird on the wing, soaring higher and higher till I can't see the people any more, can't see the earth. And then my laughter suddenly turns into terror. I feel myself shaking, and the branch under me shaking too, as if someone was shaking apples from an apple tree. In the end I break away like an apple plucked from the tree-top and tumble into the abyss, into darkness, seeing nothing beneath me, and then I wake up all covered in sweat. Even when I'm wide awake I glance distrustfully round the room, wondering where I am. God, where am I, for darkness looks the same wherever it is. And I can't believe that I'm lying in my bed, in my bedchamber, in my palace, and that my wife is sleeping beside me. I touch her in order to convince myself that I really am lying beside her. And when I wake her up sometimes, I don't know where to begin, because she just imagines that I want her in the middle of the night.

Oh, that death of his follows me around unceasingly. It has already become my own death. And so unrelenting, I tell you, so full of revenge, that it never allows me to get a step ahead. I walk from chamber to chamber, and it's already right beside me. I drop off for a while after lunch, and it's right there beside me. It fears neither the day nor the light, even when the palace is all lit up. It already comes to me in the flesh, my dear. Sometimes I can hear its rustle reaching out behind me like the rustle of a bridal train trailing across the floor. Then again it half opens the door, but doesn't come in. Then it'll ruffle the curtains like a draught. Then again it walks, oh, like now, can you hear it? That's it. It. It manages to prowl around all day like that. It won't rest, won't stop for a moment. I know it, I know that it's measuring out my time with those steps. Sometimes, listening to that walking, I wonder how many steps I still have left. Oh, listen, how it walks, how it walks. It even disregards your being here. Or maybe that's not it. Maybe it's my own penitent footsteps that I can hear.

You know, I've remembered what they say about me here. Namely, that after that man's death a terrible punishment was awaiting me. Amusing, don't you think? But perhaps it's also true. Perhaps it's true. I even found hell locked against me, and even though I beat my fists against its iron gates for three days and three nights, not even an echo answered my call, so I came back here, to earth. And since then I appear every day in the palace, and I walk, I walk constantly, now round this chamber, now round another, but most often round my bedroom. Though I've also been heard in the tower and in the attics. It's true nobody's seen me yet, but as soon as one person heard me, then they all heard me. And there's no doubt that it's me, for who else could it be? Anyway, those who knew me say I walk in the same way as I did when I was alive, like when I was giving an audience and I used to pace up and down the room with my hands folded behind my back, like when I walked in the park mulling things over, or when I inspected the village, just the same calm measured step, as though I wasn't aware that I was walking. And I was the only one here who walked like that. Even the night-watchmen recognized me in the distance from my footsteps, knew it was his lordship coming, though they were surprised I was on foot, and not in my carriage.

And they say that in the beginning I only appeared at night and walked until first light. But evidently my journey was a long one and the night was no longer sufficient for me, because since a certain time I've been heard during the day as well. And I constantly follow the same path, always walking in the same direction. I never retrace my steps, only when I reach the wall I start to walk again from the opposite wall, and so on incessantly, in this one direction, without pausing for breath, without respite, over and over again, anew, endlessly, constantly towards that same wall. So that many people were moved to pity. And all because, as a punishment, I wasn't allowed to die immediately and find myself in eternity, either in the good or in the bad as is our due, and instead I have to walk myself to this eternity, have to reach there on my own legs, have to cover who knows how long a road, for it's not the same for everyone, and I have to cover all the crimes I've committed, retrace the unending footsteps of my guilt. And the road I must follow leads me through the palace, through the rooms, chambers, corridors, floors, attics, cellars, so that everyone might hear me here, for what would be the point of my penance if others didn't hear it, didn't know about it, didn't feel compassion for me? And so that I too might hear myself and thus suffer all the more for my crimes. For I suffer more, suffer perhaps absolutely, hearing myself here; suffer more than I would walking day and night to some eternity. Maybe that's why I wasn't allowed to die at once, so that I might hear myself out to my very last step, to the last step of my penitent soul, which one day I might tread.

And I hear myself, hear myself. You have no idea how terrible it is to hear myself constantly. During the day I can somehow bear it. But when night descends, I simply can't find a place to put myself. I want to run away from here, leave on some long journey before this descending night. I shut myself in my room, I don't want to see anyone, hear anyone. That's why they also leave me in peace, knowing that night is once again thrusting itself upon me. And I wait, not knowing myself what for, I wait, all twisted up inside, tense, as though something was about to happen, though it's only the night descending, just one of those many nights which forever descend and then retreat. I imagine that this darkness doesn't come to invade the world, but only myself, me alone. That it's not darkness at all, but a whirling vortex, into which I sink minute by minute, floundering with no will to resist, which draws me into it, thickening every moment, so that if I remain a minute longer in that darkness I won't be able to raise my hand or even open my eyes.

I leap to my feet, walk over to the door, but I'm overcome by a helplessness worse than fear so that I don't even feel like turning the key in the door. I switch on all the lights, but do you imagine that brings me any relief? Then I begin to be tortured by the suspicion that the darkness hasn't vanished at all but is only hiding somewhere behind the light, skulking there somewhere, lurking in wait for me. With its thousands of invisible eyes, those of monsters, of wondrous creatures, of miraculous birds, it peers out at me from beyond the range of the light, from every direction, from every corner, as I stand there in that light as though shut in a cage, as I feign calmness in that light, that light which exposes me before the darkness to the point of transparency. And it simply waits for sleep to overpower me. But I know that until I fall asleep, nothing threatens me. This is my sole defence against it – not to fall asleep. For even the most fleeting of sleeps, somewhere on the brink of waking and resting, which strokes your face like a warm palm, which doesn't even close your eyes, which touches your eyelids at most, which filters into you like a feeling of peace, like a feeling of relief flowing into your weary body, even such a sleep as this draws you into the abyss as soon as you surrender to it. You imagine you are not falling asleep, but dying. And so suddenly, unexpectedly, that you hardly have time even to think you might be dying. You barely manage to rouse yourself by some superhuman effort, glance around the room, adjust yourself in your chair, when another kind of sleep comes upon you, more real, more cruel. It sprinkles dust in your eyes, churns up your thoughts so you can't even save yourself by thinking. This one is like a leech, it goes on sucking till you feel like a corpse. It's the worst kind of sleep to defend yourself from, for your only defence is some sudden terror, the feeling that something awful is happening to you, that you're hurtling from on high into depths of jutting rocks. But after a while you feel beset by other sleeps, other dreams. Now they flow over you one after another. More and more cunning, insidious, insinuating, yet some are almost happy. They seduce you as though they weren't dreams but wish-fulfilments. They promise you rest such as you've never known, they promise you stillness, repose to your body, respite to your thoughts. They even promise to free you from your own self. And they don't demand a lot, only that you should close your eyes, soothe your heart, show yourself a little kindness. But don't trust them, don't trust them. For who knows if death doesn't begin in this way? All you have to do is show it a smattering of trust, and it'll be down on your chest like a ton of bricks. And when you no longer hear your heart beating within you – your heart which is a constant reminder that you're alive, a bell ringing inside you whose eternal vigilance is the only thing you can trust, and in moments of the greatest fear all you need to hear to start living again – when you suddenly no longer hear that heart, then you leap up terrified and rush in the direction of the door. But the door is shut; death has shut it, not you, and you fall back into your chair, for there's no saving you now. And then for a long time afterwards you can never be certain whether you've been rescued from that terror or not.

Oh, you can't imagine what torture it is to defend yourself against sleep all night long, throughout that long, never-ending night. And time passes more slowly than during the day, slackens to a more slothful pace, stops every moment, as though it too was groping in the dark, as though it too stumbled, lost its way, yet returned many a time to the beginning of the night. You imagine that dawn ought to be breaking, but the clock is only striking midnight. For the dawn is your only hope in the throes of such a night.

Scarcely does the darkness thicken and you're already scanning the walls for some patch of limper darkness, which you could persuade yourself is the dawn, persuade yourself that the dawn will begin soon in that place, from that patch of limper darkness. And sometimes, when you suddenly snatch your eyes away from their tiredness, you catch a moon-drop in the window. Then you leap to your feet, walk over to it, relieved that dawn must be beginning, that you've obviously survived that long night of darkness. Every picture becomes your dawn as it grows more distinct, every wall that is brighter than another, every piece of furniture that looms out of the darkness – you bestow it all with your own dawn as your weary eyes spread it about the room. So when at last the real dawn begins to dilute the darkness, you feel so tired you cannot feel relief, and you even shut your eyes before its corpselike pallor.

Sometimes, when I can no longer defend myself against oncoming sleep and dawn is still a long way off, I get up, light a candle and wander about the palace like an apparition, from chamber to chamber, ever so quietly so I don't wake anyone up. And I walk round every room, illuminate every corner, as though I expected to find something there, something that might be the source of my perpetual anxiety. The chambers seem more spacious at night, somehow deeper, more precipitous. It's difficult to believe that they're empty, slumbering. And in every one, as I stand there with my candle in my hand, I feel something like a tide of death washing over me. Fear sometimes freezes me so solid that I have no idea how I'll extricate myself. I imagine that the doors have slammed behind me, that in a moment someone will blow out my candle. And I often spend the whole night wandering around the palace in this way.

Did you know, my dear, that for many years now I haven't slept on my back, that when I lie in bed I never cross my hands on my chest? And if I catch myself doing it, a shudder passes through me, I imagine I'm gambling with death. I lie instead like a dog curled up in a ball, nestling into my own body, as though I was about to be born out of my own warmth, my insecurity, my fear. I press my head deep into my pillow until I can hear my heart beating, until my whole head is full of my heart, until I feel the whole of myself in this heart, which is pounding noisily, rhythmically, somewhere in the bedclothes. And after every beat I feel relief, but before every next beat I'm gripped by the fear that this'll be the one when something seizes up, starts to growl, starts to flutter; that something in it will start to slow down, become blurred, and that the next one will slow down even more, become even more blurred, and then the next one after that will be nothing but the echo of my own hearing, and the one after that will be the last. I lie there clinging to this heart, strung up on it as though on a thread, and I wait moment by moment for that thread to be severed from me. And should it start beating more feebly, should I not hear it or hear it further away, somewhere in the depths of my pillow, then I seize it in my hand, press my whole chest against that hand, as though I wanted to shake it out of me on to the palm of my hand and convince myself that it's still inside me, that I'm still alive. Sometimes my whole body will go completely numb and I'll refuse to turn over on to my other side, fearing that on that other side I won't be able to hear my heart any more, or that it won't be the same heart and that I'll only torture myself with worry.

You say that none of us will escape death, so what's the point of all this? Besides, I know that. Yes, I know. I know that I shall die, but I don't believe in it, my dear. But perhaps it's not death itself that I'm so afraid of, but the fact that I might die without knowing about it. I'm afraid that the moment of my death might give me the slip, so that I won't even notice it, not feel it, not experience it within me, and that I'll die somewhere outside of myself, unaware of it, not knowing, for ever not knowing whether or not I was a match for it. But perhaps I'm merely scaring away this death inside me. Perhaps that's one way of coping with death, with oneself. For when I listen intently to my heart throughout the night, when I torment myself with worry, then it's easier for me during the day, I no longer think about death. In the daytime I even want to laugh at myself. And there are times when I suddenly burst out laughing for no apparent reason, and they all stare at me in amazement, wondering what's happening to me.

Now listen, you. Don't forget to bring me my drops for the

night. And don't overdo them. Remember, don't overdo them. Don't overdo them. Oh, don't overdo them.

I feel tired, sleepy. Dusk. Faint. Insecure. Alien. I wonder whether to get up from my chair. But what for? To what end? I feel I ought to. Yet I don't want to. I get up. Walk over to the window. Outside it's still not dusk. It's only inside that it's grown so grey, as though a coat of mildew had settled on the walls, the furniture. Outside the dusk is only just beginning. The sun has already set, but obviously barely a moment ago, for everywhere still brims with the cooling embers of its light. Except that out there in the park the trees have drawn closer together, huddled into flocks, and from out of the trees the shades of night are already emerging. Nowhere is there a human form, no voice, no movement, not even the illusion of one. Silence. Empty. Impassive. In this silence it seems that even the day has withered away, that it won't ever move from where it stands, won't ever free itself from the dusk; it's as though it's collapsed on the threshold of the night, and is now simply waiting to give up the ghost, sinking patiently, imperceptibly into its own death. The room too is steeped in silence, the whole palace. I can distinctly feel the boundlessness of the silence all around me, its immensity, its height, as though all the chambers, rooms, corridors had crowded together into one continuum, quivering in its own superfluousness, with me standing there by the window. Me.

I don't like such silence. I always have the feeling that something is about to happen to me, that something is secretly creeping up on me, and I don't even know on which flank, since all flanks are exposed. Such silence is beyond my patience, my indifference. I even have to summon my valet and give him a thorough upbraiding, relentless, full of hatred almost, though he's the soul of innocence and I have no idea why I'm doing it. But I have to do something so as not to be alone in this silence. Mostly I sit down at the piano and play, play, till my fingers swell. Once I even ordered my coachman to harness four horses to the coach and drive it around the palace, for I could no longer bear the ominous silence. I threw open all the windows, and he drove like a madman. Faster and faster. You could still hear the crashing echo on one side, as he came hurtling round the other in a cascade of pounding hooves, rattling wheels, bursts of gunfire. And up there on his box he cursed it all, spat out the most abusive swear-words, things you'd never think of in your worst temper, things you'd only utter in moments of such delirium. What a display of driving that was! My head was reeling from it. And the whole palace was reeling with me. The maids stuffed their ears as they rushed distractedly from room to room. But he drove on and on, ah, I'm telling you, he drove on and on, my heart was racing. You've never seen such relentless, rapacious driving. Finally one of the horses collapsed and brought the whole thing to a halt with its dead body. But after that not a trace remained of that accursed silence.

Did you know that sometimes in such silence I am seized by a strange longing to be someone else, not myself, even if it's only for a moment, someone else, ordinary, poor even, so long as it's not myself? To forget about this palace, about myself. Not even to be rich, but to be at peace instead. To be some shepherd even. Well, tell me, what's so wrong with being a shepherd? Born to live, not die. Spends his whole life tending his sheep. And if he's got a good dog, then he sleeps through more than he ever lives through. The dog minds the sheep, and he merely dreams somewhere under a hawthorn bush. And if he wants, his dreams can be his reality, reality his dreams, just as he wants. If things are bad, then he can bury himself in nature, in the birds, in the clouds, in the sun, in his dog, and what can hurt him then? Perhaps then he no longer exists as himself. Perhaps he only exists as those birds, clouds, as that sun, flock of sheep, dog, not even as his own destiny. Anyway, destiny is too grand a word for a fellow like him. You almost crease up with laughter at the thought that he could have a destiny – stinking of sheep, rancid milk, rams' semen, grass, outdoor air, his sheepskin coat. Ha! Ha! Ha! What an insult to destiny! A mockery of destiny. An outrage. Destiny. Nowadays everyone wants to have their destiny. Take any farm-hand nowadays, and he's dreaming of his destiny. He's not satisfied any more with enough to eat. He wants his destiny as well. He should be saying his prayers. Giving thanks to God. But no, he wants his destiny. This is already beginning to get threatening, my dear. You can already hear the first rumblings.

Here you don't have time even to think about yourself, yet a nobody like him has no idea what he wants. Oh, I'd go to the waters if I could. My legs keep going numb. Somewhere abroad. Someone I know has already gone, someone else. When was the last time I went? I can't even remember. But here you keep hearing that so-and-so's returned. So-and-so lost everything at cards. So-and-so had a damn good time. But here you can't tear yourself away from it all. There's always something to worry about, problems, troubles. If only I wasn't rich at least, I might know why things happen as they do. Sometimes I almost feel sorry for myself, sometimes I almost hate myself. Any stupid little blunder, and I'm unable to forgive myself.

But please, Father, do help yourself. It's old wine. Goes to your legs, not your head. It's a shame the sun's already set. For if you were to raise your glass, Father, and hold it up to the sunlight, you'd catch a glimpse of how nobly it changes colour, as though a precious stone were aflame inside it, scattering its rays of red. Perhaps you'll try some nevertheless? Please, Father, I beg you. Only first with just your lips. It's the best way to catch that fabulous taste, neither sweet nor bitter. So what sort of year did you have for corn, Father? And how are your horses keeping? Well, and what about your sheep? And how are things with me, you ask? Well, what can I say? My corn's like never before. Just grain, straw, no waste. None of my horses dropped down dead. None of my sheep miscarried. How good it is, Father, that you've come. It's good to see a genuine face in this desolation. I was feeling the lack of someone with whom I could sit for a bit, have a good chat. I was already feeling so alone, you can't imagine. You came, you say, on foot. Oh, I'm so sorry, I didn't know. I'd have sent the horses for you. Though, to tell the truth, it's not that far. You could even have recited your breviary as you walked along, prayed without worrying you'd be late. But you must be tired after your journey. They'll be bringing us something to eat in a minute. You'll only have tea? Ha, what can I do? They'll be bringing us tea.

I asked you, Father, to come here so we could speculate about the immortality of canaries. Somehow nobody so far has tried to speculate about it, but yesterday yet another one died on me. My canaries all seem to be dying of late, Father. Could there really be some kind of curse hanging over me? Oh, if you'd only seen how it died, poor thing. It wouldn't eat, wouldn't drink, just sang and sang. At one point it was transported to the skies on the wings of song, when it suddenly broke off and crashed like a stone to the bottom of its cage. And its voice was like a meadow in full chorus, like when you bury your head in the grass. What grief! With each one of my canaries, you know, Father, I too lose a little bit of my own life. I am, after all, in every canary. I almost depend on every canary. Who knows, anyway, if the divide between man and canary isn't narrower than the gulf between man and man. Especially when you think what people are like nowadays. For tell me, what do we really know about canaries? We know that they sing. Therefore we don't know very much. Almost nothing. This distressing feeling, or perhaps it would be better to say these pangs of conscience, came over me last night in fact, when, steeped in my despair, I was wondering, my good Father, how we could at least help him to be saved. Oh, I'm not talking about its body, its feathers, not even about its soul, but about its song. Specifically about its song. For it used to sing so beautifully, I simply can't bring myself to think it might not be saved. Tell me, is it really not possible to be saved through singing, does it really have to be through suffering? You, after all, spend your whole life proclaiming to people the mystery of salvation. You therefore must know, Father. And so I asked you to come over to help me out, or at least to comfort me. Perhaps this is my weakness, that I am no longer capable of suffering anything in solitude, of suppressing it within myself without uttering a word. It was only a canary, but you see what despair it's cast me into.

Confession won't do anything to help me now, Father. Once upon a time the Bishop himself used to urge me to go to confession, but I told him I didn't know why God demands humility from me. Because He doesn't want to listen to my sins, He knows them already, He has already condemned me for them. Oh, I know what you're thinking at this moment. You're thinking, no doubt, I must be very unhappy. And you feel sorry for me, sorry for me. Perhaps you even pray for me, perhaps on the quiet, not even in your thoughts, in case they should betray you, but in your heart of hearts. There's no need, my good Father, no need. As you well know, I can't complain about happiness. I don't even rightly know what happiness is, so I've obviously never been unhappy. Sometimes I even feel bored and envy people their misfortunes. Oh, in secret from myself, of course, even despite myself, even as if to spite myself, but I am jealous that they're not my misfortunes, that misfortunes do not visit me but others, that fate has chosen others to vie with, not me, that it's honoured others, not me. I too would like to experience something of that sort, some great incalculable misfortune that I can't even imagine, a misfortune that would be the will of fate, the will of chance, perhaps my own free will. That would crush me like a millstone, break me like a reed in the wind, make me experience my own helplessness, so that all I could do would be to feel compassion for myself, weep for myself, my tears and my compassion being my only consolation. I don't even know, Father, what it might be, but there's no need to invent misfortunes, is there? You imagine I'm blaspheming, that I'm only tempting fate, that maybe I even hate myself. But has it never occurred to you that this might merely be the manifestation of our longing for our own selves, like the longing of light for darkness, of darkness for light.

Besides, don't you think that a human being is never closer to himself, never feels himself more intensely to be himself, more at one with his own person, than in times of misfortune, precisely in times of misfortune, when he suffers, when he not only feels that he's him, but also knows that he's him, and can't even not know that he's him, him and nobody else? For suffering is not only pain, but knowledge as well. And he never feels himself more truly in league with himself than when he suffers; then he's in league with all the things he hates in himself, the things that humble him, that are the bane of his life, so that he's even ready to defend himself before the whole lot, and to forgive himself before the whole lot too. Maybe it's precisely this very longing, albeit cruel, vain, selfish, that is the most genuine longing a person can have, and all our other longings are but the longings perhaps of shadows, perhaps of names severed from things. Though I don't know, I don't know. I merely doubt.

I can even guess what you'll most likely say in reply, that this is our longing for God. But then I'll reply to you that it's really our longing for a fellow human being, for our union with another person, and if you want to discover it, you have to come down to the level of their suffering. For nothing unites one human being with another so much as their suffering shared. Perhaps this is precisely what's meant by happiness, Father, to find yourself with another person in a single shared suffering, and not to be able to distinguish which part is theirs and which is yours. Perhaps that's precisely why you get these moments when you long for misfortune. Don't you think?

As you know, my dear, I couldn't get married for a long time. The years went by. People were amazed that here was such a lord and yet he couldn't find himself a suitable wife. Besides, there was no shortage of available girls, and from the best noble stock too, rich and beautiful, all of whom would have married me with their eyes shut. They were even brought to me, embarrassed, dropping their eyes at my every glance. I was invited everywhere where there were daughters. But somehow none of these girls from around here did anything for me, none of these angels, madonnas, saintly maidens. It was as though they were too real for me, somehow too easy to understand. I could tell in advance that any one of them would bring tranquillity to my life, quite apart from riches, of course, and that we would live together easily, that she'd be her ladyship, and I'd be his lordship, that we would have children, our own little secrets, a few worries and that would be all. But I demanded something more of someone with whom I was going to join my whole life, and I also demanded more of myself. I don't know what, but something more. And so in the end I brought back a wife from far and wide. It was precisely this that attracted me in her, that she was from a long way away, almost foreign. It quite simply excited me, believe me. Even now to this very day a kind of shame sweeps over me when one of the servants sees us together. I'm ashamed of her in front of my guests, even in front of my family. And when there's no one there to see us, I'm ashamed that the two of us are alone together, as though that in itself was already something unseemly. I prefer to miss her in my seclusion than to be together with her. I prefer to imagine her, desire her without her knowing, in the refuge of my own thoughts. Then I don't have to feel ashamed that I am seeing her naked, stripped of her sumptuous dresses, that I am touching her in her most secret places, that when she raises her eyes and rests them upon me I see them shrouded in mist, beseeching. For when I'm actually with her, I can't even want her, can't even pluck up the courage to stretch out my hand to take hers in mine. It seems to me that when she raises her eyes to look at me – though this happens rarely, my dear, rarely – I see more compassion for me in them than affection.

You're the only person to whom I can confess all this. I know you understand, because you too took a great lady to wife. Did you know that I never go to bed until she's fallen asleep? And when I lie down beside her, I can feel such a chill emanating from her body, it's as though I'd laid myself down beside death. Her body neither stirs at my coming, nor sighs. But it's as if it's turned to stone in its sleep, in order to ward off my nearness. I bury myself in the bedclothes, and thus sink all the swifter into sleep. Yet if I could only find her one day, believe me, sleeping a normal sleep, lost in this bed, flung across it in abandon, full of trust that when I come I'll gather up that warm body, made defenceless by her dreams, strewn by her dreams among the sheets, and draw it under me, breathe into it the happiest dreams the whole night long. Not on your life! I always have the feeling that she gets into bed as though into her grave, that she doesn't dream, but controls her dreams, that she grows larger in the darkness to fill our whole bed, leaving me barely enough room to squeeze in beside her.

But I knew she'd be like that. People even told me she'd be like that. But I wanted her to be like that, this was how I desired her. For even then I was sick, my dear. No one knew about it, never suspected it in me, but I already sensed that my time was running out. And she was so young, so young, that everyone was amazed I was marrying such a rose-bud, a rose-bud whose petals had not yet unfurled. They used to say we looked like father and daughter, not like man and wife, that she'd obviously been captivated by my wealth, and I by her youth, but that there'd never be anything between us other than her youth and my wealth. And she also didn't know about the secret I was carrying with me to the altar. You'll say it was cruel. Perhaps it was. But you have no idea how afraid I was, afraid I'd have to die, unable to share this death with anyone else, only with myself, which would be like dying twice over. I was afraid I'd be unable to bear this death on my own, as it dragged itself out day after day, if I didn't have someone to die with me day after day before my very eyes, if I didn't have someone on whom to bestow just a small part of my death, even though I'd keep it secret from them. Anyway, perhaps I reckoned that someone as young as she would conquer our mutual death with her youth, this death that she shared with me. Perhaps I reckoned that she'd overpower it, and that we'd both walk out of it as young as each other. And if not, then at least her dying along with me might somehow compensate me for my own death, so cruel and unjust, so that when confronted by it, I might feel compassion for someone else, not simply for myself. And perhaps then I'll be able to comprehend it with dignity, forgive it, even love it a little, when it's not simply my own death but someone else's as well. Or maybe I wanted to endow my wife with some great and all-consuming emotion, which would be mine alone, which would be everything that I am, everything that is hidden inside me, and therefore I surrendered myself to this death in order to release that emotion from me. An emotion that would not only be joy, but suffering too – and let it destroy me, even, for what does it matter, what does it matter? Remember that only great emotion can absolve you from the sin of your existence.

Standing at the foot of the altar, above the great crowd of people, who filled the church brim-full with their thousands of eyes fixed upon us, amongst the myriad of flaming candles, in the midst of the singing, the organ, the prayers, I felt a strange kind of joy that here was I, a man singled out by death, taking to wife this young woman, who was standing here trustingly beside me, leading her into my death, binding her before God and man for the rest of her life to this death, yet nobody knew my secret, not even she. And that was the only joy I felt in that exalted moment.

Maybe it's all rather base, but how much easier it is for me to bear this sickness which, as you see, keeps me confined to my chair, to this room, to the palace. All I ever see of the world, my dear, is what I see through the window, or what I see when they carry me out on to the terrace. A life consumed like this by sickness is not a life to be envied, even though it may be a rich one, like mine. Everybody here takes pity on me, but I don't want it, I don't want it. I can't bear pity. Anyway, would you believe that this sickness isn't at all like a sickness to me, but like a mountain spring of the purest water, which gushes with my great feeling for my wife, radiates my constant unfaltering emotion at her very existence, the tenderness I experience every time she appears, every time I hear her speak, every time I think of her, suffer on her behalf. Oh, I suffer more on her behalf than I do on my own, and more than she could ever imagine she was capable of suffering. This feeling even conquers my humility in relation to her, conquers too her estrangement, her haughtiness in relation to me. I even contrive to love her youth, that youth so absolute it can afford me nothing except compassion. I contrive to love her, for she doesn't know, unhappy soul, just how helpless she is, just how dependent she is when faced with my death, which is her death as well, just how dependent solely on my love.

You'll say that it was I who made her like this, that I drew her deviously into my death, made her so vulnerable that even her youth can't protect her from me, that this youth of hers has become nothing but a charming vanity in the face of our dying. It's true, my dear. I even confess I feel a certain superiority over that youth because of the agonizing knowledge I have about us both, the knowledge that seems to have been entrusted to me, to me alone, in the deepest of secrecy, so as not to wound her to no avail. But maybe thanks to this I'm capable of my great feeling towards her, because she's so vulnerable, so vulnerable that she doesn't even know how much she needs my love, now and always. Doesn't know so profoundly, so passionately, that she suspects nothing beyond that youth of hers. Her youth has become her faith, in which she has placed all her trust. Perhaps she even believed that youth was her destiny, as though youth was the sole destiny of some in this world, and death the destiny of others.

If you could but see how she constantly examines her youth in front of the mirror. She's scarcely opened her eyes of a morning, and she's already leaping out of bed and running to the mirror to greet herself. She stands there full of excited curiosity – yet at the same time unsure of herself – opposite her own reflection, two, three paces in front of the mirror, and only after a while does she draw near and wipe her eyes as though wiping them not of sleep, but of disbelief, of rapture. She strokes her hair, her face, her neck, her arms, then she leans forward trustingly towards herself and smiles at herself, thankful that during the night she has not ceased to be young.

In the evening, however, on her way to bed, she bids a long farewell to her youth in the mirror, as if she wanted to remember herself for her dreams, confide in her dreams so that they would dream of her, only of her, of her alone, her as a young woman, and then she walks away sadly, as though she were walking away from her youth not for a single night, but for ever and ever. For days on end she just sits in front of the mirror – for what else has she got to do anyway? – and gazes intently at herself yet not at herself, as though it's not enough for her to know how young she is, but as though she must also see for herself, so that no shadow of doubt might blight the youth within her. When she sits like that, almost lifeless, motionless almost, gazing only at herself, she seems set for ever in the beauty of that youth. Suddenly she leans forward and stares into her eyes from close to, almost face to face, her eyelashes nearly touching, so she can hardly see herself any more, but she goes on staring and staring, until her eyes fill with tears and blur her image. Then she stands up, walks a few paces from the mirror, and then slowly, haughtily, step by step, she approaches it afresh, swinging her hips, surrendering to her body, which, just as haughtily, draws near to meet her. And only when she's gazed her fill, when she's reassured, relieved, does she summon her maid and allow her to brush her hair. Then she busies herself with her perfumes, powders, dressing. But just let something in herself displease her, just let something sting her there in the mirror, then she'll leap to her feet and run to another mirror, run from mirror to mirror, her face pallid, flustered, as she peers at herself with ever greater alarm, hoping everywhere and trusting none of them. Sometimes she flies into a tantrum, dissolves into tears, and then runs off somewhere, sobbing into her hands. She runs to the Rooms, where there are still so many more mirrors she may yet find one to console her. Sometimes a terrible fierceness flares up inside her. She rips off her dress and stands naked in front of the particular mirror that has insulted her. She shows herself to herself, now from the front, now from the side, then she stretches, raises her hands to touch herself, and takes her breasts in her palms, as though trying to seduce her own self, to incite the envy of anyone who might see her there in the mirror. And she has plenty to be proud of, oh, yes she has, my dear, but it's better not to say anything, for words would only mar her beauty. For what words could ever do justice to her neck, her breasts, her youth?

Yet I feel sorry for her nevertheless. I sometimes imagine that once she's been disappointed by all the mirrors in the palace she'll come to me, to the one who's been waiting all the time. She will come and lay down her head on my knees, brimming with tears, though she might not even be crying. For she is already condemned to my love, just as she is to my death. My love alone is all her defence – even against our death – all her earth, all her light, all her hope, for there can no longer be any existence for her outside of my love. Drawing her into my death, I have drawn her into my love. And when a loved one enters death's domain, even as unaware as she is, even as young as she, then you must never lose that person from your love, not even for a moment, for in the course of that moment they might easily divine the death within them.

Don't think this is my pride speaking through me. I really don't want anything from her apart from her existence, apart from her dying this one death with me, unconscious to the end, but it is, after all, only my death, only my death. I'm even going to tell you that I feel guilty towards her. I am never allowed any peace, neither during the day nor at night, by my tremendous feeling of guilt, which I can't forgive myself, can't forget, which I even rekindle inside myself every time it wears off. This guilt just degrades me all the more in her presence, but I want it to degrade me, I want it to, you understand, because I want to take nothing for myself from this love of mine, neither openly nor secretly, not even any illusion, so that I might exist only as my love for her, as my love in her, beyond which I would be nothing to myself other than continual death. So that I might exist as the love – if such love is conceivable at all – that would protect her from her own self. As all her suffering and as her death; and if it's possible for one of us to die for the both of us, then I'd gladly be the one to die. And so that I might exist also as her fear of this death, as all she knows of this death, as all her helplessness. As the love in which her every thought would flicker and expire, her every moment of anxiety, everything that might wound her fragility and cause just one tear to roll from her eyes. Leaving her with nothing but her youth, her everlasting youth, the joy of that youth.

Look, there's her portrait hanging on the wall above you. Could you ever bear it, if you suddenly saw tears in those eyes, those doe eyes, which gaze down at you, which you can no longer free yourself from? You stand here, and they're watching you, you stand over there, and they're watching you, wherever you stand, they're watching you, wherever you walk away from them, they're watching you, and so vulnerable, as though they'd placed all their trust in you alone. Could you bear it? If some sudden fear were to appear in them, if some grief were to sadden them, perhaps some resentment towards you? Oh, no, my dear, let me bear it all so that she may never be touched by even the shadow of a doubt, so that she may never stray beyond her youth, never suspect that there exists another time, which bears us all towards death. It's enough that I know, know on my own behalf, know on her behalf, know it even more painfully on her behalf than on my own. Even my own dying doesn't distress me as much as hers, whenever I gaze at her, whenever I think about her, whenever I long for her. My own dying is not so totally vulnerable as her dying is for me. At least I can confront my own dying with my unbelief, with my hatred at least; I can comprehend it, come to terms with it, and so rise above it. At worst I can feel defeated by it. But her dying is without her knowledge, so could it ever be more vulnerable than it already is?

And what wouldn't I do for her, my dear, simply to confirm her in her youth? Everyone's saying that his lordship's mad about his young wife. That he's so tantalized by her youth he no longer knows what to do with himself. That the world, people, his riches, no longer interest him, that he's being robbed left, right and centre, that the peasants no longer go out to work in the fields, but that he just sits for days on end in his palace with his young wife. And the palace is closed to everyone nowadays, nowadays the palace is extinct, no one ever rides up to the palace nowadays, no one ever leaves. No one even knows what goes on there, because the valets too keep their mouths shut tight if you try to ask them. No balls, no guests, no visits, not like it used to be. And when evening draws in, a single light burns weakly in a single room, all the rest is but a black night, a hollow, deathly night in all the windows, silent as the grave. But what have I got left apart from my love for her? My love is my whole world, all people, God, my own self. In my love I find everything, everything, even compassion for myself. My love reconciles me with myself, with myself just as I am.

I have built this love inside me like a church, out of everything I could lay my hands on, out of what I could and could not lay my hands on, out of my will and out of my impotence, out of my longing and my helplessness, out of my knowing and not knowing, out of my insecurity, fear, suffering, out of my selfishness, out of everything I imagined to be inside me, till I felt I'd reached the extremities of my being. For remember, love is never granted to anyone as a free gift, it's not enough to crave it in order to be smitten by it, you've simply got to construct it within yourself. And it's an edifice that often transcends the boundaries of our strength, our patience, our comprehension, even our wisdom. I constructed it like a blasphemous creed, for there's no room in it for any god, no room for any person except her alone, my wife. Like the truest of creeds – though because of that the most severe, for it knows no separation of joy and suffering. But it's also the most lonely of creeds, for it exists for no one to believe in but me.

When evening comes, when the palace drifts into slumber, only then can I calmly surrender myself to this love of mine, which I seem to have been hearing inside me, as though I'd been confiding in it, conversing with it secretly, certain that no one else was listening. Sometimes it's only the dawn that rouses me from it, the chirping of the birds outside the window, the shouts of the early risers in the village. Whenever I sit up like this at night, and my great love sits up with me, not even death seems so dreadful to me, I almost feel reconciled to it. Though don't imagine that a happy tranquillity descends upon my soul. Sometimes a terrible doubt engulfs me, suddenly, from out of the blue, which I then can't stifle for weeks, months on end. Doubt whether she is really dying with me. For time passes, and yet she remains perpetually young, just the same as she was when I brought her here years ago. Doubt that perhaps her youth has managed to protect her from my death. And once she is beyond the reach of my death, then she's also beyond the reach of my love. Panic pounces on me like a wild beast, fear that she no longer needs me at all, fear that my secret love does nothing for her, fear that my love is nothing but my humility, the common humility of a sick man, the mere forgetting of the death within him.

Ugh, how I hate it then, how intensely, how fervently, the whole of this great love of mine, injured, redundant. All I want then is to live to see the moment when her youth begins to abandon her, when she won't be able to hide it from herself. When the first hint of fear flickers in her doe eyes, and then the next, and then every day, till all trust vanishes from those eyes and only astonishment peers out. And one day she'll examine herself and no longer perceive herself to be young, but simply scared. Perhaps without realizing it she'll start to avoid the mirrors, and eventually she'll be offended by the fact that there are so many mirrors in the palace. After all, it's improper, it only encourages vanity, stimulates pride, and that, as the priest said in his last sermon, is all a sin. After all, one mirror is enough.

When the radiance of her body pales like the morning sky. When she starts to take good care of herself, make sure she's no longer visible through her sumptuous dresses, no longer lets you suspect that somewhere under there she's naked, without shame, like she always used to be, like she always will be. When her breasts begin to sag like the bags beneath her eyes, her eyes where spiders now weave their lace-line webs. When from the depths of those eyes, immersed in their own reverie, startled birds take flight every time you glance at her. This will be the time when the rings on her fingers will burst into flower, blossom forth with a redoubled sheen, a sheen imparted by her sorrow and her helplessness. When she begins to hide from me not only her body, but her thoughts as well. For this will be that special time, conceived long ago because of my death, welling up inside her at last. And perhaps one day, when she's in the chapel saying her prayers, she'll suddenly realize that God can afford her no support other than His own helplessness. And then she'll remember me. And she'll come to me, I believe she'll come to me, if not of her own free will, then because fear will impel her towards me. She'll come and rest her head on my knees without uttering a word, and I will say to her, What beautiful hair you have. People used to say it did your hair good to rinse it in oak bark, adding a few hops to the water. But do you hear? I think someone's knocking. Who on earth could it be at this hour? In the middle of the night? I'm not expecting anyone. I don't remember inviting anyone. Besides, I don't want to see anyone now. I'm tired. I've had a long day. No one has the right to intrude on me. Oh, do you hear it? No, it's not a mouse scratching about. Why is it so dark in here? What's happened to the lights? Put on the lights, for God's sake! Or bring me a candle at least! Isn't there a valet around somewhere? Tell him to go and tell them that I'm not at home. That I'm not here. Perhaps I'm already asleep. It's already quite dark and no light burns in any window of the palace. A hollow, deathly night in all the windows, silent as the grave.

Ah, it's you! I had a feeling you'd come, though. But why now, at this time at night? So suddenly, unexpectedly, without even letting me know you'd be turning up? Oh, I've been expecting you, I've been expecting you all right. I'm even pleased that you're here. You just caught me a bit unawares. But come on in, please. It's dark in here, I'm afraid, but it saves me having to introduce you to anyone. We're all sitting by the fireside because it's always cosier somehow than with the lights on. And perhaps it's better this way, when all we can see of one another is what the fire lights up. For everyone sits with everyone else, yet at the same time we're all hidden from everyone else. It's not so exhausting. But just let one of the logs go pop, oh, then you'll see the flames shoot up, suddenly illuminating all our faces, even the saddest, even the most depressed, wretched, suffering. Oh, there the Prince has been lit up! Bow to the Prince! But why are you all dressed up, my child? What's that, you've been celebrating somewhere? It's summer, and yet you're in an overcoat with beaver collar? Can't you feel this oppressive heat? We're expecting a storm any minute. The birds are fainting, dropping out of the trees. I feel like peeling off my own skin, and here you are in top hat, gloves. And how your boots shine! And with a cane too? Take a look at this, ladies and gentlemen, such a whippersnapper, yet he's got a cane already. In my day you had to be an old gaffer to walk around with a cane, and even then you had to be really old, or a cripple. You haven't crippled yourself, have you? Ha! Ha! Ha! Or perhaps it's just the fashion nowadays?

So tell me what brings you here at this hour, so suddenly? And don't try and deceive me, don't try and deceive me. Perhaps you want to make me believe that you've been missing me. So you decided to pay me a visit, hence the formality, and now you've arrived out of the blue, because your missing me drove you here. But no doubt you've lost again at cards and need money. And a lot of it. No doubt you've knocked up a few debts there, what? And not just on cards, but on wine, women. Ha! Ha! Ha! Perhaps you've even pledged your honour. Come on, admit it, admit it! And now you want me to buy it back no doubt? Yes, yes, honour is a great thing, a serious thing. The only trouble is, when you've got no money, then you've got no honour either. And you, so they say, are skint, on your uppers. Ha! Ha! Ha! Well, what the hell, I'll give it you, only remember that this is the very last time. I can't keep up with you any more, and you no longer have a conscience. It won't be long before I'll have to sell the palace. You'd even strip me of my soul if you could.

What's this, you're not after money? Then perhaps you really did miss me. I am prepared to believe it. Ha! Ha! Ha! He missed me. Listen to this, ladies and gentlemen, he missed me! So, give me a kiss. Give me a kiss. I'm touched. Only remember, it's not that easy to pull the wool over my eyes. You can try the proverbial third time lucky, but you won't fool me. You don't know me, you don't know me, I can see that. But as you've turned up, you might as well stay. I was just telling them how gay it used to be in the old days. And as we've got nothing better to do, and it's dark in here, we're all having a good laugh. So sit down and have a laugh too. Hey, you there, take the young gentleman's coat!

So where did I get to? Aha, I wanted all the world to be gay. If the world's got to be as sad as it has been so far, I think to myself, then it's about time it was gay. May all the people in the world be gay, and their wives too, their children, their cattle, and everything that brings forth fruit and multiplies, may it multiply with gaiety, not with sadness. So at least there'll be plenty of it, like sunshine in the sky, water in the river, trees in the forest. For what God in His love has failed to provide, man should strive with all his might to put right, even if it means damnation. So everybody might go to bed with gaiety in their hearts, and rise to salute it in the morning. And so I might be the gayest of all, for I can't abide sadness, I avoid it like the plague.

All well and good, you'll say, my dears, but how do you bring this gaiety into the world? After all, I'm not the first to want to do it, but nobody has yet succeeded. But I didn't have to rack my brains for long. Human nature itself came to my aid. It was human nature, my dears, that came to me as I sat in my chair one day, lost in thought, and whispered in my ear that there's quite enough gaiety in people already, you just have to shake it up a bit, rouse it from its slumber, and it will take possession of them. For people are made to be gay, though they don't realize it, made to make each other gay, made to make the God above them the gayest of all. And all the sorrows that they bear within them, all the bitternesses, hates, fears, are but fallen angels from the throne of gaiety. And this human nature urged me to set up taverns, then laws – and then everything would happen of its own accord. And one tavern next door to the other, so no one could claim later that he'd got far to go. And I introduced laws that said they all had to drink what was assigned to them, so that no one, God forbid, would cheat himself. For people don't know themselves that they want to be gay, and even if they do know, then they don't know how. Laws, too, that said that no one must stint himself on gaiety – for you often got some Judas who worked against his own interest – and that anything they earned on my estates could only be collected in the tavern, in vodka, in beer, in salted herrings. Perhaps that surprises you, my dears, those herrings. What's a herring got to do with gaiety? But it's got a lot to do with it, a lot to do with it. Why, herrings increase your thirst. And the more thirsty they were, the more they drank, and the more they drank, the more thirsty they became. And the best thing for thirst is herrings, because they make you thirstier still. And thirst should never be quenched, for then it only ends in sorrow. It's like when you're on fire, everyone rushes to save you whilst you're still ablaze, but once you've been put out, no one even wants to sympathize with you. Though when you were actually alight, you seemed to have the whole world behind you. But I must say, I hope you never live to see the end of a fire like that. It's the saddest of ends. You don't even know where to put your hands, and there's no one to stand by you any more. But hang on a moment, where was I? Aha! So there was no end to the gaiety. And the gayer they became, the more truly they felt themselves to be human. Till in the end they got used to the fact that they could only be human when they were drunk.

And they drank, oh, how they drank! I tell you, I never came across a single one of them sober, just a bunch of buffoons. As though a never-ending carnival had come to pass. An eternal holiday. The absolution of all their sins. As though they'd gained their freedom. For, I tell you, there's nothing like vodka for raising the spirits. Vodka is the one answer to everything. With vodka, God never seems so distant nor hell so full of dread. With vodka, your desires are realized more quickly than in dreams, prophecies, hopes. With vodka, a certain nobility even descends upon you. So you feel ready to save the world, destroy the world. With vodka, they say, you even forget your own memory. And so everything grew as gay as the world grows green in spring. Grew gay as though all the people had suddenly become happy, as though all creation rejoiced along with their happiness, both the good and the bad, all heaven and earth, all the fowl of the air and every creeping thing that crawls upon the earth, all the water in the rivers, and all the fish. Oh, I tell you, how the people mellowed, became trusting, submissive, no longer remembered whether life had treated them well or ill, whether they'd been born in squalor or in luck, whether they were who they were, or who they were not. And how the children multiplied in that time of gaiety, my God, how many new souls! People bred like wildfire, as if they'd been relieved of all sin, all shame. And everywhere there were weddings, weddings, weddings.

You ride through this world of gaiety, and even though you may have been steeped in the saddest of sorrows, sunshine streams into your soul. You simply don't want to believe they're the same people who until now harboured hatred in their hearts instead of gratitude. Every one of them now implores me with his gaiety to pardon his innumerable sins. Every one of them is stricken by the sorrow I carry on my countenance. Every one of them wants to ease my sorrow lest it turns into a cloud of hail, into a cruel storm of anger. And every one of them tries to be gayer than the next. One of them hangs from a fence, and when I draw near, he raises his head and crows like a cock. Another has climbed a tree, and when I ask him what he's doing up there, he says he's waiting to take off. Then again some wretched fellow, drunk as a lord, blocks the path of my carriage and shouts, beating his breast, What have I done to offend you, your lordship, what have I done to offend you, when you're so good towards me, so generous to me, to my wife, my children? What have I done to offend you?! There's more and more of them all around me. My horses can hardly move in the crush, and in the crowd there are women too, children, old men. Staggering, giggling, singing. Softly at first, just amongst themselves, so as not to insult me. But when they see I don't object to their singing, they become bolder, raucous, running one song into another as though they were quarrelling, getting it all off their chests, swearing at each other, everyone along with everyone else, with God, with the whole world. And the more delirious ones rip open their shirts, revealing to me their sincere hearts, beating their breasts as though they wanted to smash all their sins in front of me. They touch my carriage, the horses, the harness, even the coachman on his box, crossing themselves as with holy water. And the children even lick their fingers after touching. Every few paces the horses stop, and already a dense throng presses against them. I almost feel myself to be one of them. I feel as jubilant as they. I take the whip from the coachman and fling it into the crowd. And there they squeeze towards it, one after another, snatching it from each other's hands, from each other's mouths, kissing the end of the strap with reverence. Until at last someone screams in a frenzied voice, Lead us to the tavern, your lordship! Hey, lead us to the tavern to our only joy, to vodka, to beer, to our salted herrings, so that our thirst might never desert us! And you laugh along with the people, rejoice gaily with their gaiety.

You ride along, yet you hardly recognize the world around you.

A peasant is pulling a cow on a leash. His grandparents in tow, his wife with baby at the breast, several other children.

And where are you off to, my good people?

To the tavern, your lordship.

What with a cow, children, grandparents?

So let them all enjoy themselves. Why should we stint ourselves? There's still plenty of drink to get through, so let the beast have a good time too, let the children have a good time, let my grandparents go a bit crazy before they have to face the life eternal. For a man can't cope with it all single-handed. Can't cope, your lordship, even if he drank day and night, even if he drank himself to death. And the innkeeper threatens you too, saying that if you don't drink your portion then you'll have to drink twice as much, as a punishment. And neither tears nor pleas will help you then, it won't help you even if you're sick, even if you die, for they'll still pour it down your throat. And apparently now's the best time, for the herrings are just right, your lordship, neither gone off nor bony, but thirsting. So thirsting that after one of those you could down as much vodka as there's water in the river. And their heads aren't too big either, for it's nothing but a swindle when half the herring's its head.

And farther on in the gaiety a peasant rides bareback on another, spurring him on with his heels, grasping the man's hair in his paws like a mane, till the horse's eyes pop out.

And what has your companion done to offend you, my good fellow, that you have to ride on his back?

Nothing, your lordship, only I carried him to the tavern, and now he's carrying me home. For both of us wanted to have a good look at God's creation even if it's only from a horse's back. But don't let your charitable heart show him any mercy, your lordship, for it's easy to get us mixed up, even though it looks as if he's the horse and I'm the rider. For I'm the one who's collapsing from exhaustion, all he does is carry me, I'm the one who takes pity on him, I'm the one who suffers for him, and all he does is groan. But it's easier for us this way, your lordship! For neither of us knows if he's carrying his own destiny or the other's. And because of that neither of us knows which one he really is. Each of us feels he's more the other than himself. We thought and thought about it, till the other day we were struck by the brilliant idea that one of us should become a horse and the other the rider, and then we could take it in turns, because there's too little of us to make two people. And so the two of us became one person. And even you, your lordship, won't be able to tell which of us he is, for we can no longer tell ourselves. But guess which one of us is his soul, and which his body. Which one of us is immortal, and which is temporal. Which one is damned and which is saved. Which one is fate and which is free will. Which one of us is the heavier and which the lighter. And so you see. For wherever we are, it's all so gay that we no longer feel anything inside ourselves. And even when we have a drink we don't feel it inside ourselves, but as though it was round about us. As if we didn't exist at all and there was only round about us. In that round-about-us you could even get on a stick and ride it too like a horse, except that it wouldn't neigh beneath you. And that stick, if you don't mind the comparison, your lordship, would be stiff as your stallion eager to mount your mare!

Oh, birds are congregating in the sky. A great cloud of birds. The sun rocks from their flight like an apple shaking on a branch. And its light is all churned up. Now it grows dusky, now it brightens up, wheeling into swirling coils, into spirals of smoke, flying away somewhere high in the sky, casting shadows over the earth, but after a moment, when it already seems to be night, it bursts forth again with a dazzling brilliance. Almost blinds your eyes. You can't see anything. And the birds fly as though propelled by a power other than their own, as though borne on the wind. Their wings seem to die whilst still in flight. They lose height with nothing but their terror to save them, clamorous, mournful. Somebody kneels down. Then somebody else, and somebody else. Then others too. People at work in the fields stand and straighten their backs, then they too fall on their knees. Even the ones with disbelief written on their faces. Somebody whispers in alarm, It must be the plague wind blowing our way, or the war. Suddenly my coachman begins to laugh. He shouts. Look, your lordship! I see some peasant arguing with a poplar tree. Sobbing with his arms round the trunk. Muttering, wailing in self pity, making threatening gestures, bashing his head against the tree till it almost resounds. He snatches his scythe from the ground and hacks with all his might into the poplar, as though it were a clump of grass, but the scythe sticks in the wood with a hollow thud and leaves the man grasping the handle, at a loss what to do. He leans against the tree and cries out to his woman, grovelling to her name, to her body. He hails her fair hair, praises her blue eyes, her breasts, her belly, her loins. Promises to forgive her if she'll only appear, even on this last of all nights.

And what might you be up to, my good man, doting on a tree?

He wipes his eyes, looks at me in fear:

I can't placate my woman, your lordship. She disappeared somewhere in this poplar by the roadside when I was chasing her through the night with my scythe and promising that, come what may, I'd chop off her head, the bitch. I was trying to get to her all night long, your lordship, but she wouldn't let me have her because I was drunk, and because I'd make her another bastard. But how can I be drunk, look at me, tell me what's drunk about me! What did I have to drink that could have made me drunk? I am drunk, but on her. And if she's having it off with someone else, then I'll really make her suffer. How can I be drunk? I followed the road back home. The long straight road. And there wasn't even a moon to guide me. Not even the palest star. It was overcast. Gathering for rain. So dark, I walked like a blind man. But I made it. So how could I be drunk? And I looked forward to her as a child looks forward to a sweet. I saw her, and her alone, in all that darkness. She lit my way with her shining body. With her breasts like little suns. The night all around me was full of her, and I carried her in my arms through the darkness to our hovel, to our bed of straw. My insides were all aflutter. I got tangled up in my own legs. But she awoke and ran away. Disappeared, as if she'd been nothing but a fleeting vision. She was here, but now she's gone. I can still feel the thrill of her body in my arms, but she's gone. My hands still burn in the baked rye of her hair, but she's gone. My palms still burst with her breasts, but she's gone. I plunge them in her belly as if in a stream, but she's not here any more. What have I done to deserve this? I'm drunk? I am drunk. But obviously not drunk enough, if she appeared to me and then ran away. Besides, I carried her in these very arms all the way from the tavern. Along the dark and bumpy road. Rocking her as if she rode in a carriage. And I didn't let fall a single hair from her head. And as I walked, I wanted her so much I could have burned down our hovel. Together with us, together with our children, together with our poor wretch of a cow, which coughs like a ghost in the night and never gives us any sleep. I'd have burned it down, believe me, your lordship, I'd have burned it down in order to save her, save her from what I can't protect her from. And when one day I really do get drunk, then I will burn it down, and let that be the end of us. But I'll have to get so drunk I won't even be able to feel myself, so drunk I can do nothing but desire her, desire her so sorely it'll be like the hovel burning down, her, myself, our children, all our sufferings together with us, all our tears together with us, with God, with our death, with all human oppression. Perhaps such a desire is too vindictive, but perhaps it's the only thing that has the power to redeem us, to deliver us from the curse that has been inflicted upon us, upon our children and upon our grandchildren, as yet unborn but whose wails of complaint already reach us. For no one else, good or bad, will ever redeem us if we don't redeem ourselves with what powers we have. Though I am nothing, your lordship, scarcely a poor beast, yet I too have no power within me other than the power to destroy myself. But that is a great power, like the divine power in man, so that when one man perishes, the whole world perishes with him, all other people perish with him, as though out of loyalty to him, as though other people can't go on without him, whoever he is. For the rivers too dry up, along with him, and the forests bow down, and all green things turn yellow, and all creatures become extinct, and the birds fall from the sky, and the whole earth crumbles to dust, even the sun and the stars are snuffed out – and God too, if He was ever within him at all.

But one day I must get really drunk, so drunk I'll forget about myself, for otherwise I'll live in constant fear of my own power. And when one day I do get drunk, then you'll see, your lordship, I'll enter your estate, enter your palace, and I'll spread the news that there's no longer any sin, that sin was merely the invention of one lot of people to destroy another. That they're all free, if they're still capable of being free. Oh, one day I'll get really drunk, really drunk. Oh, I'll get so drunk, and then, your lordship, you'll rue the day you ever tried to cheer me up.

But here's a wedding, a wedding party rolling towards us like a trailing cloud, tossing about, singing hoarsely, raucously, yet mournfully, as though all they wanted to do was make a noise. But the bride is being led by the hand weeping, drenched in tears. And the groom nods his head as though he was half asleep.

And who's marrying whom, my good people?

Nobody's marrying anybody, your lordship, but since you ordered there to be weddings, we're having a wedding. There's nobody else left, so we're all getting married all over again, just so we can have a wedding. As soon as Sunday comes round we all assemble, go to the tavern, and then parade round the village like a real wedding, across the fields, through the meadows, till sometimes we almost imagine we *are* a real wedding. But all this gaiety is beginning to pall, our brides have grown old, it's sad to make such a mockery of ourselves, some are already widowed and ought to be in mourning, not in wedding veils. And there's not many grooms left either, still less eligible ones, so we've got to wait till they grow up. And when will that be, your lordship? For wars and injustices have devoured us like wolves. And no one wants to be a bride any longer, or a groom, or a bridesmaid, or a best man, no one, for we only poke fun at each other as we would at our worst enemy, and our children just laugh at us. Now and again someone still wants to be a wedding guest, part of the procession, part of the wedding throng, the onlookers, but not the bride, not the groom, no one, and yet we're forced to have a wedding. So each time we have to call on the village elder to appoint the bride and the groom and the bridesmaid and the best man. But none of us knows any more what true gaiety is really like. It's only the blessed vodka that still keeps us gay. It's already become our bread, our salt. It's already our God, the one thing that binds our affections, our sorrow and our joy; it's no longer blood that throbs in our veins, but vodka. If there's still anything we hate, your lordship, then it's vodka. If there's still anything we crave, then it's vodka. But at least the more we drink, the more we feel ourselves to be people. And so we somehow go on getting married, but no one wants to any more, even if they could, because every wedding just turns into more sorrows and more worries, and these just go on multiplying because of our wives and children. Release us from these weddings, your lordship, and leave us to our misery! Release us, for we already bear so much more than was intended, so much more than was simply unjust, so much more than if God just wanted to punish us, yet you still order us to be gay. But you won't make people out of us like this, for we weren't born to be people. People will only come after us one day. For how will we ever muster the strength, your lordship, to go on with our perpetual wedding processions? This gaiety of ours has already become our nightmare. We're even afraid it'll make us forget our sins, our sentences, our destinies. And what will become of us then, when our sins are no more, our sentences are no more, our destinies are no more, and all we have left is a perpetual wedding? How will we ever endure it, your lordship?

But the gayest of all, my dears, was my blacksmith. He never knew whether he was drunk or sober, happy or sad. Ha! Ha! Ha!

But how come you're taking so long to think, my dear Judge? After all, it's your turn. Mine? How can it be mine? I said pass. His Excellency threw down the ace, and now we're waiting for you. Come on, I beg you, put something down. Anything will do, it won't make any difference. The game was lost long ago. What you're about to remind us of was last year. Last year, my dears, I lost my entire stud with precisely that card, yet I'm not making any mention of it. Hurry up, we ought to be finishing. Do you hear the music? The voices? The ball's already in full swing. We cannot not be there. We disappeared without telling anyone, and I'm sure the valets won't know where to find us. We were only going to play one round, just one round, before the ball began, but here we are playing on and on, and none of us knows how long it'll be before we finish. Not very nice of us, gentlemen. Moreover let us not forget that when we're not there, we're more conspicuous by our absence than if we were there. I vouch that more than one lady has already noticed us. No doubt there's already plenty of pouts, offended looks, awkward questions. So finish, my dear Judge, finish. Just put down anything and give up. We can't hide anything from the ladies, gentlemen, we ought to know that. They can feel our absence out there. Perhaps at this very moment their sparkling eyes are searching for us in the crowd, in the dancing. Perhaps they're sad because we're not there. And that radiance in their eyes, which someone here once described so beautifully as the radiance of rising stars, has already begun to dwindle. One could say the ladies are fading away because of us, gentlemen, like those stars before the dawn, though the ball is only just beginning. Even the glitter of their dresses is dwindling. What a shame, what a waste of such sumptuous dresses! No, no, I can't agree with you, *Voivode*. I'm prepared to concede you're a connoisseur of horses, but not when it comes to women. So remember, my dear, that women's dresses are more seductive than their bodies. You'll uncover more nudity in their dresses, if I may put it that way, than you'll ever uncover in their bodies. Ah, so you weren't aware that their dresses too can be naked? Yes, my dear, a woman's dress is naked before it's anything else. I'd say the nakedness of a dress is without end, mysterious, it's a nakedness that knows how to torment you, that will never let you into its secret, even if you let it lure you into hell, even if you tear it to shreds, so what is the nakedness of the body beside that? The nakedness of the body ends on exposure, my dear. It's only thanks to her dresses that every woman is different, but she's only different until she undresses. Ha! Ha! Ha! Even His Excellency confirms it, you see. And I'll even go as far as to say that a woman only dresses in order to seem more naked to us, to men. And thanks to her dresses her nakedness varies, confounds us, protects itself against us and against its own sameness. With every dress she assumes a different form and excites you anew, because she's so commonplace in herself that if you were to stop and think about it, you'd be quite amazed that you go on desiring her. Thank you, thank you, you flatter me. But hasn't it ever happened to you, my dear, that when a lady undresses in front of you, you've experienced – well, I won't say embarrassment – but something akin to disappointment? And perhaps you've even been gripped by a feeling of guilt that you've exposed her unnecessarily to her own ordinariness, so carefully concealed from you. What? Come on, admit it, *Voivode*. Ha! Ha! Ha! Yes, yes, if only you knew, the dress is the woman. That's what they say. The dress more than anything. And that's why, gentlemen, to be quite honest, I often prefer the dress on its own. Ha! Ha! Ha! But don't breathe a word. That's only between us. We'd be storing up trouble for ourselves if they were eavesdropping. And even these thick walls have ears. Ears. Believe me.

So how are you getting on there, Judge? Had a good think about what to throw down? Not yet? Then I see that you too are planning to recover your losses. Though I don't understand what for. I really don't understand. What resentment could you be harbouring in your heart towards me? I'm not surprised at His Excellency – forgive me, Your Excellency – or at the *Voivode*. They're beaten. And that's tough. I almost feel sad for them. The *Voivode*'s lost everything but his soul. And His Excellency's even been relieved of his rings. Look at his hands, glittering only with their own whiteness. Do excuse me, Your Excellency. If you'll allow me, I'll make a present of one of those forfeited rings to your wife. I'd never forgive myself if your grief were to sadden her beautiful eyes. Oh, we must take pity at least on the ladies, gentlemen, even if we can no longer take pity on ourselves. Then we could say we're playing for nothing. Ha! Ha! Ha! For nothing, gentlemen. That really would be fine play. That's what real play's all about. For nothing, and therefore for what? For even our honour no longer comes into play. So you're torturing yourself in vain, Judge. I told you, just throw down anything. For if I was to divulge to you the whole truth, I'd simply give His Excellency and the *Voivode* their last chance, if they want it, to win everything back. But what of it, even their cards have let them down. Don't let that ace deceive you by any chance, Judge. His Excellency has just pulled it out of his sleeve. Only I haven't seen anything, Excellency. His Excellency's honour doesn't permit me to see anything. Oh, no, no, not because of my friendship towards you, my dears. It's not even my magnanimity. It's simply some instinct telling me that you've lured me into a trap, so I'm letting you recover your losses. With you lot, even when I win, it's all entirely up to you. But as far as I'm concerned, it has to be up to me. Up to me alone. Today I've got nothing to lose. You've excelled yourselves with your cunning, gentlemen. No, no, we're playing on, we're playing on, my dears, playing to the end. Only if you don't mind, our dear respected Senator will take my place for a while. Please, my dear

Senator, and I'll disappear for a moment, at least show that I'm here. Do you hear the music? The voices? Out there the ball's in full swing. I'll be back right away, of course I'll be back, certainly I'll be back.

I clap my hands.

Hey, orchestra, play, play! Give it all you've damned well got! Bring wine for the orchestra! Wine for the orchestra! It's not the end yet, ladies and gentlemen! Daylight hasn't caught up with us yet. And it won't until we want it to. No, don't put the lights on! Let the darkness be our light. We've never had a party in the dark. But maybe this is in fact our proper hour? We won't have to see each other, so perhaps our interest in each other will be rekindled. So let the darkness come to our aid. Every couple on their feet! A waltz! A ladies' waltz! Ladies inviting the men!

What's this I see, you're off home already, sir? But fie, this isn't very nice of you, my dear. The ball isn't over yet, there's still no sign of the dawn, yet you're off home already? What do you mean, yes? But we're all exhausted, my dear. Cast your eyes about in the darkness, sir. They're all staggering around, but they're still dancing. Semi-conscious, drunk, barely alive, yet no one's forsaking the ball. Even the ladies are fainting from exhaustion. Look, sir, at the weaker ones expiring in the chairs, on the couches, panting like drooping dogs, grappling with sleep. But they too, once they recover, will join in the dancing. Some of them, even though they're still watching, look on with unseeing eyes. Others already have one foot in the grave, yet they still call for wine and fresh air. Some are already snoring, splayed out as though in their own beds. It's a shame you can't see it all, sir. They're already dreaming about this ball. Dreaming about their horses and their hounds. Their skies of ploughed land. Eternities of naked ladies and maidens. What a shame! Some are already bulging like fish out of their frock-coats. And those splendid frock-coats no longer seem like frock-coats, but like funeral robes. Why not have a good laugh at them, if you can? That man there's dropping off his lady on to the parquet like a leaf falling off a tree, but the valets are there ready to save him. Ugh, those valets! How obscenely dignified they are! Just carrying on pouring out the wine, whether you want it or not. Can you hear that laughter, sir, those cheers, the music?

You must be able to hear them. Well, I ask you, someone's telling a valet to guide him to his lady because his legs can't carry him any more. And the valet's guiding him across without a word, without a smile, without any understanding, without any condemnation. Ugh, those valets! Why don't you go and woo yourself some little dove, sir? In darkness like this she'll simply throw herself into your arms as soon as you lean over her. You'll dance with her once, twice, and she'll be yours without it even being a sin. Ha! Ha! Ha! Look, there sits the Countess, drunk already. She won't even recognize you. You could go up to her, invite her to dance. And you want to leave the ball already, sir? You want to tear yourself away from us so soon? Not very nice of you, my dear, not very nice of you. Anyway, all the doors are bolted. Nobody will open them for you until the ball's over. Even I don't have the right. We've locked ourselves in. So dance, sir, drink, dance, it's the only thing you've got left now, and the ball will finish in its own time. It's a shame you can't see them dancing, the ones who no longer know what they're doing. Exhausted, yet happy nevertheless. Maybe this is our very last ball, my dear, so maybe it ought to outlive us. We can only go on as long as the ball goes on.

Hey, orchestra, a waltz!

I can see you now, Princess, I can see you again. But only for a moment, and again you vanish into the darkness. I can hear you laughing somewhere, but I can't believe it's your laugh, for I always remember you as sad. And again you appear, and again you vanish. And I follow in your wake, not knowing how to ask you to dance. Even though it's such a simple thing. Even though others ask you all the time, and so unceremoniously that I shut my eyes in disbelief. They just walk up to you and bow, raising your hand to their lips, elegant, delicate, like the neck of a swan. And I don't know if I even know how to approach you. Whether I wouldn't stop half-way across the floor, frightened by my own anxiety. For in your presence I feel the diffidence of a child. The dread of a sinner. So I'm waiting, Princess, for when we'll be alone, just before dawn maybe, when life will have drained from all the rest. Because this ball was meant only for us, for us two alone. And perhaps then you'll deliver me from my diffidence. Perhaps you'll even say, How good it is that we're alone at last, for now I can have a proper look at you. And now dance with me, dance with me, whilst the day remains unbroken, whilst I'm still drunk, drunk, drunk. And whilst you, my lord, remain unsure.

Oh, I'm dancing, dancing with you, Princess. Could you really not feel me? For my arms are full of you. I carry your slender body in my hands. Press your tiny palm in mine and feel each one of your fingers. Bend over your hair and touch its softness with my face, touch it with my lips, but so reverently you'd never even suspect it. I breathe in your whole self like the fragrance of wild grasses. I'm full of the thought of you. Your mournful eyes glow within me, I can hear your heart beating inside me. And yet you aren't even sure of me. Oh, that's not fair, my unkind, beautiful Princess.

From the very beginning I've been dancing only with you. Ever since you first appeared at the ball I've been dancing only with you. If it wasn't for the darkness keeping us hidden, they'd all be talking by now. And your lord, the Prince, would have taken you home no doubt. And perhaps he'd have locked you up in a tower, bricked you up in a windowless chamber. Your stern master, the Prince. So praise be to the darkness. No one will spot us. Not even the Prince's owl eyes. For we are nothing but shadows to everyone else, just as they are but shadows to us. We are here with all the rest of them, but it's as if we were alone at this ball, in this ballroom, in the palace, in the world. Yet I must confess, their gaiety irritates me. Hurts me almost. I'd prefer not to hear it, but I can't not hear it. I'd prefer to be indifferent, but I can't be indifferent. Oh, I know, I know, it's a ball. But I get the impression that they're trying to stir up this gaiety inside themselves, yet they haven't really got it in them. That they're trying to evoke this gaiety, but inside they're sad and lifeless. Maybe fear has come to haunt them and they want to lose themselves in gaiety. Perhaps they're dragging us into their gaiety, too, only we don't know about it. But if we're here alone, we have no need to be afraid of them.

If we're here alone, then it's of no consequence if we're alive or dead, for the boundary falls away between this world and the next. That's why I ordered them not to put on the lights, so we wouldn't have to know anything for certain, only that we're dancing, dancing together, Princess. Perhaps we oughtn't even to see one another, you and me. Or know any more than we know from intuition, from our dancing, from our longing for each other. For I'd never forgive myself if I saw your face scarred by pain, or the vaguest hint of death in your eyes. I'd probably curse all light for having done you such an injury.

Believe me, Princess, you're the only person here I really feel sorry for, the only one out of all the others. And out of you and me too. Though all I know of you is that I'm holding you in my arms, that I can feel your fragility, that I'm bending over you, listening with rapt attention to your hair, your mournful silence, that I'm dancing with you. For beings like you should, by their very nature, be free from death. Free from suffering, from tears, from everything that is vulnerable in man. They should be eternal, for something in this world has to be eternal so that those of us who are merely passing through can still hope that our admiration might last for ever, if nothing else. So that this world doesn't constantly have to end with every person and begin anew with the next. And if God is not eternal, what is, if not beings like you, Princess? If only I could save of you just a fleeting moment of your sadness, or just one memory of this ball, you'd already be eternal. If only I could. But what can I do except dance with you, dance with you? Let's forget even that we're alive, since it's only our helplessness that binds us together. And let's enjoy ourselves, enjoy ourselves like the rest of them, till we're out of breath, till we're oblivious. Let their empty gaiety sweep us away in its embraces, let us lose ourselves in it.

I'm dancing with you, Princess, dancing with you. In my head I can hear the sweet sough of the trees. And I feel so light, so exalted, as if we were waltzing through the night, sailing on high between the stars and the earth, so that I want to say to you, look down below, can you see the palace? We're not there any more. I don't know why, but it seems to me that the whole ballroom is spinning in time with our waltz, the people, their whispers, their laughter, their shouts, even the walls of the palace and all this immense darkness, spinning along with us, with you, with me, all around us. Yet if we were to miss a single step, it would all come crashing down at one fell swoop and nobody would ever get up again. I feel like laughing, Princess. Foolishly, emptily, laughing unrestrainedly at the top of my voice. Forgive me. I don't feel gay at all. I'd just forgotten what they were playing. As though I'd suddenly lost awareness of the music. But I can hear it again now, I can hear it. I'm with you now. Perhaps some other memory was trying to draw me into it. A memory from some other ball, some other waltz. Or perhaps I'm just tired of this ball all around us. These balls, continual balls, so crowded, clamouring with the brilliance of the lights, the laughter, the bodies, the music. So possessed by gaiety that I often wonder what despair must be lurking in people's hearts, if gaiety sweeps them so easily off their feet.

Look, can you see that there's more and more of them, that it's getting noisier and noisier all around us, that the darkness is getting denser and denser. Oh, how good it is to feel you beside me, inside me, Princess! How I'd like to be with you at this very moment somewhere far away, far away from this ball, far away from all these people. Where we would no longer have to hear this music, nor the conversation, nor the laughter, the cheers, the dancing couples. Where not even our recollections of the ball would torment us. Where we could lose our memory, so that not even the slightest remorse for those recollections would linger within us. But where there would only be us, the two of us, even if the only thing that bound us together was our mutual suffering. I don't know why, but I'm seized by panic at the thought that we might have to wait until dawn along with all the rest of them. Oh, the dawn will afford us no mercy. The livid light of the rising day will transform us into corpses. We won't recognize ourselves, won't be able to tell that only a short while ago we were still gay. Each of us will feel ashamed in front of the other, we'll shut our eyes before each other, we won't even recognize each other because of our shame. For what a ghastly sight it will be, when we suddenly catch a glimpse of our ashen faces, clouded by the shadow of death, our sightless eyes devoid of expression. It's as though I can already feel that death inside me. It's they who have infected me with it, they, so that I would remain loyal to them. To them and to myself. No, it's not even a trick on their part. They had the right, they had the right. After all, I'm one of them. I feel as though a strange kind of inertia has stripped me of all desire, Princess, of all hope, and of all my hatred too. I have nothing left inside me except my sadness. And I don't even feel any resentment towards them. I can't feel resentment any more. Only you and you alone, Princess, could save me from this inertia. You remain my only hope, my last resort. Say that it was because of me, only because of me that you turned up at this ball. That you knew I needed you. Say it. Don't you think it's strange that I found you so easily in the darkness? That I didn't have to search for you in the crowd? That you almost fell into my arms of your own accord and nestled up to me?

I'd elope with you, Princess, if only you'd agree to it. But hear me out before you utter a word. And if you're going to refuse, better not say anything. No one would notice our disappearance. The darkness too would come to our aid. Just agree to it, and I'll burn for you with a great love, a love such as you'll never find with your lord, the Prince. For only my great love for you can rouse me from my inertia, wrest me from this death lurking here in wait for me, restore me to myself. All I have left is my love for you, Princess, my wonder at your existence. And I shall love you with all the love that you crave. Even if it be blind, submissive, reciprocated only by your compassion. Even if my love does nothing but flatter your vanity, fuel that vanity. I shall love your vanity. I shall love it indulgently, tenderly, for perhaps you're no longer capable of any feeling, only of this proud vanity. Perhaps someone once cast a spell on you, carelessly, in one of your vainer moments, and thus you remained. Perhaps someone gazed only at your beauty, so you became nothing but that beauty. Gazed at your enigmatic smile, so you became nothing but that smile. Gazed at your haughty glance, so you became nothing but that glance. Perhaps someone once saw in you his own futile desires, and so you became those desires, never to be fulfilled. But I shall love you just as you are. You can be as vain as you like, as haughty as you like, an unattainable dream, but I shall be totally at your mercy. Unbeknown to you, I shall hanker for you, long for you, suffer because of you, yet you won't even know what it means to suffer. I shall bear our love for the both of us. I shall offer up prayers to your hands, to your eyes, to your brow, just as we humans in our helplessness offer up prayers to a single God, so that my love for you will never cease throbbing. I shall be forever filled with my wondering at you, until one day

I might even feel your eternity within me. Though I don't know, perhaps I won't be able to bring you happiness, but maybe I can give you just a little of its illusion.

Let's run away from here, Princess, before the darkness pales. Listen, a four-horse carriage awaits us on the north side of the park, there where the roads part to east and west, under the old oak tree. Don't be afraid of the dark, you'll find it easily enough. The horses will sense your approach and whinny softly. Neither the clatter of the hooves will betray us, nor the wheel marks on the road. For both hooves and wheels have been bandaged. And rest assured that the coachman got his share of land, his stretch of forest, his gun, his purse of money, and he's had his eyes put out too so he won't recognize you. You'll slip away as soon as they start the next dance. As soon as the couples begin to sway from side to side, you'll slip away unobserved, you'll disappear, but as innocently as if you'll soon be back. You'll turn right into the corridor, go right to the end – but, God forbid, don't ask anyone the way – and you'll come out through the back door. The servants' door, Princess, but you'll have to swallow this indignity, for it's the only way out. Imagine you're laying a sacrifice on the altar of our feelings. And walk through it. No one has any right to recognize you if they see you wish to pass unrecognized. And cover yourself securely, your black shawl would be best, so you won't shine in the darkness. And walk right up to the door with your head bowed, so you're not taken for someone who's lost their way. The door will be open, you'll just push it gently, and if it scrapes, don't be alarmed for it'll only be the door. Then a white path will lead you across the park to the little gate hidden beneath the wild vine. No one remembers it any more. No one knows about it. And thus you'll come to the carriage. I shall be waiting for you there, Princess. Full of uncertainty, bad premonitions, disappointed dreams. I'll have been looking out for you for a long time, catching your every step as it comes to me out of the darkness, counting the hours between each one. I shall be watching out for you from all corners of the night, taking all the night sounds to be your footsteps. I shall trust that you won't let me down, yet at the same time I shall expect the disasters that will stop you ever coming. And when you come at last, you'll fall into my arms, terrified, breathless, and then we'll disappear into the night, our happiness complete. But remember, this night will never end unless you appear beside me.

Princess, you're crying? You're really crying? Have I done something to hurt you, Princess? Oh, forgive me, forgive me. I didn't mean to. How could I ever forget, unhappy man that I am, that you can't even give me any hope because you yourself are so unhappy? That being no longer of this world, you too do not belong to yourself? How could I forget? Obviously I got carried away by our dancing, possessed by it, and forgot what I was doing with you by my side. Now it's all over and all that remains is the remorse, the remorse and the frustrated dreams. We met just this once, at this ball, yet we'll go on parting for ever. Isn't that cruel? They've even stopped playing, do you hear? But we go on dancing, dancing, dancing. We've forgotten ourselves, Princess. Forgotten ourselves, but how sweet it feels. Princess, where are you? Where are you? Princess? Princess?!

I can hear my voice, but it's not me calling out, it's the emptiness calling with my voice, the walls, the chamber, the palace, the darkness. I can hear myself somewhere in the darkness, round about myself, above my head. I don't know what's happening to me. There was a ball going on, there was a princess, and now all that remains is darkness. I stretch out my hands like a blind man and finger the emptiness, hoping I might bump into a chair, a table, a wall, it doesn't matter what, so long as I can find myself again. But is it me? Is this really me? I'm still dancing after all. I can hear my own confessions, my hope, my bitterness. I hold the Princess in my arms, caress her, kiss her hair, console her tears. Don't cry, Princess, your tears are like precious stones, it's wasteful to weep them away. And I dance, dance, dance.

Suddenly the room is illuminated by a brilliant flash of light. A massive boom and then even greater darkness. Something crumbles, collapses. Plaster flies from the ceiling. Dust clutches at my throat. For a moment I hardly feel anything, can't see, can't hear anything. But the booming noise gets louder, roars, splutters, rampages in the darkness, as if it can't find a way out. I retreat before it. Squeeze my eyes tightly shut, put my hands over my ears. I'm not here. Not here. After a while, however, I cautiously open my eyes. In the corner of the room some brilliant light has not gone out after that great flash. It's the grand piano. I hurl myself through the darkness to lay my hands on it, then I come crashing down with all my might on to the bared teeth of the keyboard. They seethe with anger, lashing out at that booming above me like a whip mowing down leaves. Now it's gone, not the slightest echo remains.

The darkness swells with sounds. They vibrate, ring out. And the darkness too vibrates with them, the room, the palace, myself. I imagine them tearing the darkness to shreds, and at any moment the darkness growing lighter with the pale dawn, with the early morning, with the sun coming up. I listen and I can't believe that it's me who's making these sounds with my own hands, that the rippling sounds resounding above me are the product of my blind and anxious hands, as scared as baby birds fallen from the nest, and that it's me who's hearing them, hearing them in the darkness, in the palace, in my own self. I raise my hands to my eyes, I can't see them, but I stare at them in amazement. I squeeze them together, then straighten my fingers, then squeeze them again. I place one hand on top of the other, then swap them over. They're warm. I clasp them together. Squeeze them tightly, then harder still, till they hurt, till I have to bend over them. I want to feel even more painfully that it's really them. Because I can't believe in them, can't believe in them. But I'd like to, God, how I'd like to! I could unfold them, raise them up. Only to what? I could dig them into my knees and grind them, grind them till the blood spurts out of them. But now I can really feel these hands of mine, now I have them, now nothing can take them away from me. Now they've grown heavy. I can even feel them in my arms. A kind of strange longing engulfs me, not me, but these hands. A kind of temptation. Oh, not me, but my hands. They're inciting me to follow them. Pulling me with them. I can't resist them. Though I'm afraid that confounded brilliance might flare up again any moment, break upon my ears, burst forth in a clap of thunder, and punish my pride. Anyway, let it happen, whatever wants to happen.

I sit down at the piano. I stare at the row of white keys shining before me in the darkness, and for a moment it looks like some monster flinging wide the gaping chasm of its mouth. But should

I try to touch any one of those fangs, that mouth will clamp shut, taking my hand with it. However I feel a flush of confidence, of faith. How easily it comes over me! Not only do I believe in myself now; I envy myself that I'm here sitting at the piano. Me. With my hands ready, poised above the keys. And my own hands too. And after a moment, if I manage to survive it, my hands – these ordinary hands, which I've had since the day I was born, which I don't even have to touch in order to sense, feel their roughness, their shape, which go everywhere with me, which sleep with me, which will die with me, with which I eat, scratch myself, shake hands, which I clench in my anger – these hands will hover for an instant in the darkness, freeze in mid-air, then swoop down on the piano like the talons of a buzzard, digging themselves into the white keys as if they were made of flesh. And the music will gush forth from them like blood, and the darkness will quake with fear, and the walls will start to shudder.

I can feel the music inside me, hear it inside me. Immense, sublime, reverberating throughout the palace, throughout my fear, which still smoulders somewhere within me. Intensified by my elation, it resounds over and over again. I hear it outside in the park, among the trees, somewhere high in the sky, on the very limits of my being. I don't know whether I exist any more, or whether this music now exists instead of me. For I can't feel any memory inside me, can't hear my heart beating in my breast. It's already become myself. It makes me ache. But I long for it. It sends shivers up my spine. My hands are tingling, itching to be stretched out, stretched out to catch it and squeeze it in my fingers till it hurts. And now it's even more immense, even more powerful than those first sounds that formed its opening bars, that mowed down that terrible booming only a moment ago. I can hear it so clearly now that all I have to do is lift my hands, – what could be simpler? – just lift my hands, order myself to lift my hands, order myself to lift them up and up, and then lower them on to the piano, and the music will mount and soar of its own accord, even guide my hands of its own accord, and I'll be nothing but my hearing of it, my merging into it, nothing but its pain, its anxiety.

I can even see myself playing now, my eyes closed, my head uplifted, entranced, towards the music, which hangs over me somewhere like a cloud, like the vast dome of the sky – yet I am totally possessed by it, I am flung wide by its vastness, I am ecstatic. I. I. God, how agonizing it is, yet how exhilarating! I rock in time with my hands as they slip, glide over the keys, lightly, unrestrainedly, drifting from shore to shore. I can't feel them at all, my pussy paws, no longer my hands, my butterflies, no longer my hands, scarcely brushing the surface of the keys, scarcely vibrating as they skim over them. Suddenly a devil enters into them and they gallop, gallop, startled, breathless, like dogs, dogs, dogs bounding from all directions, dogs pouncing on one another in their blind fury, biting each other in their obsessive panic. They stand still for a moment, a brief moment of humility or of doubt, but then they begin to sink into the keys again, so warmly, like sunshine drenching the earth. They splash about, the water barely lapping over them. Suddenly they leap in the air, then plunge into the abyss.

Ah, how beautifully you play, your lordship! What a pleasure it is to listen to you! What happiness! You're miraculous. The whole world is becoming your music, and anyone who's been bewitched by it feels as if for ever sealed in a crystal ball. Bravo! Bravo! Well, what can one say, you're a true master, my dear. A master, I tell you. And I thought, if I might say so, it was just horses and women. He! He! He! I don't know much about music, it's true, forgive me, my friend, but having been at the waters one year.... Oh, may the grace of God protect you so you never fall victim to the sin of pride, for none of us can ever tell which is stronger in you, God or Satan. Listening to you is like listening to Nature. Trees, wild herbs, the soil, the sun. And the night, Countess, the night, above all. What do you mean, you can hear wild herbs? The blood curdles in your veins when you hear music like this. And how is it you've got so much pain in you, your lordship, so much love, so much intuition? It's simply excruciating. I've heard it, I've heard it. Thundering away. One can't tell if one's experiencing grace or profanity. Do let me congratulate you. Why, my dear, our dear beloved! I was moved to tears. Trembling all over. So touch me and calm me down. Or play something else. Eh, Cousin, Cousin, where did you get those hands? Where did you get that soul within you? Oh, you've cast me down into hell, I've found myself in hell, now I shall never know any peace. You have horses, horses in your hands. Let me give them a squeeze. I imagined a flock of birds flew out of them, fluttering their wings. Clouds of birds. It's a premonition. I don't know whether to laugh or cry. Tell me, all of you, should I laugh or cry? Tell me, my lord, should I laugh or cry? Deer, stags, hares. Troubled waters. No. I won't forget. I shall die with you. One of the damned, one of the damned. You're killing us. Hell. Heaven. A thunderbolt has struck. Ah, play us something else, your lordship. Play for us, we beg you. Implore you. Don't reject our pleas. Play us something else. Play, lord and master. Play. For whenever you play, it's as if our hearts opened up and our sins crawled out of us like vermin. Play, lord and master. Play. For the only thing we live for now is to be able to listen to you. We bow down before your feet, before your conscience.

I raise my hands. A moment of concentration. I'm about to bring them down on to the keys when a feeling of doubt comes over me. I hold them there in front of me, yet I can't make them spring into action, dive on to the keys or even give up in despair. I'm even afraid to move them, I even put them back on my knees. I hold them steady, for they were supposed to sweep down from the heights of exaltation, but now fear has imprisoned them there. They tremble. Fear seeps into me, robs me of my will, fills me with humility. And they feel heavier and heavier, as if I'd picked them up laden with earth. I feel I can't cope. I clench them into fists, into stones. Then I smash them. Smash the living daylights out of them. And then I tap a key with one finger, timidly, as though knocking on a door. It reverberates with the scuffling of a mouse. And even though it falls silent immediately, I listen to it intently, as I listen intently to the silence which follows. I tap a second time. It whimpers just the same and then falls silent. Then I try somewhere else. A bit louder. But it's not the same. It's not the same. It's disappeared somewhere, my great music. But I heard it after all. I heard it everywhere, within myself. Won't it ever come back to me? I feel most sorry for my poor hands. They don't even suspect the helplessness I'm condemning them to. The humiliation. The derision. I can hear them all making fun of me. Chortling away. I raise them to my eyes. My poor hands. They look exhausted, sore. I bring them to my lips and breathe on them with my warm breath. Blow on them. After a while I feel them coming to life again. Thawing from their frozen state. Freeing themselves from themselves. Sprouting wings. They're mine again, mine again. The same old hands. I place them on the keys. The sounds ring out, but what's up? Somehow it grates, somehow it's empty. I strike again in another place. And again, the same. I slide over all the keys, starting from the left with the lowest notes, dull as the thud of falling trees; moving to the very high ones, fine as a hair's breadth, so faint they fade away as soon as they're struck. I strike yet again. This time deep down. On those low notes. They're the closest to my heart, loud, tremulous. And everything vibrates with their trembling. The darkness, the walls, the palace. I begin to suspect that maybe this music of mine has hidden itself from me. But I shall unearth it, I shall extract it, no matter how deep I have to dig, I shall tear it up by the roots. I strike again, but so deep I almost hit rock bottom. I can hear myself playing. But it's not my music, not the music I long for, not the music that makes me ache, that sends shivers of fear through my body, thrills of joy. That I sing inside myself. I am singing, singing, shouting, screaming, praying. But the sounds are wrangling beneath my fingers, ranting, raving, tussling with one another, pouncing on each other like baited dogs. They flee from under my fingers, take flight, take fright, leaving behind only their squeals, their gnashing teeth, their gibes. But I go on playing, go on playing. I must play on till I reach that music which is inside me, which is brimming over inside me, which is already bursting out of me. Till I reach that special music, that sublime music, that music which is mine and mine alone. I can't give in to it. That would be beyond my powers. Beyond my faith, beyond all my longings. And so I go on playing, go on playing, just so my patience doesn't abandon me. Playing if not with longing then with hatred. Out of revenge. I might curse myself, but I'll go on playing. I might hurl myself into hell, but I'll go on playing.

Suddenly my fury spurs me into action. It's the piano, the piano that is bent on destroying me. The brute's got it in for me, his own lord and master. I lay into it with my fists, furiously into that bloated body till the strings howl in agony. Oh, you, you! You're a beast out of hell. I'll sort you out, you'll see. I'll do you over without mercy. Without the slightest twinge of remorse – I'll do you over like a dog, like a thief, like a rebel. I'll have you flogged. I'll summon my strongest farm-hands and let them loose on you with their whips till they drop down dead. And I've got men like that. I have, and here they all tremble at the very thought of them. And I'll throw you out into the yard, into the muck, so you'll become a laughing-stock. Let anyone who wants thump all over you. Let children infest you like flies, stamp on your music. Jeer at you for having lost my favour. Mice will breed inside you, hens will lay eggs among your strings, and the cocks will crow, crow – and you won't even have the power to startle them with a single sound. Even the village girls walking past will knock their buckets against you. Ha! Ha! Ha! Let cows rub against you. Horses bolt at the sight of you. Or no. I'll cast you into a dungeon. Have you locked up so no one will draw any sound from you ever again. You'll be superfluous, abandoned, empty. And you'll see just how unhappy you can be, more unhappy than a man could ever be. So unhappy that perhaps that music inside you will start to weep of its own accord. You used to flatter everyone here, even those whose fingers were dead, whose eyes were cold and lifeless. They couldn't even hear themselves, yet you would flatter them. You were lord and master to anyone who wanted to play. Even drunks found favour with you. Even mockers. Traitors. Sinners. Guzzlers. Even idiots. Even the simplest valet, chambermaid, anyone who could wring something out of you, even if it was by stealth. So what have I done to offend you? Is there something wrong with my fingers? Do I have no soul? It's causing me such pain. Understand that. Save me from my humility. From my fear. From my impotence. Give me back my great music. Give it me back from out of every song – song of man, song of earth, song of beast. Give it me back from out of the heavens. Let this darkness pass away in that great music. This palace. Let me too pass away in it.

I want to implore the piano. I want to kneel before it, pray to it. But I don't know how. I don't know how. In the same way that I pray to God? And supposing, like God, it doesn't listen to me? Whatever will I do then with my humility? With my hands? They'll become even more helpless. They'll become hateful to me.

And whatever will I do then with hands like that? With hands that have known such impotence? With such cursed hands? What shall I do then?

I clench them till they hurt and unclench them till they hurt. Clench and unclench. Clench them till my nails dig into my palms, till I feel nothing except the pain. I throw my whole weight on to the keys, but there too I feel nothing but pain. The only thing I can hope for is the sound ringing out on high, yet all I can hear in it is mockery, not my pain; I can hear my humility, my futility, but not my music.

Suddenly I thrust my fingers into the keys like claws into the earth, into a mane of hair, into someone's throat. And I play with nothing but my anger. With my impotence. Blindly. Wherever my hands carry me. And fast, as fast as my hands can keep pace with my anger. So fast that one sound cannot extricate itself from another. So that one sound vents its spleen upon the next. The sounds smother each other, bite into each other. I can't hear, feel anything inside myself. Even my longing has deserted me. Perhaps I'm not even playing any more. Perhaps I just can't come to terms with myself. Now all I do is simply pound away, pound, pound at these sounds, resistant, hateful. At this conceit called music, which has dragged me deviously into its own hell. For the most I can do is to get my own back. I have to. I can't walk away from it without getting my revenge. My hands ache as though I'd rammed them into a tree, into a stone. But I feel joy at their pain. I can't even get enough of this pain inside them. I could hit them till they fall off, till I'd reduced them to pulp, shake the living daylights out of them to make up for my own impotence.

I snatch them away from the piano, shove them between my knees and squeeze them, squeeze them. Oh, you, my accursed hands! And then I raise them to my eyes. Whatever's happened to that pain of theirs? Where is it? Well, where is it? They're trembling. They're afraid of me. They're cringing. I can feel they're afraid. They're pleading with me. Weeping. I feel sorry for them. After all, they're my hands. After all, it's my impotence, not theirs. Our impotence is one and the same. Our helplessness is one and the same. I cover my face with them. They're feverishly hot, they're scalding me. Oh, my poor hands! So that's what you're really like? My own hands, and yet so accursed, you sons of bitches! And who could have punished me so vengefully by giving me hands like you? And whatever for? All I can do with you is smash you, smash you, and then weep over you. Lift you up towards God, but to no avail. Shove you in the straw-cutter one day and shut my eyes, even though you're my own hands and I feel sorry for you. I've done everything for you, yet you're so ungrateful, prodigal. When the frosts used to bite, I used to enfold you in my warmth, breathe on your decaying stiffness like you were baby birds. I used to pluck out the thorns so they wouldn't sprout all over you, I used to heal your blisters, used to suck the blood from your wounds till I'd made them clean, used to lay my lips on your bruises. Or perhaps you're not mine. Perhaps I inherited you from a condemned man who'd been deprived even of his hands. Perhaps you're not hands at all, but scythes, forks, axes, yokes, prayers. Perhaps you no longer know how to return to your own shape. Oh, you stupid things, you stupid things! And whom did you offend so cruelly that they hate you so much? Wake up and play! Only through will-power, only through longing, can you redeem yourselves. Only through your hatred, until your hatred becomes your love. It doesn't matter that it hurts you, it hurts me as well. Oh, play to me, play to me, let them all make fun of us, jeer at us. Let them all curse us. But you must go on playing, go on playing till you probe that great sensitivity within you, that butterfly touch.

I'm playing, I'm playing. I can hear myself playing. Feel myself playing. Though slowly at first, as if I was kneading dough, it's so thick, so heavy, so deep.

Suddenly it's as though a chasm opens up beneath my fingers. An incredible lightness enters into my hands. I imagine I'm touching water, sunlight, green leaves. I fly, fly over the keys. Hit whole handfuls at a time. And I hear myself, hear myself. Still a long way off, still hesitant. But it's my music. I recognize it. Hear it. For the first time in my life I hear myself so loudly, so clearly, so painfully. I almost don't want to believe that these sounds are really me, yet some strange fear excites me, because it is all me. Me. And I play, play more and more furiously because it's me. Play with hatred, play with love, because it's me. And I feel I want to weep for myself because it's me, my own self, me at last. I feel I want to vanish without trace, dissolve into oblivion, into non-existence. And as for my hands, oh, they no longer feel like hands, like my heavy aching hands, but like wings wheeling on the wind. Now I hear nothing but them. In this darkness, in the palace, within myself. Louder and louder. Fiercer and fiercer. Greedy for this ascending music as though they wanted to rake it all up and bury themselves in it, as though they wanted to be transformed into its sublime and noble sounds. Pulsating with music. Shedding music like blood. Now they no longer plead with it, no longer whimper before it. They tug at it like dogs tearing at a carcass so as to rouse it from its dignity, bite at it so as to awaken its fury, force their way into its whole being, penetrate its shame, its weakness, its wrong notes, its lies, scratch out its helplessness, its soft angel sweetness.

Till at last the sound of a bell rings out above me. And after it, all the bells in heaven. Bells bewailing bells, bells lamenting bells. I hear cattle lowing behind me, dogs barking on their jangling chains, sheep bleating – sensing I'm no longer there under my hawthorn bush. I'm no longer anywhere now. Not anywhere. All there is now is the endless tramping of innumerable human feet, shod in shoes of stone. Some kind of prayers – yet not prayers – resound throughout me, clumsy, lame, uttered not from people's throats but from their parched lips, whispered through their teeth as they grind on their hunger. The roar of water gushing from a mill. The scraping of carts. Clouds bursting asunder. Thunder. A wedding! A wedding! Raucous cries, laughter, giggles, squeals. A hailstorm of hooves. The shrill clatter of wheels. It's the horses bringing me my bride, pure, jasmine-scented. Nestling beside me – where I no longer am. I can hear her heart racing, excited, frightened. Beating against my own heart. The drum rolling behind us. A wedding! A wedding! Somewhere people are weeping. Tears come cascading down from the stars on high, shattering on the earth, clanging like buckets cast down a well. Suddenly the water, the water from these tears bursts from the sky, streams down in torrents, felling the trees, the houses. It roars in my fingers. I can hear it, I can hear it. But I am above it now, indifferent. And in the distance I can hear someone singing, in a piercing, clamorous voice. It's me who's singing. Me. Me. A song – yet not a song. A string of deformed, disconnected words, laughter, curses, whatever comes to my lips, for it's not words that I'm singing but my own jubilation, my own love, my own pain.

Suddenly I see my music transformed into a brilliant light. An intense radiance floods the room. But I go on playing and singing, playing and singing. The radiance swells inside me with the music, prays inside me, cries inside me out of happiness. It's my own radiance, my great, my sublime. And this radiance penetrates all the windows, doors, ceilings. It grows in strength, proliferates, hisses, spreads over all the walls. A luxuriating vine, hops running riot. Engulfing the furniture. Till its seething coil crashes with a thud on to the piano, on to my hands.

Fear clutches at my throat. I tear myself away. Fire! Fire! I run to the burning window. Fling it wide open. Fire! The palace is on fire! No, it's not the palace. The whole world is going up in flames. The village, the barns, the sties, the stables. The park too is ablaze. The flames shoot upwards into the sky. The trees writhe in pain. And in the midst of the fire the animals run amuck, terrified. Horses, cows, dogs, sheep. Neighing, lowing, howling, bleating piteously. My God, my sheep! My poor sheep. They're on fire. Their fleeces all singed. All lit up. Fire-balls, not sheep. Bright stars, not sheep. They squeeze in amongst the other animals. Rub against the trees. Kindling their own sparks. And bleat, bleat. My poor sheep! I'm almost suffocated by my rage, by my frustration, my helplessness, my remorse. Something forces me to stare at them, as if it were a punishment, to see if I can bear to watch them burning, in my eyes, in my thoughts, in my great guilt at having abandoned them, to see if I can endure it till they burn to death, till they put themselves out, to see if I can last out to the final flame. I can't. I shield my face with my hands and flee into the room. Oh, how I would love to forgive myself, but I'm afraid of the word that would forgive me. I'm choked by my crying, yet not crying. By my laughing, yet not laughing. I feel sick. What's the matter, your lordship? What is it? Oh, you poor thing, you poor thing! Where's the night-watchman? Where's the night-watchman? Where's that wretch who never sounded the alarm?! He was supposed to sound the alarm when there was a fire! Sound the alarm. I instructed him to. Instructed him like a son. Where is the traitor? God, God, and I bought him a new trumpet too. A brand new little trumpet. Pure gold. Yet where is he now? I struggle to free myself. It's as though I'm being held on a leash. I don't want to. Stop pulling me! I don't want to go away from here! This is where I belong! Here and nowhere else! Nowhere else! It's my palace that's on fire. Can't you see?! My palace! All of it! Huge! Vast! How beautifully it burns! How brilliantly! And I'm supposed to abandon it? At such a sublime and happy moment? And I'm supposed to abandon it? And who'll stay on when I am gone? I am the last of the line. Me! Me! Here is my memory! Here is all I have! And I'm meant to run away? And where to? Leave me alone! Get out of here! Get lost! The flames are all around me now, coming from all directions, flames, flames, flames. From the windows, the doors, the walls, fanning towards me. Ah, how bright it is in here! The brightness is blistering my eyes. Can't you see where we are, Princess? In heaven? Ha! Ha! Ha! Ha! Ha! Ha! Ha! You didn't guess, my melancholy one? Now we won't have to elope anywhere. Won't need our coach and horses. Besides, the coachman's recovered his sight, Princess. Ha! Ha! Ha! Make yourself at home. Can't you feel how warm it is here, how blissfully sweet? How could we feel better anywhere else? Just look how beautiful it is all around us. Oh, the clock's on fire! So not even time poses a threat to us any more. You say we're in the garden. Yes, indeed – here it blooms yellow, now red, the blossoms burgeoning forth. And how fragrant it all is! Ah, it takes your breath away. Stings your eyes. I don't know quite how to tell you, Princess. Run away? But where to? Where to? I'm surrounded on all fronts by foxes, foxes, ravenous red foxes, rabid red foxes. Oh, God have mercy on me, the sinner! Poor wretched God. Helpless God. My mean and insignificant God. Don't shut your eyes to me. Can't you see how your stars burn? Your seas? Your suns? Me? Is this your light eternal? The ladies are asking the men! A waltz! A ladies' waltz! Ha! Ha! Ha! And where are those valets off to? With their flaming candles? Whom are they going to welcome? Me? Ha! Ha! Ha! What's this, a ball in their lordships' rooms? Oh, no, Count, I shall never consent. We must remain at odds in the next world too. Where are my hands? Where are my poor hands? Haven't you seen my hands? I immerse them in the

flames and sacrifice them to you. May they be the last bright light you ever see. Oh, it doesn't hurt me any more. Look, look! The day is dawning from out of my hands. Hey, orchestra, play! Bring wine for the orchestra! And as for you, my faithless God. Well, can you feel anything? It's not hurting me. And can you feel it now? Can you feel it's not hurting me? Nothing hurts me now. Not any more. Nothing ....
....
....

20453074R00112

Printed in Great Britain
by Amazon